Critical Praise for J.G. Toews' Stella Mosconi Series:

"Toews builds interest in Stella and other characters as she mingles their personal conflicts with a mystery that will force Stella to face her deepest fear and keep readers guessing to the end. It all bodes well for what looks to be a promising series."

– *Publishers Weekly* review of *Give Out Creek*

"Toews has a nice eye for details that give charm to the B.C. outback… this one shows promise to come."

– Margaret Cannon, *The Globe & Mail* review of *Give Out Creek*

"A tale of crime, passion, friendship, family and, as is often the case with a crime story, jealousy. This entertaining read…takes readers on an enjoyable journey to discover the truth behind two untimely deaths."

– Aleesha Harris, *Vancouver Sun* review of *Give Out Creek*

"I owe J.G. Toews a tremendous vote of thanks for reigniting my interest in B.C.-authored crime fiction – and I look forward to the next book in the series."

– Bill Engleson, *Ormsby Review/BC Booklook* review of *Give Out Creek*

"*Give Out Creek* is unusually mature for a debut work, showing Toews' insights into the multifaceted life of a small town."

– Jim Napier, *Ottawa Review of Books* review of *Give Out Creek*

Give Out Creek Shortlisted for the 2019
Left Coast Crime Lefty for Best Debut Mystery Novel

Give Out Creek Shortlisted for the 2016
Arthur Ellis Award for Best Unpublished Crime Novel

T0170949

LUCKY JACK ROAD

Library and Archives Canada Cataloguing in Publication

Title: Lucky Jack Road / J.G. Toews.
Names: Toews, Judy, author.
Description: Series statement: A Stella Mosconi mystery | Sequel to: Give Out Creek.

Identifiers: Canadiana (print) 20200196537 | Canadiana (ebook) 20200196545 |
ISBN 9781771615082 (softcover) | ISBN 9781771615099 (PDF) |
ISBN 9781771615105 (HTML) | ISBN 9781771615112 (Kindle)
Classification: LCC PS8639.O3885 L83 2018 | DDC C813/.6—dc23

Published by Mosaic Press, Oakville, Ontario, Canada, 2020.

MOSAIC PRESS, Publishers

Copyright © Judy Toews 2020

Printed and bound in Canada

Cover design by PolyStudio (www.polystudio.ca)

Author photo courtesy of Lisa Seyfried Photography

ONTARIO ARTS COUNCIL
CONSEIL DES ARTS DE L'ONTARIO
an Ontario government agency
un organisme du gouvernement de l'Ontario

We acknowledge the Ontario Arts Council
for their support of our publishing program

Funded by the Government of Canada
Financé par le gouvernement du Canada | Canada

MOSAIC PRESS
1252 Speers Road, Unit 2
Oakville, Ontario L6L 5N9
phone: (905) 825-2130
info@mosaic-press.com

LUCKY JACK ROAD

J.G. TOEWS

A STELLA MOSCONI MYSTERY

For David

1

HE SCOOPED HER UP in his arms and threatened to toss her in the pond, laughing when she shrieked and clutched at him, turning her head to avoid his big open mouth. She clawed at his face. He dropped her. Touched his cheek and stared dumbly at the trace of blood on his fingers.

Coughing and spluttering, she scrambled up and out of the pond, water streaming from her clothes. "Bad girl," he said, catching up, slamming her against the big shade tree, his hand on her throat nearly crushing her windpipe. She tried to yell but choked on the words. Kneed him and he howled and let go.

She ran for her bike. "What the fuck?" he called after her, as if the whole thing had been nothing, a minor misunderstanding. She pushed off, careened down the hill and across town barely touching the brakes until she reached her street, her house.

Her mother was on her knees in the garden. "What happened to you?"

"Nothing. Rode through a couple puddles."

"Look at you – you're a mess. Where's your helmet? I'm not buying you another one."

"That's okay," she said, leaning on the handlebar to catch her breath. "I know where it is."

2

Twenty-two years later...

STELLA GRABBED HER BICYCLE and raced to the courthouse to get the story when the verdict in the logging standoff came in. Media types from as far away as Vancouver jockeyed for position as protesters waved anti-logging placards at passing cars. No sooner had she parked the bike and pulled out her camera than – *bam* – the big wooden doors swung open and men in suits stepped out, flanking the defendant. He bellowed to his supporters, raised his arms in a V for victory. Stella nailed the shot, then jumped into the fray to catch quotes from the lawyers.

Minutes later, she was back on the bike, pumping up Stanley Street standing up. Wheeling a sharp right onto Nelson's main drag, she cursed under her breath. Jack Ballard, the last guy she wanted to see, was sitting outside the Dominion Café. He'd tipped back on his chair to lift his tanned, chiseled face to the sun, black curls grazing the collar of a scarlet bike shirt open to the waist. Long, muscular legs stretched halfway to the curb where a high-end mountain bike leaned against a Victorian lamp post.

Eyes straight ahead, she upped her pace.

"Yo, Stella."

Goddamn.

"Lookin' good," he called as she sped past. Taunting her.

Most days it seemed everyone in town loved Jack Ballard, everyone except Stella. She'd known him forever, but thought she'd seen the last of him when she left Nelson straight out of high school. But she'd found her way back, settled in with a family and job. Readjusting to the small-town fishbowl had not been easy, though she had managed to fly under Ballard's radar for a while. Now it seemed every time she turned around, there he was.

Shoving Jack Ballard to the back of her mind, she carried on to the old railway station that was home to the *Nelson Times*. Upstairs, editor Patrick Taft was holding a draft of the front page. "Give me the camera," he said as she rushed into the newsroom. "I'll size the photo while you fill in the blanks in your story." Stella handed over the camera and woke up her computer. "Nice," Patrick said, clicking through the images. "This the guy who chained himself to a bulldozer? Looking pretty chuffed now. But that verdict could have gone either way."

"Definitely." Stella transcribed the lawyer quotes and forwarded her copy.

"Visser," Patrick called across the room to the paper's only other reporter. "Check out this front page. This is how it's done."

In her head, Stella Mosconi did a little victory dance. No sense letting Ballard spoil her day.

* * *

Joe never tired of the view of Elephant Mountain through his classroom window. If he squinted, he could make out the CBC tower up top where the aspen and birch were still in full leaf. At his previous school on the Coast, he'd be sucking stale air in a science lab in the bowels of a building that dated back to the 1920s. Now he only had to look up from his desk to drink in an outstanding panorama of mountains, lake, and sky. Within minutes he could be hiking, cycling, or out paddling on the lake. And as a newly minted volunteer with Nelson Search and Rescue, he had upped the ante. Going after lost hikers and skiers in places that fed his soul – it couldn't get any better.

Joe graded the last Biology 12 lab report from the stack on his desk and locked his classroom door. If no one waylaid him at the office, he'd have time to stop by his favourite bike shop on the way home.

At Ballard's Cycles the front door was wide open, the owner scrolling through pictures of bikes on his computer. Jack Ballard had cycled professionally in his late teens and twenties, making a living doing what ordinary schmucks only dream about. After retiring from competition he'd come back to his hometown to set up shop. For all the things he'd done and places he'd seen, Jack seemed happy enough to kick back in sleepy old Nelson. For bike nuts like Joe you couldn't ask for a better guy to run a bike store. Anything you needed – support for a cause, a prize for a race – Jack was your go-to guy. Now he looked up from his screen and boomed, "Joe. What's happenin,' man?"

"Just another day in paradise. But here's a question: What can I put my ten-year-old on that'll challenge him without freaking out his mother?"

"Hey, happy wife, happy life." Jack sauntered out from behind the counter, a master of timing, never rushed, never stressed. "Speaking of. How's she doing, your lady? She blasted past me on her bike today. Every time I see her, man, those legs are working overtime to spin those wheels."

"She's good," Joe said, squelching a flicker of jealousy. Ballard had a way of turning the conversation to Stella. But then in a town the size of Nelson they would have known each other growing up. "Thing is, with less than two months left in the season," Joe continued, "she won't be keen to buy the kid a new bike. He's ready for a real technical ride though, champing at the bit."

"I hear ya," Jack said. "And I can cut you a deal, my friend. Our end-of-season sale starts early this year, a birthday gift to myself. Hey, you and Stella – you guys free Friday night? Party at my place. Help me celebrate the Big 4-0." Jack's cell rang and he reached for it. "Yo, babe," he said, then covered the mouthpiece and turned back to Joe. "Take a look at that red and gold stunner on the sidewalk. Your kid'll love it. I guarantee it."

Joe went outside. The all-terrain bike with front and rear suspension was a stunner all right, as was the price tag. Matt would be all over it. Stella, not so much.

Back in the store, Jack was still on his phone. He winked at Joe. "Jeez, babe," he said to the caller. "It's a zoo in here. Haven't taken a break all day. Better you go pick it up anyway – make sure they sized it right, yeah? One sec, okay?" To Joe, he said, "So?"

"Nice machine. Bit over the budget though."

"Hold on," Jack said. "I got another idea." He ended his call and pointed to a fat-tire bike that hung suspended in the front window. "Now that's too heavy for a ten-year-old but I can get you a lighter model, no sweat. A fat bike won't break the bank yet the wow factor is there, know what I'm saying? Your boy'll be able to take it anywhere. Hell, he can ride it when the snow flies."

Joe laughed. "Now I want one."

"Hey, do it. Meantime, don't forget: Friday night. Be there. You and the lovely Stella."

As Joe left the shop, he almost bumped into a dark-haired teenager who looked vaguely familiar. "Sorry about that," he said, taking a closer look. "Do I know you from the school?"

"Don't think so," the boy said. "I was there for a bit last year. But now I'm, ah, doing my senior year online?"

"Well, good luck with that," Joe said. "Give me a shout if I can help. I'm Mosconi, by the way, science and biology. What was your name?"

"Kieran. Uh, thanks." The boy loped to the back where he and Jack greeted each other with some sort of convoluted handshake.

Joe was quick to forget the kid as he drove home, April Wine blaring on the sound system, his mind on fat-tire bikes and Jack's party invitation as he tapped out the rhythm on his steering wheel. A relative newcomer to Nelson, he was flattered to be on Jack's A-list, if indeed he was. No mention of an address for the party but then everyone knew where Jack lived. It occurred to Joe "the lovely Stella" might have had a crush on Jack back in the day – maybe Ballard had the hots for her too. Thoughts that damped down Joe's mood as he crossed the bridge over Kootenay Lake. He couldn't see them as a teen couple though. Stella would have been too wholesome for Jack, and even as a kid he would have attracted the foxy girls at school.

* * *

Stella Mosconi was at her desk hammering out the first instalment of a two-part story about panhandling in the downtown core, a concern that had a lot of people in Nelson riled. She wasn't sure where she stood on the issue, personally. In her humble opinion, everyone had a right to be downtown, but safety concerns had been raised at City Council. She was checking her notes from an interview with the mayor when banter from the sales office leaked into the newsroom. At a burst of laughter, she got up to shut the connecting door and caught a glimpse of Jack Ballard, likely there to order a display ad for his next bike sale. Typical of Ballard to appear in person when an email would have done, but then the sales staff showed him the sort of respect normally reserved for pillars of the community.

Minutes later the newsroom door flew open and Stella's fellow reporter Jade Visser paused on the threshold to speak to Ballard on his way out. "How's the new bike?" he roared. *Did the guy even have an inside voice?*

"Love it," Jade said. "Gosh, with all your customers I can't believe you remember my little purchase."

"You kidding me? I personally made the match. That bike was built for you. Fits you like a glove."

A tinkling laugh from Jade Visser. "You know what? I almost believe you. The suspension is incredible. I can ride it anywhere."

"Fantastic." Ballard followed her into the newsroom. "Stella, hey," he said, his voice softening. "How you doing? I hope Joe told you about the party."

She glanced up from her computer. "Oh, yeah, the party. Don't think I can make it."

"What?" he said. "You gotta be there, right Jade? Help me out here."

"I think the lady's blowing you off, Jack," Jade said.

"Jeez, you guys ganging up on me?" Ballard propped his well-muscled rear on the corner of an empty desk, settling in. "Gimme a break, eh? I'm turning forty – I need all the help I can get. Listen, Stella. Your old man tell you we had a tête-à-tête about a fat-tire bike for your son?"

"He mentioned it," Stella said. "Um, I hate to be rude. But I'm on deadline, so –"

"And here's me, barging in. My bad." Jack managed to look rueful without budging an inch. "I want to talk to you too about a bike for your boy though. How 'bout you stop by the shop when you're done here?"

Without looking up, she said, "No can do, Jack."

"Stella, c'mon. You're the cyclist in the family. Don't get me wrong – Joe knows his stuff. But you and me, it's in our blood from growing up here. We speak the same language, know what I'm saying? Promise you'll stop by. Promise and I'll get outta your hair."

"Bye-bye, Jack."

"Okay, okay, you're busy. I can take a hint. We'll chat at the party." He stood up to leave and included Jade in a big smile. "You ladies take care now."

As the door closed behind him, Jade clamped a hand over her mouth to stifle her laughter.

"Was I too mean?" Stella said.

"The meaner you got, the more he grovelled. God, Stella, he is *so* flipping into you."

"Please," Stella said. "He's into whoever'll buy a bike from him."

"You don't see the way he looks at you?" Jade said. "Or you don't want to talk about it? I understand if you don't want to talk about it. I mean, you're married and Jack has a girlfriend. You met her? She's what my grandpa would call a pistol. I heard Jack popped the question. Danielle Stone – know anything about her?"

"Hey, did I mention I'm on deadline?" Stella said, keeping her tone light. She was pounding on the keyboard now, hoping Jade wouldn't come close enough to see the gibberish on her screen.

* * *

Later, on the ride home, heady aromas from an Indian restaurant on Baker Street got Stella thinking about what to cook for dinner. Curry seemed too ambitious. She mentally ran through the contents of her fridge, trying to recall how much leftover chilli there was and how long it had been there. The last thing on her mind was a stop at Ballard's Cycles, but the boss himself was out front by a rack of bicycles, talking to a pharmacist from the drugstore. Sadly, Ballard spotted her too. "Stella," he cried, as if she'd recently returned from the dead. "You're here. Fantastic." He stepped into the street to seize her bike and all but dragged her into the shop, the pharmacist nearly forgotten. "Take it for a spin, man," he said, over his shoulder. "Kayla here'll hang up your white coat and grab you a helmet."

"Great to see you still riding, Stella," he said, leading her by the hand to the fat-tire bikes on display. "I mean it. Makes me feel like time's stood still. The two of us still back in school."

He seemed so needy she found herself thawing a little. Could it be he only wanted to please her, to try to make amends for the past? Her gut said nothing was ever that simple, not when her body still held the memory of him pawing at her. She cleared her throat. "So, you'd put a ten-year-old on a bike like this?"

Ballard held up his hands, palms out. "I know what you're thinking. But a boy like yours? Absolutely. Now correct me if I'm wrong, but your son's a talented cyclist, a keener. Kid like him needs to keep up his skills over the winter. Know what I'm saying?"

The bell over the shop door jingled and Ballard's attention shifted to the stunning blonde crossing the threshold. She was dressed in black yoga tights and a partly unzipped, sparkly gold top, a pouf of platinum hair contrasting with her bold dark brows and pouty red lips. This would be Danielle Stone, the famous live-in girlfriend, whose beautiful face twisted into a scowl as she approached. Rumour had it she and Ballard had met on the mountain bike circuit and she'd followed him to Nelson from Cincinnati. It was hard to picture her blasting down a gnarly trail on a mountain bike, but as a reporter Stella had learned how much people can surprise you. "Hey, babe," Ballard said. "You two met? Stella, Danielle. Danielle, Stella."

"Nice to meet you," Stella said, offering her hand.

"Hey," Danielle said, ignoring Stella's hand, her eyes fixed on Ballard. "Are we going for an early dinner or what? The movie starts at seven."

"Jeez," he said. "Whole thing skipped my mind. Why don't you go grab us a table at the diner? I'll join you in a sec."

Danielle took on an aggressive stance, feet a shoulder width apart, hands on hips. It was getting easier to see her as a competitive cyclist. Stella found herself standing up a little taller too. "I know what a sec means," Danielle said. "I'll be halfway through my first cocktail before you tear yourself away. Maybe Kayla could help uh . . ." She fluttered her hand in Stella's direction.

"Stella," Ballard said, firmly. "Stella Mosconi, she's an old friend of mine. She's a reporter at the paper. Listen babe, Stella and I got some business to discuss. Be a sweetheart and go grab us a table."

"I don't think so." Danielle plucked a chartreuse jersey from a display table, held it to her chest, and tossed it aside. "C'mon, baby. Chop-chop." Impeccably manicured fingers caressed Ballard's neck. "Let Kayla look after the customer. That's what you pay her for."

Stella was already backing away. "I should run," she told Ballard. "We can do this another time."

"Gonna hold you to that, Stella," he said, rushing to swing open the door for her.

But Danielle Stone almost knocked her aside to sashay through the doorway first.

3

IT WAS FRIDAY AFTERNOON and the newsroom was eerily quiet. Patrick had disappeared and Jade was watering a jumbo philodendron that nobody liked. "I wonder what you'd have to do to kill this thing?" she said.

"You'd have to stop feeding and watering it for a start," Stella said. She was fuming about the previous day's encounter with Danielle Stone as she tied up loose ends at the close of her work week. What *was* the woman's problem? They'd never even spoken before the incident in the bike shop, yet she had treated Stella like dirt. Joe was still pressuring her to attend Jack Ballard's party but after the run-in with Stone she was even less inclined to go.

Jade Visser broke into her thoughts to gossip about the birthday boy. "Can you believe he's *forty*? He seems so young." Jade actually *was* young. Twenty-five tops. Getting no response from Stella, she added, "Or is forty young to you? You guys went to school together, right?"

"He was two years ahead of me," Stella said, annoyed at herself for rising to the bait. "Don't you have time to copy edit Patrick's editorial for Monday?"

"I suppose," Jade said. "Where is he anyway?"

"No idea. The managing editor doesn't have to explain himself to me."

Major eye roll from Jade, but she set down the watering can and brought up the editorial on her computer screen. "He's probably duking it out with the publisher. I heard she wants to cut staff. Have you heard anything?"

Stella shrugged. "Haven't given it much thought." A whopper, but Jade left it alone.

Stella made minor changes to a submitted piece about a benefit concert and cropped the accompanying photo. The day was winding down. She happily would have stayed late if her story list had justified it, any excuse to sidestep the party.

Joe called to pester her again. He'd spoken to Cassidy Pickering, their sons' much-admired swim instructor, to see if she could pinch-hit for their regular sitter, who was already booked. He told Stella he could pick up Cassidy and take her out to the cabin, then swing by the *Times*. He'd bring her something nice to wear.

Stella finally caved.

Later, in a closet-like restroom down the hall from the newsroom, she peeled off her cycling shorts and jersey, slipped into skinny jeans and a blush pink pullover, and touched up her makeup. An adult night out. Had the party been for anyone other than Ballard she would have clicked her heels together.

* * *

Cassidy Pickering was crossing her fingers the babysitting job for the Mosconis would be a go. At least then she might hear something about Jack Ballard's party when Mr. Mosconi drove her home. By rights, she and her mom should be front and centre at the celebration.

Cassidy knew for a fact Jack Ballard was her biological father, even if no one on the planet was willing to admit it. She held the proof in her own two hands: a secret scrapbook full of faded snapshots and poems her mom had copied or clipped from magazines as a teenager. The poems were mostly lame. What interested Cassidy were the margin notes, handwritten in a code that was easy to crack. The transposed initials "BJ" must have stood for Jack Ballard – her mother had been crazy about him.

Luckily, they had never lost touch. Last week at the farmers' market, Jack had invited her to his party. "At least stop by, Karen," he'd said. "You'll know a tonne of people. Lot of the old gang is still around."

Cassidy had begged her to go, but she only said, "You know me – I hate big crowds." Cassidy hoped she hadn't given up on Jack. She'd recently met a guy online and was talking about having him over to the house. Whenever her mom mentioned him, Cassidy changed the subject.

Her legal father had died working on the trains when she was a baby, so she'd grown up without a dad. Kids teased her in elementary

school, the crueller ones calling her a bastard. Cassidy closed her eyes
and pictured Jack and her mother as a couple. Apart from making
her mom happy, Jack would be such a great dad. He would cycle
and swim and work out with her. There'd be no end of parties and
getaways to cool places. No daughter of Jack Ballard's would have to
live out her teenage years in excruciating boredom.

Cassidy had been born seven months after her parents' wedding
day, and at age fifteen she no longer bought the family myth about
a premature birth. Premature baby girls don't grow into teenage
athletes almost six feet tall. Like Jack, Cassidy had long legs and was
good at sports. But the clincher was a page of photos from her mom's
twenty-fourth birthday, an event that took place *exactly* nine months
before Cassidy was born. Jack appeared in as many birthday pictures
as her legal father did and in every photo, he smiled at her pretty
mother as if they were the only two people alive.

Well, today was the big day – his fortieth birthday – and Cassidy
had a plan. First, she rushed home right after school to wash and blow-
dry her hair, which took forever now that it reached the middle of her
back. Then, before her mom got back from work, she left the house
and headed for Ballard's Cycles on foot. It would have been faster to
take her bike, but she didn't want to wreck her hair with a helmet.

At the store, Jack greeted her with his usual ginormous smile.
"Hey there," he said. "Cassidy, right? Man, you are the spitting
image of your mother as a teenager. Seeing you two gorgeous gals at
the market the other day really took me back."

"My mom's the reason I'm here," Cassidy said, feeling herself
redden at the compliment. "Her birthday's coming up and I know
she would love a bike, her being a fun-loving person and, like, way
more youthful than most women her age."

That made him laugh. "Yeah, Karen's great. So, would this be a
gift from you and your grandparents?"

"No, just me," Cassidy said. "I thought if you had a bike that
wasn't too expensive I could swing it myself."

"Good on you." He led her across the store. "This hybrid's a
beauty, isn't it? Lightweight but tough – know what I'm saying?
Great on any surface – roads, trails. The tag says five hundred, but
for you, let's say three ninety-nine. Would that fit your budget? You
want to try it out?"

"No, that's okay. I know my mom would like it, and that discount would be amazing. But I was wondering . . . do you maybe have some kind of instalment plan? I could put two hundred down and pay the rest before Christmas. I'm planning to get an after-school job."

"You remind me of myself at your age," he said, making her blush again. "You want something, you make it happen. Tell you what. You put down the two hundred and pay me the balance when you have it. Before Christmas, after Christmas, whatever. How does that sound?"

"Awesome. That's very generous of you, Mr. Ballard."

"Jack. Please."

"Well, okay," she said. "Jack. Thanks. Thanks a lot."

"You want to ride it home? I can lend you a helmet."

"I'd rather leave it here for now, if that's okay. I could call you about picking it up. I want to surprise my mom on her birthday."

"Hey, I'll deliver it myself. Just make arrangements with Kayla over there."

It was like he had read her mind.

* * *

Jack Ballard's birthday party was held at what locals called the big house, a chalet that his father Richard built at the top of Lucky Jack Road. The steep, winding road had begun as a prospector's trail, one of many that criss-crossed the mountains in the mining heyday early in the last century. It wrapped around a water feature known simply as "the pond," a dammed-up stream that served as a private reservoir for the property.

As Joe pulled into the driveway, Stella couldn't help contrasting what must have been the small footprint of an old miner's shack with that of the extravagant holdings of the Ballard family. Apart from the imposing timber-frame chalet, all three levels ablaze with light, there was a massive garage no doubt full of cars, snowmobiles, skis, bikes, and what-have-you. Above the garage sat a studio apartment Jack's father had built for him when he turned sixteen.

Jack wasn't his real name. His mother had named him Charles, after her father, then soon left him with *his* father to return to her roots, plus an old love interest, in Oregon. Richard Ballard called his son Jack, Lucky Jack the inevitable nickname, because the boy was not only privileged, he was good-looking, athletic, and smart in ways that count.

Stella felt sheepish turning up at the party after telling Ballard she wasn't going to show. While Joe attached himself to a mountaineering crowd in the front room, she slipped out to the main deck to watch the lights come on in the town below. She'd just buttoned up her denim jacket, crossing her arms against the evening chill, when Ballard materialized in black jeans and a grey linen shirt, his dark hair still damp from the shower. "Oh, hi," she said, instinctively looking for an escape hatch. "Happy birthday."

"You came," he said, tenderly. "But hey, you're shivering." He tried to wrap his arm around her but she glided out of reach.

"I'm good," she said, edging toward the oversized French doors. "We should go inside though. Your guests . . ." She shoved open a door and forced a smile over her shoulder as she joined a knot of women in the kitchen. Bottles of wine and spirits cluttered a mammoth granite-topped island overseen by a bartender who bustled between the island and a sideboard stocked with tubs of Nelson Brewing Company beer. Servers in black pants and shirts circulated among the guests with trays of fancy appetizers.

Ballard followed Stella in and asked if anyone had seen Danielle. His stepmother Pamela, elegant in snug, bronze-toned pants and a cream silk shirt, said she hadn't come over from the studio yet.

More guests started to arrive. By eleven o'clock, the number of party goers had swelled to about one hundred when a tall, gaunt woman wobbled toward the drinks station in killer heels. Like the servers, she was dressed entirely in black, but there was no mistaking her for hired help with her shaggy, blue-black hair and dark-rimmed eyes. The bartender seemed eager to please, but she declined a glass and helped herself to a frosty can of beer. Jack must have noticed the exchange. He touched her elbow and steered her to a quiet alcove, but when he whispered in her ear, the woman in black stared straight ahead and shrugged off his hand.

Danielle Stone chose that moment to make an entrance. "Hey," she said to no one in particular, her heavy-lidded gaze sweeping the crowd. She wore a sheer muslin shirt over a slinky, low-cut body suit with matching high-heeled boots in silver tooled leather. The hefty diamond solitaire on her left hand glinted under the pot lights as she brushed back a thick strand of platinum hair, prompting several women to squeal over the ring.

Jack's buddies pushed him up onto a straight-back chair and he would have toppled if Joe hadn't steadied him. "See, this is what happens when you turn forty," he said, to general laughter. "So, thanks for coming, people. But birthday-shmirthday, I guess we got something bigger to celebrate." His voice caught and he paused a moment. "What can I say? This lady and me – we're gettin' hitched."

"A toast," someone cried. "To Jack and Danielle."

A disjointed chorus of "To Jack and Danielle" rang out as guests refilled glasses and swarmed the flustered host and his new fiancée. Stella wondered how long the lovebirds had been living together. Danielle looked younger than Jack, late twenties, maybe.

Now Jack's father – a craggier version of his son with a leathery tan and curly grey hair – struggled to get up onto a chair. Richard appeared close to tears himself as he began a long rambling speech about the son who had filled his life with joy, making him prouder than any man had a right to be. "So now my boy is going to take a wife and – can I tell?" He grinned down at Danielle and she glanced quickly at Jack. Seemingly oblivious to Danielle's reaction, Richard crowed, "There'll be a child in the house again. Isn't that wonderful?" The news brought happy murmurs from the crowd, along with more hugs and backslapping and toasts. The woman in black helped herself to another can of beer and teetered out of the room.

Pamela Ballard smiled indulgently at her husband, seemingly at ease in her lovely home. She was one of those ageless women with delicate features and flawless skin, always beautifully groomed, always gracious. Richard carried on, comfortable now up on his perch. "With the little one coming, maybe Pamela and I should make way for the future. Let Jack move back into the big house with his bride. What do you say, Pammie? You're always talking about downsizing, going off to see the world. Should we trade digs with these kids? You and me move into the studio?" Pamela's smile became strained.

More women clustered around Danielle to admire the ring and Jack poured shots for all takers. New guests arrived and the engagement announcement was repeated. Doors were flung open as the house got warmer. Stella spotted Joe across the room and waved; he raised his beer to her. Then she skirted through the crowd to use the powder room just in time to see the woman in black rush inside and noisily bolt the door. Ten minutes passed and the mystery woman hadn't emerged. Stella gave up on waiting; she was ready to go home anyway. She was in the foyer searching for her husband's jacket when Jack stormed by, frog-marching a young guy toward the front door.

A party crasher?

Stella did a double take. What in God's name was Kieran Corcoran doing there? She hadn't realized he was even back in town. Jack caught her watching as he came inside. "Stella! Havin' a good time?" he said, putting on his happy face. "Hey, c'mon, let me freshen that drink."

"No, that's okay," she said. "But that guy you just escorted out – I think I know him."

"Just a kid I kinda took under my wing. I warned him tonight was adults-only. No underage drinkers allowed."

"But it was Kieran, right? I thought he was still at the Coast."

"He *was* down there – doing time at some reform school." Ballard grabbed a bottle of Pinot Noir and refilled her glass to the brim. An old grandfather clock began to chime for midnight.

"Youth custody centre," Stella said, ditching her glass on a side table. "They're called youth custody centres now. So how long have you known Kieran?"

"Couple months? Never mind the kid. Let's sit down and catch up."

"Not tonight, Jack. It's late. The babysitter will be looking for us." Her head began to throb in time with the chiming clock.

"Stella, you kidding me? You can't go – it's barely midnight." He shook a beefy finger at her. "You've been avoiding me, young lady. Look, maybe I was a tool back in the day, but that was a long time ago and I never stopped liking you. I never shoulda let you go – seriously. Come and wish me a happy birthday. For old times' sake." He tried to pull her into an embrace.

"Uh, happy birthday," she said, using Joe's jacket as a shield.

He put an arm across the doorway. "I know what this is about, you know. Don't think I don't just 'cause I had a couple drinks. You think I'm the same ol' party boy. But now I'm gonna be a father and all, I better fuckin' grow up, know what I'm saying? Be more like Joe.

Climb mountains like a real Kootenay man, eh? I don't even ride like I used to, tripping back and forth to the coffee shop is nothing. Oh Stella, I've gotten so fuckin' soft."

So this was Jack doing self-pity. His little speech did nothing to soften her heart. "C'mon, Jack. You're all right. Listen, I have to go." She tried to duck under his arm but he blocked her like a drunken linebacker.

"Hold on now, Stella," he said. "C'mon, give me a sec. One second of your *val-u-ble* time. Your opinion counts, know what I'm sayin'? If you tell me to go climb a mountain, I'm gonna go climb a mountain."

"I'm not going to tell you what to do, Jack. Now I have to –"

"No, Stella, c'mon. Don't go. You don't have to go. You tell me what I gotta do to win your respect. I'm not trying to cut in on Joe. Joe's a good guy. I jus' want your respect."

"Maybe we'll talk about climbing mountains another time, okay? Now –"

"I'm gonna hold you to that, Stella. You and me, we'll grab a coffee."

"Sure, but right now. . ." How to get past without having to touch him? Even surrounded by people, she was beginning to feel panicky. She scanned the crowd for Joe and couldn't see him. After a couple of deep breaths, she plotted her escape.

"Promise we'll do that, Stella," Jack said. "We got history, right? Jeez, at first, I didn't even know you were back in Nelson. To me you were always Stella Hart. Who was this mysterious Stella Mosconi working at the *Times,* eh? But one look at you on your bike and there was no mistaking the girl I knew."

So her married name had been her cover these past months. "Gotta go, Jack," she said. A woman with tattooed arms and shoulders appeared and Stella smiled and said, "Hi, did you want to get past?"

"No, that's okay," she said, retreating. "Just looking for someone."

Jack didn't acknowledge the guest. "Stella. Promise we'll talk real soon."

"Yeah, sure," she said. "We'll talk."

"Promise."

"I promise," she said, lying through her teeth. He dropped his arm.

Now all she had to do was find Joe and get the hell out of there.

4

THE DAY THAT FOLLOWED Jack Ballard's birthday party was a gloomy Saturday in September. Rain fell in sheets outside the Mosconi cabin, turning the lake a dull slate colour and blurring the view of velvety green hills on the far shore. Joe cranked up the volume on the TV to hear a football game over the noise of rain pounding on the metal roof. In the tiny kitchen, Stella whirred bananas and raspberries in a blender to make smoothies for her sons. Ten-year-old Matt and eight-year-old Nicky were sprawled underfoot creating elaborate boats from untold quantities of Lego. Nicky had headed off to see if his boat would float in the bathroom sink when the landline rang and he picked up. "For you, Mom," he said. Stella gave her hands a quick wipe on a tea towel.

"Stella?" The voice on the line was strong and self-assured. "Pamela Ballard."

This was a first. "Pamela, hi."

"Listen, I hate to trouble you, but Jack has taken off and we don't know where he is. I'm certain there's a reasonable explanation, but Danielle is beside herself. She woke up at noon to find him gone. Vanished. None of us has seen him since last night. The cars are all accounted for and so is his bike. Danielle claims he had a long talk with you just before you and your husband left the party. Afterward she thought Jack seemed, well, distracted. The girl tends to dramatize, but I thought I should try you. He's a grown man of course." She gave a short laugh.

"I guess you've called the store." Stella stepped into the bedroom to escape the sound of the TV. She glanced at her watch; it was 1:15 p.m.

"He's not there and his employees haven't seen him since the party. He hasn't been to his favourite coffee shop either, and I've left three messages on his mobile. Danielle couldn't rouse any of his buddies. Sleeping it off, I guess. Where on earth would he go in this rain? I don't suppose you have any idea?"

Stella didn't care what Jack Ballard was up to, but she cared about Pamela. His stepmother had been kind to her when she'd visited the big house as a teenager. She'd asked about her interests, offered refreshments, never seemed frazzled or cranky like her own mother. "It might have been the booze, but when we talked last night he kept going on about climbing mountains," Stella said, "although I think that was more of some mid-life goal than a plan for today. As you said, the weather hasn't been great. Sorry I can't be more helpful."

"No, don't apologize. I knew this would be a long shot." Pamela's voice quavered despite her brave words.

"Wait a second, Pamela," Stella said. "Let's say Jack did decide to go hiking in the rain. The trail up Elephant Mountain would be an obvious choice. Close to town and easy to bail if the weather got too intense. You mentioned his bike was still in the garage, but does he have an old one? Joe takes a beater if he's going to leave a bike at a trailhead."

"Oh, now Jack might have done that. And our garage is full of old bikes. A note would have been nice, but that's not Jack, is it? Never mind. You're right, he's probably off on some jaunt to shake off last night. You've reassured me, Stella. Thank you."

* * *

At 2:06 p.m. Joe's mobile vibrated. He muted the TV and took the call; a recorded page-out from Nelson Search and Rescue alerted him to an incident on Elephant Mountain. An adult male had gone over a cliff at Pulpit Rock, landing on the rocky slope below. A trail runner had called 9-1-1. Adrenalin pumping, Joe fumbled to press the correct button to confirm he was on his way to the rallying place at the base of Elephant Mountain.

"SAR," he announced to the family, jumping to his feet. "A guy fell over the edge at Pulpit Rock."

"What?" Stella followed him to the closet where he kept his gear. "Who falls off Pulpit Rock? People take their babies and toddlers up there."

"First time for everything," Joe said.

"You gonna save his life, Dad?" Matt said. "Do you think he'll be all covered in blood?"

"Don't *you* fall, Daddy," Nicky chimed in. "I don't want you to get all covered in blood."

"Don't worry, guys," Joe said, reaching into the closet. "We'll look after whoever fell. Nothing'll happen to me." He knocked coats off hooks and scattered shoes and boots as he hauled out his ready-to-go backpack.

Stella dropped her voice. "I just got off the phone with Pamela less than an hour ago. She's been looking all over for Jack. You don't think it was him, do you? He might still have been drunk this morning. God, his parents will be going out of their minds."

"Hold on, hold on," Joe said calmly, although his fingers trembled as he laced up his boots. "It's not Jack. Jack was more likely hungover than drunk this morning. He's probably at a buddy's place watching the game. Forgot to call home – happens to the best of us."

"Mom, can you help me?" Nicky said.

"In a minute, honey." She turned back Joe. "Pamela and Danielle must have rung all the usual suspects."

"Don't worry about it," Joe said. "I gotta run."

"This won't stay on!" Nicky said, flinging his boat on the floor. "Matt has all the good pieces."

"Do not," Matt said. "Don't be a baby."

"Hey, guys, there's plenty for both of you," Stella said, getting down on her hands and knees to sift through the Lego. To Joe, she said, "Call as soon as you know anything, okay? And stay safe."

"Always. Bye, boys. Love ya!" He sprinted to the car.

Joe tossed his pack into the back of their old Pathfinder and spun up the drive, but at the highway, he made a point of slowing down. Rule number one for a SAR volunteer: Don't risk your neck or anyone else's by racing to a search site. Nearing the big orange bridge over Kootenay Lake, Joe made a right onto Johnstone Road and proceeded to the approach to Elephant Mountain. The overflow parking area was full, a ragtag bunch of hikers all over the place. Ahead, two SAR trucks, two fire department vehicles, an ambulance, and a police cruiser occupied the right side of the two-lane street, now closed to traffic. At the trailhead, a firefighter was stopping civilians from going up the mountain. A second was directing road traffic and wouldn't let Joe through. He made a U-turn among the crush of bystanders then backtracked half a kilometre to park his SUV on a marginally safe bit of shoulder. Praying he hadn't forgotten anything, he strapped on his ten-kilo backpack and walked briskly up the road, pushing his way through the crowd.

* * *

At the Mosconi cabin, competition for the Lego had gotten out of hand and Stella made a deal with her squabbling sons. If they apologized to each other and returned every tiny plastic block to the appropriate bin, she would take them to the climbing walls in town. It was the best rainy-day activity she could think of and always a hit with the boys.

Near the bridge into town, there was a jam at the turnoff to Johnstone Road. Cars had been abandoned, the occupants heading off on foot. "What are all those people doing?" Nicky said.

"I guess the road is closed because of the accident at Pulpit Rock," Stella said. "I bet your dad had to park back here too."

They were crossing the big orange bridge over the lower part of Kootenay Lake when Matt yelled, "Hey. Cassidy."

The cyclist had her head down and was moving fast. "Yeah, that's her," Stella said. "We'll stop and say hello." At the south end of the span she steered into a pullout. The car had barely come to a stop when the boys jumped out to flag down their swim teacher.

The girl was pale and teary-eyed when she came to a stop. Stella said, "Cassidy, what's wrong?"

"There's been a terrible accident," she said, choking on the words.

"We heard about it," Stella said. "Joe was called out by Search and Rescue. Did you see him back there?"

"No, but I saw the person that fell," she said, between sobs. "Nobody else was around. I called 9-1-1."

"Oh my gosh," Stella said, putting an arm around the girl. "But there must be plenty of people around now. Didn't anyone offer to drive you home?"

"A fireman asked my name then I just got on my bike and took off."

"For goodness' sakes, you're soaking wet. Get in the car. You too, guys. C'mon, let's go. I'll put the bike on the rack."

As she got back into the driver's seat, Stella heard Nicky say, "Was the guy all covered in blood?"

"Zip it, Nick." She glared at him in the rear-view mirror. "Cassidy has had a big shock and we're going to *quietly* drive her home."

At the Pickering residence, Stella told the boys to stay in the car. Cassidy got out and banged on the front door, collapsing into her mother's arms the instant it was opened. "Oh, honey, what happened?" Karen Pickering said. She looked over her daughter's head at Stella and invited her inside.

"No, that's okay, Karen," Stella said. "I have Matt and Nicky with me. There was an accident up at Pulpit Rock. Someone went over the edge and Cassidy had to make the 9-1-1 call. Is there anything I can do? Anyone I should call for you?"

"I think we're good, Stella," Karen said. "Thanks for bringing her home. I'll get my mother to come over later. Right now, I better get Cass out of these wet clothes and into a warm bath."

When Stella got behind the wheel, Matt and Nicky were roughhousing in the car and she waited for them to settle down before she drove to the climbing centre on the college campus. There she found a place to sit and watch the boys scale the walls while she tried to make sense of what had happened at Pulpit Rock.

* * *

At the base of the mountain, Joe signed in at the Search and Rescue command truck and joined the other volunteers for a briefing by the Ground Search Team Leader. The SAR team was to follow the trail up three hundred and twenty vertical metres to the place where the victim had gone over the edge. Rain had fallen almost continuously for several hours, the leader warned. Keeping their boots dry was going to be next to impossible.

Joe shifted his pack – his shirt was already sticking to his back – and fell into line alongside a fellow volunteer the others called Mo.

Monique Thibaudeau was a petite woman, forty-ish, with a reputation as a keen mountaineer. Her slightly weathered complexion was likely the result of an outdoorsy lifestyle, or maybe she just didn't wear makeup. Either way, Joe respected her. She was fit, experienced, and by all accounts, over-the-top dedicated to Search and Rescue.

Today Mo didn't have a lot to say, at least not to him. She seemed more interested in the rope crew and the guy carrying the litter, a two-piece clamshell that would be used to transport the victim.

At the upper rallying place, first responders from the fire department milled about while a cop from the Nelson Police Department took charge. Joe recognized him as Ben McKean, the lead in a recent murder investigation. Stella had managed to get herself embroiled in the enquiry, ostensibly in her capacity as a reporter. Joe had been uneasy about the whole situation, particularly Stella's involvement with McKean, although he couldn't say what he didn't like about the guy. In any case, today he would have to suck it up. McKean would probably be the official Incident Commander, although Joe would likely take his orders from the SAR leader.

Joe stepped toward the brink to try to get a glimpse of the fallen man and McKean shouted, "Back away. We don't need another set of boot prints over there." The cop's concern seemed ludicrous considering the number of personnel up there and the fact the site was already a mud bath. No one had said anything about a crime scene, and who fusses about boot prints when a life is at stake? Insult to injury, McKean's outburst had prompted Mo to shoot Joe a dirty look.

Meanwhile Search and Rescue volunteers were proceeding to unwind ropes, debating where to place the anchors, finally deciding on a vertical rope rescue. The rain had let up but clouds were building again when Reilly, an experienced SAR volunteer with advanced First Aid training, stepped over the edge and began to rappel down to the scree where the victim lay.

So, okay, no search was needed, but the integrated team was going to have to pull out all stops to transport the injured party back up to the trail lookout. In minutes, Reilly confirmed that the victim was an adult male and began a step-by-step assessment, reporting his observations over the radio to his colleagues up top. The guy was face down, he said; from what he could see, his face was red and blotchy, a possible sign of lividity. "Can't find a pulse," Reilly added. "I'll try to open an airway." Then, "Oh, shit. Trismus."

The Ground Search Leader spoke into the radio. "Recommend you don't start CPR."

"He's not even going to try?" Joe muttered.

Mo hissed at him to be quiet. "Lockjaw. Rigor's starting to set in," she whispered. "Plus, lividity – you ever heard of it? Maybe you heard of gravity. When the heart stops beating the blood pools in the lower parts. Reilly's down there dangling on a fucking rope and he has to get the victim into a bag and onto the litter before full-on rigor sets in. He's not going to waste time on a useless procedure."

Over the radio, Reilly said, "Code 4."

Everyone went still.

"Dead?" Joe muttered. "But he didn't fall that far. . . and there's all that vegetation to break the impact."

Mo said, "Shut up and focus, Mosconi."

A second man rappelled down to help Reilly bag the body and strap it onto the litter. Then all personnel worked together to haul up the litter and the two men guiding it. The process took more than two hours' time – longer than Joe would have expected. He supposed things might have been different had the victim been alive, the urgency to save a life spurring them on. At least the general mood wouldn't have been so damned depressing.

Apparently, Reilly had recognized the man, which was not all that remarkable in a town the size of Nelson. Soon whispers of his identity reached Joe's ears.

Jack Ballard.

Joe waited for someone to say there'd been a mistake. No one did.

The ground at Pulpit Rock was a quagmire now but Ben McKean seemed to have more important things to do than rag about boot prints. Joe tried to keep out of the way as newly arrived police officers snapped photos and took measurements and conferred with McKean. The coroner appeared (was anyone in Nelson incapable of huffing it up three-hundred vertical metres?) and proceeded to huddle with McKean and Reilly. Finally, it was time to take the litter down the trail, a process that would require the efforts of everyone present. While they bumped the heavy burden down the steep, twisting path to the road, the heavens opened again and rain battered the rescuers as two more gruelling hours crawled by.

At the bottom, Joe overheard McKean assign a colleague to accompany the body to the morgue so as to maintain the chain of evidence in the unlikely case a crime had been committed. Now

McKean, poor bugger, would have to notify next of kin and interview the trail runner who had discovered the victim and called 9-1-1.

To Joe, the scene down on Johnstone Road felt like the aftermath of a macabre sports event, a contest with no winners. Personnel hung about changing clothes and talking in hushed tones, gulping water, gobbling snacks, looking guilty for being alive. Joe took out his phone and texted Stella to tell her to put the boys to bed without him. No one would be going home before a lengthy debrief of the incident, made even longer than usual because a death had occurred.

He was still holding his phone when McKean passed him. "Watch what you say, Mosconi," he said. "It's a serious breach of protocol to divulge the victim's identity."

"I know the drill," Joe said, biting back the urge to add, "you asshole."

5

PROPPED UP AGAINST THE headboard of her bed by heaps of decorative pillows and one well-worn stuffed bunny, Cassidy clicked on Snapchat for news about the accident. Predictably, her friends were regurgitating what she'd already told them. The doorbell chimed. *Shit.* She dove under the covers.

The front door creaked open and she heard a man's voice. Then her mom said, "Yes, come in. I've been expecting the police. But you do realize she's only fifteen? She's shattered. Is it really necessary to see her today?"

"Just for a few minutes, Ms. Pickering. While the event is still fresh in her mind. Is there somewhere I could talk to you before we disturb Cassidy?"

They must have gone into the living room because Cassidy couldn't make out what was being said anymore. After a few minutes she heard them rustle down the hall. Her door swished open and her mother whispered, "She's asleep."

"*Are* you asleep, Cassidy?" The cop's voice again. Cassidy lifted her head. Now she was going to have to talk to him. "I'm Sergeant McKean," he said, and he looked nice, which made her relax a little. He was tall with dark hair. Good looking for a guy about her mom's age. "I'd like to talk to you about the incident you reported."

"Okay." Cassidy sat up, reaching under the covers to straighten her clothes. Her mother suggested they move to the living room, which gave her a chance to pull herself together.

When she joined them, her mom was handing the cop a cup of coffee and offering cream and sugar. They both looked up. Cassidy took a deep breath and said, "What do you want to know?"

"Start from the beginning," McKean said, smiling kindly. He put down his cup and pulled out a small notebook.

"So, Elephant Mountain. I run up there three-four times a week to get some cardio. This morning I biked to the trailhead, pretty much as usual. I never expected –" She had to stop.

"Sorry, Cassidy. I know this is hard. Was it raining when you left home on your bike?"

"The rain had let up a bit. That's why I took the bike."

"So, you cycled over," the cop said. "And you started on the trail at what time?"

"Ten or so? It was quieter than usual, probably because of the rain. The only person I noticed was another trail runner, a guy in a hoodie who passed me. He must have gone all the way to the flagpole because I didn't see him at the lookout on Pulpit." Cassidy paused to decline her mother's offer of juice or milk.

The cop had stopped scribbling. "This runner – did you know him?" he said.

"Never seen him before. Anyway, I got to the viewpoint and that's. . . I guess that's when I noticed the person who fell. Down below."

"Where were you standing, Cassidy?"

"I don't know, the viewpoint, like I said." Her mother pursed her lips at her rudeness, but Cassidy didn't like the way the cop looked at her now. Accusingly. Barely blinking.

"What made you look over the edge?" McKean said, leaning forward as if he wanted to reach over and pull the words right out of her throat.

"I guess I just happened to look around. I might have seen some colour? Red, maybe. Yeah, the person down on the rocks was wearing a red shirt or jacket. And I thought, he must have gotten off the trail. You know, on the way up. I called down to see if he needed help."

"You could tell it was a man?" McKean said.

"Well, I couldn't tell for sure, but I guessed it was. Maybe the figure looked a bit, I don't know, bulky? Anyway when I called, no one answered. I didn't know what to do. I wanted to know if the person was okay, but, well, if I tried to like go down there myself maybe I'd slip and fall too." She couldn't help it – she started to cry again.

McKean stopped writing in his notebook and leaned back. "You did right not to endanger yourself, Cassidy. And your guess was correct. The victim was a man, and I'm sorry to have to tell you he was someone familiar to you and your mother. It was Jack Ballard."

"Oh my God." Cassidy covered her face with both hands. She couldn't stop crying.

Her mom passed her a tissue and said, "I think this is enough for today."

The cop must have told her mom it was Jack when they spoke in the living room, yet she looked incredibly calm and composed. How did she do it? She'd just found out the love of her life had been killed – her heart had to be breaking. McKean said, "Sorry, ma'am. I won't keep her much longer. Cassidy, do you think you could answer just a couple more questions?"

"Okay." She took a swipe at her nose with the tissue and stole another look at her mother.

Karen Pickering lifted the coffee pot to refill the cop's cup, then spoke directly to him. "Did you have to notify his family?" Slight emphasis on 'you.'

"I did," McKean said, and you could tell from his face how terrible that must have been.

Her mother shook her head. The room was quiet for a moment before the cop continued. "Just to be clear, Cassidy, you didn't see Mr. Ballard fall, is that right? He was already down below when you got to Pulpit Rock and looked over the edge."

"Yeah, like I said. It was all like I said." She stood up. "Could I go back to bed now. Please?" She wiped her eyes with the backs of her hands.

"Sure, of course. I'll want to talk to you again, but for now get some rest. Thanks for answering my questions and for calling 9-1-1."

"No problem."

"I like your attitude, Cassidy, but an experience like this can affect you more than you might expect. You may want to talk to a counsellor at school or from the health department. I'll get some contact information and pass it on to your mother."

"Like I said, it was no problem. But thanks." Cassidy went back to her room, checked her phone, and put it aside. She was in no mood to snap with anybody.

* * *

Kieran Corcoran kneeled over the toilet he shared with the junkies down the hall, the smell of his own puke adding to the usual stench of piss and mold. Some dick kept banging on the door. "Hey, you die in there or somethin'? Open up."

"Fuck off."

Kieran closed his eyes but he couldn't shut out the images from Elephant Mountain embedded in his brain. The whole day had been a screw-up from start to finish. First, he'd still been smarting from Jack throwing him out of his party. Shit, he'd only wanted to drop by, lots of people were dropping by. The fact he was under the legal drinking age was a bogus reason to keep him out.

No, his age wasn't the problem. The problem was Danielle Stone. Flirting and flaunting her porn-star body, coming on to him every chance she got. She seemed closer to his age than Ballard's, but she had this habit of calling him baby-cakes or baby bro, which bugged the hell out of her so-called fiancé. And it wasn't like Kieran encouraged her. He didn't even look at her when Ballard was around.

But try explaining that to the man. How do you tell a guy you're not interested in his woman without insulting them both? Particularly when the woman is as hot as Danielle. He'd tried to reason with Ballard up there on the mountain. But when it was clear the dude wasn't going to let it go, he should have backed off. But, no. He had to keep on yammering until they both lost it. Afterward, he just took off, running higher and higher until he was alone at the top of the mountain, his hands shaking.

On the way down, he nearly ran into the cop, McKean, jogging along the switchback right below him, followed by guys in uniform carrying a stretcher like they were soldiers in a war. He slowed down so he wouldn't catch up, then bushwhacked to the road, stupidly wondering why the victim's face was covered until the horror of what had happened sank in.

Now you've done it. He could hear his loser uncle's voice echoing in his head. The old stoner never used to miss a chance to remind Kieran of his screw ups. Still, he'd been there for him when the shitstorm hit a few months back, scraping up the money for a lawyer when his own mother turned her back.

The lawyer got him off with two months in custody, and it wasn't as horrific as he'd thought it would be. He had his own crib and the use of a half-decent gym, and he made friends with another inmate called Loki, the smartest, hippest guy he'd ever known. Loki was a screw-up too but he taught Kieran some amazing shit about old Norse myths, stuff as meaningful as ever in today's fucked-up world. Too bad inmates weren't allowed to take calls because he would have given anything to talk to Loki right then.

Ironically, with Jack gone, there was no one he could really relate to. His mother was still drinking herself to death in Toronto, his uncle still dealing weed on the East Shore, refusing to diversify even though legalization was putting guys like him out of business. Kieran was done with living to hell and gone over on the East Shore, busting his ass doing yard work and selling nickel bags of weed to get by. When Jack Ballard had come into his life, he thought he'd won the freaking lottery.

Jack gave him a bashed-up bike and goaded him to ride like a warrior. The man was merciless. The cycling nearly killed Kieran – whacked elbows, gashed shins, he'd ached all over – but then before he knew it, he was hanging with Jack, running his errands, smoking a doobie or two under the bridge with him – no hard stuff. Life was sweet until he had to go fuck it all up.

He leaned over the stained bowl and brought up the last thin stream of yellow drool. Done then. He wiped his mouth and drank from the faucet. Nothing bad should have happened up at Pulpit Rock, but more to the point, had anyone witnessed it? A girl had started up the trail just ahead of him but he'd passed her like she was standing still. No way could she have made it as far as the viewpoint in time to see him and Ballard lock horns.

* * *

Back after the outing to the climbing centre, Stella reminded the boys their dad wouldn't be home till way past their bedtime. They grumbled a little but seemed mollified by an extra half-hour of screen time and cups of hot chocolate. A few minutes after she'd tucked them into bed, she caught a call from Jade. "It was Jack Ballard," she said, her voice breaking. "I just heard it from a very reliable source on Johnstone Road."

Stella exhaled. If she had to be honest, Jack had loomed in her mind as a possible victim ever since Joe's call-out from Search and Rescue. "How the hell could that have happened?" she said.

"It doesn't make sense, does it?" said Jade.

Nicky chose that moment to wander out, clutching his pillow. "Can I snuggle with you?" he said. "I miss Dad." Stella made room for him on the couch and drew him close.

"Jade? Thanks for the call. I need to get my kid back to bed. Try to get some sleep, okay?"

She steadied her voice to reassure Nicky. "Five minutes, honey. You'll see Dad in the morning. How 'bout we have a special breakfast tomorrow? What would you like me to make?"

"French toast, I guess. Dad never makes pancakes anymore. Cassidy acted like the guy who fell was dead. Why couldn't Dad save him?"

"I'm sure he tried really hard to do that. He'll tell us all about it tomorrow. C'mon. I'll tuck you in again."

Stella returned to the front room and collapsed on the couch.

Jack Ballard dead. Why would he have hiked up there that morning – and how could he have fallen? After weeks of trying to avoid him, he was gone – just like that. Stella's next thought was for Pamela and Richard and how devastated they must be. Someone from the police would have notified them. She wondered if that terrible duty had fallen to Ben McKean.

Sergeant Ben McKean. Stella had known him as long as she'd known Jack; they'd all gone to school together. On her return to Nelson after two decades away, she and Ben had connected over a murder inquiry some months ago. The reporter and the cop, each with a professional stake in the case, yet neither of them able to keep their feelings for each other fully in check, feelings that had lain dormant for twenty years. Now Jack Ballard was dead and Ben McKean would probably lead the investigation into his death. Stella would likely cover it for the paper. How the hell was she going to be objective about either one of them?

Stella checked that both boys were asleep and went outside to wait for Joe, watching as the moon drifted from east to west in a purple sky. It was late when a single kayak cut through the water close to shore, the paddler wearing a small headlamp to light his way. Later still, Joe's car coasted down the driveway with the headlights off. He started when he came upon her sitting on the porch in the dark. "Hey," she said. "Didn't mean to surprise you. Are you okay?"

"Yeah, fine. Just need a bit of shut-eye." He walked past and held the screen door open behind him. She followed him into the kitchen and turned on the cold-water faucet.

"So, it *was* Jack." She filled a glass for him.

"It was Jack." He drank the water in one long swallow. "How'd you find out? Cops were paranoid about releasing his identity."

"Jade called. News like that spreads fast. So, lots of people at the scene, I guess."

"Oh, yeah." He kicked off his pants and climbed into bed. "Your pal McKean was there, throwing his weight around."

"I wouldn't call him my pal," she said, picking up the clothes.

Joe grunted and rolled over. In seconds he was snoring.

* * *

McKean fell into bed at midnight. Too revved up to sleep, he went over the events of the day, beginning with the Chief's order to report to Elephant Mountain and followed by the fiasco that led to the recovery of Jack Ballard's body. Maybe fiasco wasn't the right word. Both the SAR crew and the first responders knew what they were doing, and despite some initial chaos, everyone who turned up made himself useful.

All day, tension had built on Elephant Mountain with speculation as to how Jack Ballard had fallen to his death and why he'd gone up there in the first place. Several of the personnel, including Joe Mosconi, had been at the victim's birthday party the previous evening. Stella must have been there too and McKean wondered what she'd be able to tell him about Ballard. Talking to Stella was the only part of the case he anticipated with any degree of pleasure. He knew he would have to watch his step. That was a given with the press, although it was never easy to keep his mouth shut around Stella.

The worst part of his day had come after the recovery of the body. The dreaded drive up Lucky Jack Road to tell the victim's fiancée and parents their loved one wouldn't be coming home. Then the interview with the badly shaken teenager who had called 9-1-1.

McKean rolled over and tried to get some sleep. The last time he glanced at the clock the display read 3:07 a.m.

Sunday morning came and he caught a break. He was up ahead of his wife and toddler, quietly brewing a cup of coffee, when a member on desk duty phoned with a message. Seemed the local rumour mill had been operating on overdrive. By the time the body had been carried down the final stairway of the trail, it was no secret who had died that day, in spite of efforts to keep the victim's identity under wraps. Now someone had come forward with information as to how Ballard had gotten himself to the trailhead. McKean returned the call of the good citizen and asked how soon he could come by to talk to her.

Two large Dobermans rushed McKean's cruiser when he pulled up in front of a small cedar bungalow at the bottom of a long dirt drive off Johnstone Road. He remained in his car until a woman appeared at the door and called the dogs. She invited him into a cluttered kitchen that smelled of wood smoke and offered him coffee, which he declined with thanks. Waving him to an armchair that provided a sweeping view of Kootenay Lake, she got to the point. She'd first seen Jack Ballard at around nine o'clock Saturday morning in front of his bike store. She had been across the street in the parking lot of the Kootenay Co-op, schlepping a case of organic kidney beans and a bag of groceries when Ballard waved and called her name. He'd crossed the lot and relieved her of the canned goods. "Well, you know Jack," she said. "Or maybe you don't. But he was as friendly as ever. He didn't have his bike and he knew I lived on the North Shore. Said he needed a lift to the trailhead so he could hike up to Pulpit Rock."

"Was it raining at the time?" McKean said.

"Pissing rain, and him in shorts and a flimsy red shell. I told him he was nuts. Day like that even the hard-core types wait for the weather to lift. But there was no discouraging Jack. He wanted to climb a mountain. A 'frigging mountain,' if you want a direct quote."

McKean said, "How was his mood, compared to other times you've spoken to him?"

"Normal, perfectly normal. I heard he'd partied hard on Friday night, but other than a serious case of booze breath he seemed okay. He said he and a buddy had popped downtown for a drink after the party, but the bars were closed so they'd gone to the guy's house and liberated his parents' scotch. He ranted a little – 'try to buy a beer in Nelson after two ayem' – stuff like that."

"Do you know the name of the buddy?"

"I didn't ask and he didn't say. Who'd have thought I'd be sitting here talking to the police this morning?"

McKean thanked the woman for her help and headed downtown. At the top of Baker Street, he parked in front of Ballard's Cycles where a hand-written notice taped to the inside of a window read, "Closed until further notice." He was about to take off when he saw movement in the background. He got out of his cruiser and rapped on the door.

The young woman who let him in introduced herself as Kayla Chau. A long-time employee, she'd just come by to put up the sign. McKean offered his condolences and asked if she felt up to answering questions. "I guess that's the least I can do for Jack and his family," she said. "Let's go to the office in the back. The looky-loos are already starting to come by the window."

Kayla said Ballard must have stopped by the shop to change his clothes at some point. The black jeans and rumpled grey shirt he'd worn at the party were draped over the back of a chair; a pair of leather loafers had been kicked off. McKean asked Kayla for an unused bag and pulled on gloves to pack the clothing.

To Kayla's knowledge, Jack Ballard had never hiked up to Pulpit Rock before Saturday. "I'm a regular," she said. "I hike that trail most days before work. I used to tease Jack about what a good workout you get just walking to the first viewpoint. But Jack never walked anywhere. Took his bike to go a couple of blocks to the coffee shop." She looked away for a moment. "It feels weird talking like this. I mean, he was a good guy. It sounds like I'm putting him down."

"Not at all. It's helpful to get a sense of his routines," McKean said. "What do you think changed his mind about going up to Pulpit? Why Saturday?"

She shook her head. "I've been wondering the same thing. Someone might have dared him. There was a lot of drinking at his party the night before – anything could have set him off. Like I said, Jack wasn't into hiking, but he was an impetuous guy. He wouldn't have turned his back on a challenge."

"Even if he'd been partying the night before?"

Kayla laughed half-heartedly. "*Especially* if he'd been partying the night before."

"I heard he had a nightcap with a buddy after the party. Any idea who that might have been?"

"Rory, probably. I suppose Danielle would know. She'd have his number."

McKean made a note of that and glanced around the shop. "How's business these days?"

Kayla shrugged. "Building's mortgaged of course, and Jack used a line of credit to maintain the inventory. But retail isn't for sissies. Lot of shops like ours pretty much limp from one month to the next."

McKean prodded a little, but Kayla had nothing significant to add. He closed his notebook and thanked her. Then he drove uphill toward Lucky Jack Road, dreading his second intrusion on the bereaved family.

6

MONDAY MORNING STELLA TOOK refuge in her weekday routine, tidying her family's small lakeside cabin, packing lunches, finally setting out for town on her bicycle. As she pumped along the lakeshore road, she passed a flagpole flying Canada's red maple leaf at half-mast. By the time she'd crossed the bridge over Kootenay Lake and arrived at the newspaper offices in Railtown, she'd counted five similarly lowered flags, testimony to Jack Ballard's position in the community, she supposed, or that of his family. In any case, word of his death must have spread fast.

Upstairs at the *Nelson Times*, the mood in the newsroom was sombre. At the story meeting, Jade Visser wept openly. Twice, editor Patrick Taft stopped mid-sentence to pass her a tissue.

Patrick assigned Stella a short piece about Jack's death based on the sketchy facts available to date, a more comprehensive story to follow. A local radio station was still airing comments from so-called eye witnesses interviewed Saturday at the base of the popular trail. But none of the bystanders seemed to have anything newsworthy to say, and like the Search and Rescue crew, emergency personnel would have been ordered to stay mum.

Stella rang the Nelson police station to try to reach Ben McKean. The receptionist confirmed he had been assigned to work the Ballard case, but was vague about when he might return the call. Well, a cop never made it easy for the press. She wondered if he would get back to her that day. She hadn't seen much of Ben since inveigling her way into his two related murder cases last year. She could count on one hand the number of times she'd seen him in the meantime – at the movies or in a restaurant or just striding down Baker Street – each passing encounter a vivid memory, damn it.

To escape the pall hanging over the office, Stella took her lunch outside and found an empty bench in front of the building. She wanted to be alone but didn't say anything when Jade Visser crossed the street from the coffee wagon and plunked down beside her. "Sad about Jack," she said. She was dressed in torn jeans paired with a loose-knit, pale-blue sweater over a purple sports bra, her curly auburn hair attractively mussed. Jade's version of business casual. But then, who was Stella to judge? She rarely took the time to change out of her cycling gear, although she kept an outfit in a desk drawer for occasions that called for something more respectable.

"Very sad," Stella said. "Forty years old and about to become a husband and father for the first time." She unwrapped her sandwich and bit into it.

Jade sipped at her coffee. "I wonder if he's the first one from his grad class to pass away," she said. "Is this a first for you – losing a friend from school?"

Stella looked away. "I'm sorry he died, of course, but to be honest, I didn't think of him as a friend."

"Seriously?" Jade said. "How would you define a friend? I think of people I went to school with as friends. Maybe not first tier, but a step up from, say, someone you say hi to in passing. Plus, everyone liked Jack. He was always so out there. I bet people he hardly knew thought of him as a friend."

"I guess." Stella absently rewrapped her sandwich.

"You guess? Hey, wait a minute. I get it. You and Jack were an item back at school." Jade peered at her. "You were! I knew it. What happened? Was the break-up ugly?"

"Look, I dated him a couple of times when I was in grade 10 and he was in grade 12. It was a bump in the road. I'd be grateful if you'd keep it to yourself."

"Goes without saying." Jade mimed zipping her lips, turning a lock, and throwing away the key. "Still, though. You must be a teensy bit more upset than if a regular classmate died. Now I know why I caught that vibe between you guys when he was in the office the other day. Aw, Stella – I'm really sorry." She reached over and patted Stella's knee.

"Listen, there was no *vibe* between us – there was no *us*. We were an item, as you put it, for about five minutes more than twenty years ago." Stella put her half-eaten sandwich back in her bag.

Jade held up a hand. "Don't try to explain – I can see you're hurting. And you know what? You probably believe every word you're saying. But memories can be tricky. I mean, *twenty years*. How can you trust anything you remember from *twenty years* ago? *God.*"

Words of wisdom from the twenty-five-year-old.

* * *

McKean was impressed with how quickly Dr. Ralph Antoniak had gotten himself to the hospital in Nelson and settled in to perform the autopsy on Jack Ballard's body. The death was unusual enough to warrant a post-mortem, no question, yet the coroner must have pulled some strings to get the Vancouver-based forensic pathologist on a Sunday flight into the West Kootenay Regional Airport. Now it was late Monday morning and the pathologist had called to say he'd performed the autopsy.

McKean parked his cruiser in the hospital lot and nodded at a man pushing an IV pole along the covered walkway, a cardigan draped over his standard-issue nightshirt. Inside McKean waved at a neighbour who was arranging knitted booties and toys outside the hospital auxiliary room. She beckoned him closer. "Any word on that accident up at Pulpit Rock?" she said.

"Still investigating," Ben said, not stopping but smiling to soften the brush-off. He made his way downstairs to the morgue, more than a little curious about what the forensic pathologist had found. Over the past day and a half, McKean had thought of little else besides the fatal incident on Elephant Mountain, and he obviously wasn't alone. Everywhere he went, people were talking about it, wondering aloud how Jack Ballard had fallen to his death at a place where, almost daily, dozens of hikers stop to admire the picture-postcard view of the lake and town and surrounding mountains.

McKean had no theories as to how Ballard had taken a tumble, but an even bigger mystery to him was why the fall had killed the man. The area directly below Pulpit Rock had plenty of vegetation to break a fall. When the coroner unzipped the body bag back on the mountain, McKean hadn't seen any obvious evidence of a head injury, and the SAR volunteers who'd handled the body had remarked on how little blood had been spilled at the scene.

The door to the small office used by visiting specialists was open and McKean tapped on the frame. Dr. Ralph Antoniak stood up and thrust out his right hand. He was a short, agile man with a rapid-fire manner of speaking and thick white hair that tended to fall over his right eye. He greeted McKean like an old friend. "Wish I could say 'long time no see,'" he said, clasping McKean's hand in both of his. "But it's not many months since my last visit. And now you have another unusual death to keep you busy."

"I'm bracing for it," McKean said. He was also bracing to view another dissected body, a duty he hadn't gotten used to and likely never would. Now as he followed Antoniak to the covered trolley that held Jack Ballard's body, he made a point of steadying himself.

Dr. Antoniak pulled on gloves and drew back a sheet to expose an open chest. At least McKean had been spared the peeling and sawing. With a fine-tipped instrument the pathologist pointed to a place near the heart. McKean was never sure what he was looking at when he peered into an open cavity. The insides of human bodies reminded him of slaughtered animals, carcasses of deer and mountain sheep shot out of season and stashed in the back of suspicious pickups he stopped on the highway. "Burst aortic aneurysm," the doctor said. "Not what you'd expect in a forty-year-old."

"No?" McKean said.

Antoniak continued. "Most aneurysms are caused by atherosclerosis. Hardening of the arteries in plain speak, a condition usually associated with old age. But aneurysms can be congenital or caused by trauma. I'd guess trauma was the probable cause here since I read in the file that this man was a competitive cyclist. He would have taken more than a few serious spills in his time. You ever see those guys ride? They're maniacs."

"Ballard would have been no exception," McKean said. "But how would the aneurysm have affected him? He looked fit."

"Often there's no warning, no obvious symptoms. But a bulge in a major blood vessel is a time bomb waiting to go off. *Bang*, and the victim dies from internal bleeding."

"It burst with the impact of the fall then?"

"Most likely," Antoniak said. "Although these things have been known to rupture spontaneously."

"In that case, would he have died instantly?"

"Not necessarily. Here, take a look at the bruising. See these small marks with the distinct edges?" Antoniak pointed with his probe. "He likely got these as he tumbled down the slope with his heart still pumping. When the heart stops, the blood stops oozing into the surrounding tissue so the bruises remain small."

"The guys that bagged him didn't see much blood, but I guess there must have been internal damage."

"Oh yes, obvious trauma to the spleen and liver."

"So, to be clear, the aneurysm could have burst spontaneously, making him lose his balance and fall," McKean said. "But it's more likely he fell first – for whatever reason – and the aneurysm ruptured as his body tumbled down the scree, is that right?"

"I'd say so."

"Then you'd have to wonder what made him go over the cliff. Did he jump? Was he pushed?"

"Ah, you've been entertaining dark thoughts, Sergeant. Okay, have a look at this scar near the waist." Antoniak pointed to a ridged line, about two centimetres in length. "And this one a little higher up. Look at these marks on the trunk and upper arm." Antoniak moved his probe from one contusion to another. "There are more on the buttocks. All distinctly different from the bruising sustained as he slid down that slope."

"Given, as you say, he'd done some extreme mountain biking . . ."

"Right. A few are old scars. But other marks are more recent, and he might have gotten them at different times during the past couple of weeks."

McKean looked up. "Two weeks?"

"You familiar with the system for classifying bruises according to colour?"

McKean nodded. "I've heard it discussed in court in cases of possible abuse."

Antoniak continued. "The classification has its uses, although the accuracy is questionable. In situations where abuse might have occurred, it shouldn't be taken as sole evidence. In any case, this victim's body has bruises that likely predate his fall on Saturday. We can only speculate as to how he got them."

"Minor accident, maybe?"

"The variety suggests injury on more than one occasion. And if someone roughed him up on any of those occasions, then you'd have to wonder if he was complicit. The line between abuse and rough sex, for example, is thorny. Takes us down the murky road of consent."

McKean said, "If Ballard's lifestyle was violent or otherwise dodgy, that might have increased the likelihood that someone pushed him. Have you talked to his doctor?"

Antoniak looked down at his notes. "A Dr. Liam Sparks. The fellow wasn't aware of the aneurysm. No surprise there. Our victim didn't see much of his GP, again no surprise since he was young and fit. Probably not the type to run to his doctor every time he had a sniffle. The doc wasn't aware of any unusual scars or bruises, but then our victim had never seen him for a complete physical. Oh, and by the by, the blood alcohol level was significant despite a time of death between about 10:00 a.m. and 1:00 p.m. They'll do a drug screen at the lab, but you can expect that to take a while."

"Big bash at his house the night before," McKean said. "Rumour has it he stayed up drinking half the night, yet headed up the mountain around nine o'clock the next morning. In a rain storm. Seems like a strange thing to do, unless someone lured him up there. He caught a ride to the trailhead with a woman who lives nearby. She heard him say he wanted to climb a mountain."

"Since he must still have been under the influence, I suppose we can be thankful he didn't drive his own vehicle." Antoniak snapped off his gloves and tossed them into a bin. "Well, Ben, give me a shout if you find anything interesting. I assume you looked for evidence of a scuffle up there?"

McKean shook his head. "Scene was a mud bath. Forensics guys from the regional RCMP tried to get footwear impressions, but I don't know how useful they'll be."

"Too bad. Well, unless new evidence crops up, I'll deliver my report to the coroner tomorrow morning. As things stand now, I expect he'll classify the death as accidental."

McKean left the hospital, grateful to escape the reek of disinfectant in the morgue. It was tougher to shake off the image of Jack Ballard's defiled body. On the walkway by the parking lot, the man with the IV pole was sitting on a bench now, next to a lady with a toy poodle on her lap. As McKean passed, the patient whispered something to his companion. Times like this, a big anonymous city held a lot of appeal.

McKean headed back to the station to review the photos and measurements taken at Pulpit Rock, regretting he hadn't posted a reserve officer to guard the taped-off area 24/7. At this point, God only knew how many people had traipsed up to Pulpit Rock after the fact. He was still mulling over Antoniak's findings as he set out to revisit the site. The pattern of bruising on Ballard's body had been a surprise. It wasn't proof of foul play, but it nagged at him all the same.

7

FROM A SHELF IN the newsroom, a white bakery box beckoned to Stella. So far, she'd resisted temptation, but it was three o'clock and she was hungry. A half-eaten sandwich still languished in her bag after the lunchtime chat with Jade had killed her appetite. Almost against her will, Stella opened the small box and lifted out a cupcake topped with pink frosting and tiny silver balls, compliments of the editor whose wife worked at a bake shop. "Thought you were made of sterner stuff," Patrick Taft said, coming up behind her as she sank her teeth into the sugary treat.

"A body requires calories," Stella said, mid-bite. "It's a survival thing."

"Can't understand you when your mouth's full." He waited a moment. "How's it going on the Ballard piece?"

"His friends have circled the wagons," Stella said. "This town is too damn insular. Everyone on my interview list is only one or two degrees of separation from the next guy. Case in point, the girl who discovered the fall and made the 9-1-1 call? She's my kids' swim teacher and – wait for it – she was babysitting them while Joe and I were at Ballard's party the night before he died. Now I see she's started a Facebook page as a memorial to him. Is there anyone more earnest than a teenager?"

Patrick, the parent of a toddler, had no response to that.

Stella called the Pickering home and Cassidy's mother Karen answered. "Cass seems to have perked up a bit," she said, "probably because she's thrown herself into a project. I hear the new Facebook page is getting dozens of likes. Apparently, Pulpit Rock is already heaped with bouquets and stuffed toys. Cassidy and a bunch of her friends trouped up there after school."

Stella reached for her camera. "Sounds like the place to be this afternoon." She thanked Karen and rang off.

It took Stella about twenty minutes' time to cycle across town, over the bridge, and along Johnstone Road to the trailhead. After an additional half hour of tramping up the trail, she reached the viewpoint on Pulpit Rock where a cluster of teenage girls stood around taking selfies on their phones. It was a disturbing scene. The police tape had already begun to sag with the weekend wind and rain, and under it several bunches of supermarket flowers, some stuffed into canning jars, others lying on their sides still wrapped in plastic, comprised a shrine of sorts. A hand-printed cardboard sign declared "Love U Forever Jack." Scattered about were a dozen or so teddy bears and other plush animals – clean, but not new – probably culled from long-neglected toy boxes.

No one objected to posing for a group photo for the *Times* and, without any prompting from Stella, the girls held up flowers and toys and looked suitably downcast. Cassidy said she appreciated the publicity. "We want to raise money to put up a barrier where Jack fell," she said. "It'd be great if you could send your readers to Facebook for details on how to contribute. I don't think anyone would want a tragedy like this to happen again. Like, little kids come up here with their parents. Dogs run around off leash."

"How do you think it happened, Cassidy?" Stella said, firing off more photos. "As you say, people come up here every day. Why would Jack Ballard have fallen over the edge?"

"I guess there's a first time for everything," Cassidy said. "With no railings, it was an accident waiting to happen. The Grand Canyon has railings. My mom and I went there on vacation once. That's what gave me the idea. I mean, it's human nature to want to get close to the edge."

"Can you see a possible downside to having a railing though? A barrier might detract from the natural setting. Did your page get any posts that raised objections to the idea?"

Cassidy lifted her chin. "I don't think anyone would be that selfish. Saving lives is more important than a perfect view." One of her friends pulled her into another selfie, and Stella put away her camera. Each girl paused to look at the shrine again, Cassidy and several others wiping away tears. Then, one-by-one, they slipped away.

Within minutes the sounds of chatter and laughter came from the direction of the trail. Stella had to smile at the resilience of kids – one minute weeping crocodile tears, the next laughing like hyenas. She sat down on a large, smooth boulder, not too close to the edge, and took a deep breath. "Well, Jack," she said quietly, "I wish I knew what happened up here. By rights you should be in your shop gabbing with your customers and I should be anywhere but." She closed her eyes and hit replay on her lunchtime conversation with Jade Visser. Yes, memories could be tricky. But Jack Ballard had scared her once, and she'd never quite gotten over it.

* * *

McKean checked his phone for messages as he hiked up Elephant Mountain, looking up as a posse of teenage girls brushed past him on their way down the trail, among them Cassidy Pickering. She didn't meet his eyes so he didn't greet her. No doubt it wasn't cool to appear friendly with the police.

The trail had dried out since Saturday and it felt good to stride along, boulder hopping at the corners, jogging on the straight stretches. The air was clear in spite of a faint scent of smoke; some eager beaver must be burning branches and garden waste. A little early for that, in McKean's opinion; the trees were only beginning to drop their leaves. For no apparent reason, an image of Jack Ballard's chest cavity came to mind but he brushed it off. His memory of Ballard was of a man in motion, a guy with the grace of a professional athlete – no wasted moves. Not someone likely to stumble over a cliff, even if he hadn't quite sobered up after a night of heavy drinking.

At the last switchback before the viewpoint, McKean realized he hadn't met or passed anyone on the trail other than the teenagers. A quiet day then – that should make his job easier. But at the top, a lone female, possibly a lingering teen from the group he'd passed, sat on a rock outcropping with her back to him. She was dressed for cycling but must have left her helmet on the bike because the wind was having its way with her long chestnut hair. Recognition pierced him like an arrow. Stella Mosconi. It was too late to retreat. Not wanting to startle her, McKean called out a greeting.

She turned and stood up. "Ben, hi," she said, her lips curving in a smile. "Returning to the scene of the crime?" Pleasure washed through him like a drug.

"There's no evidence it *is* a crime scene at this point," he said. *Officious ass.*

"Right." Stella remained standing. "But since you're in uniform I'm guessing you're up here on business."

"Who's the detective here?" Another groaner. Particularly since the title didn't apply to him or anyone else in Nelson's small independent police force.

Stella Mosconi was generous enough to laugh, and the faint lines by her eyes made her even prettier than usual. "I've been trying to track you down, actually," she said. "What can you tell me about the incident?" Ever the reporter.

"Waiting for the coroner's report." He hesitated. With anyone except Stella he would have left it at that, but he blathered on. "Shouldn't be long – the autopsy is pretty much done. You remember Antoniak, the pathologist from the Coast. I spoke to him this morning."

"And?"

"Stella."

"I know. You're waiting for the coroner's report." She still didn't walk away. He was rooted to the spot. She could probably tell he was sweating – Stella never missed a thing. Perhaps as a kindness, she looked out over the lake before she spoke again. "Did you know him? Ballard, I mean. Were you a card-carrying member of the Jack Ballard fan club?"

"Knew him to see him from back in school. I talked to him once about bikes, but found what I wanted at MEC in Vancouver."

"Joe wants to buy a fancy bike for Matt," Stella said, "although the one Ballard suggested seems over the top for a ten-year-old. I wonder what'll happen to the shop now? There's a handwritten 'closed' sign on the window. I guess his family will have to decide whether to let the staff carry on or sell the business." She shook her head then met his eyes again. "Did you come up here to try to figure out how he fell?"

"Routine follow-up," he said, but he didn't want her to leave. "I saw your husband with Search and Rescue on Saturday. I might have hassled him a little."

"Yeah? Well, Joe's a high school teacher. Teflon-coated." She smiled again. "So, what do you think happened? *Was* it an accident?"

"Hard to say. What's your theory?" *Shut up, McKean. Don't engage with the press.*

"I don't really have one." Stella looked out over the lake again. "Jack Ballard always struck me as one of a kind, so maybe it's not surprising his death was out of the ordinary."

"Sounds like you knew him pretty well."

"I wouldn't say that," Stella said, hastily, making McKean curious about what had gone on between them. "I do know he had a lot to drink at his birthday party the night before, which might have affected his judgment." She met his eyes. "Yeah, I was there. He was already wasted when Joe and I left around midnight, and we were among the first to leave. Hey, and get this, Kieran Corcoran tried to crash the party. Did you know he was back in town?"

Ben hesitated. "We were advised of his release, but I haven't seen him around."

"I asked Ballard about him," Stella said, "He didn't say much except that he'd taken Kieran under his wing – that was the expression he used. Yet he threw the kid out of his party, supposedly because Kieran was under the legal drinking age. Seems weird, doesn't it? And don't you find it strange that Kieran would get involved with Ballard so soon after returning to Nelson? That kid seems like a magnet for trouble."

"I'll track him down and have a chat with him," Ben said. "Any other thoughts about Jack Ballard?"

Stella paused. "I guess accidents happen all the time, but this one – I don't know. At the party he ranted a bit about climbing mountains. But why would he have trudged up here on a miserable day after all that partying? I suspect he might still have been drunk the morning after, but even so, he was an athlete in the prime of life. I can't see him being clumsy enough to stumble over the edge."

So Stella had come to the same conclusion as he had. And she'd referred to him as Ballard rather than Jack, which seemed significant. For a whole bunch of reasons, McKean couldn't bring himself to end the conversation. "You didn't say whether you were a member of the Jack Ballard fan club."

"Definitely not. But I have an alibi for all day Saturday." She smiled. "Seriously though, don't you find this death curious?"

McKean shrugged. "Any unusual death has to be investigated." *Way to kill a conversation, idiot.*

"Right. Well, better leave you to it," she said.

He watched as she disappeared down the trail.

So, Stella had "definitely not" been a fan of Jack Ballard – there was a story there.

8

PAMELA BALLARD WAITED UNTIL Monday afternoon to carry a florist's bouquet of white lilies up to the viewpoint known as Pulpit Rock. She'd been nervous about venturing up the mountain for the first time and dreaded the possibility of running into someone she knew. But she had to get out of the house – the walls were beginning to close in on her. She hoped the effort of hiking up a long, steep trail would help her sleep at night. She'd barely gotten a moment's rest since opening the door to a policeman Saturday evening. They had just sat down to dinner, she and Richard. Danielle had chosen not to join them. Dinner was leftovers from the party, along with a rather nice Cab a friend had brought as a gift. She and Richard had been conducting their own little post-mortem on the party – they'd actually used that term. The wine was loosening their tongues and at one point Richard had her almost doubled over with laughter. That moment would likely stay with them forever, the line of demarcation between happiness and despair. Certainly, Richard would never get over losing Jack. Never.

She'd gotten up to answer the knock at the door, and one look at Sergeant McKean had told her the news would be bad. But she'd invited him in as if a visit from the police were perfectly normal – she had to believe nothing truly awful had happened, nothing awful *could* have happened on such an ordinary day. Richard was still holding his wine glass but he put it down carefully. She'd picked up the phone and called Danielle over from the studio and the tension in the room mounted as they waited for her. Danielle would have seen the police car as she crossed over to the house and her face was drained of colour when she burst through the door saying, "What happened? Where's Jack?"

The sergeant suggested they all sit down. He was gentle but forthright as he told them about the fall from Pulpit Rock that had taken Jack's life. They'd all been too stunned to ask any sensible questions. Richard had shattered before her eyes. In a flash, her protector, her rock, her funny, lovable best friend seemed diminished beyond repair. Even his strong-featured face looked blurred and flattened. Danielle, despite her usual bluster, barely reacted at all. She simply stood up and retreated zombie-like to the studio.

Then they had to get through the night and the following day. At times like this, a couple should turn to one another, to hold each other up. But Richard withdrew to his La-Z-Boy with a bottle of Glenfiddich. Sunday morning, he reconnected an old VCR and began to spend his waking hours watching jerky old family videos of Jack on the oversize TV screen. Danielle barricaded herself in the studio, admitting entry to no one except Jack's best friend Rory. Not that Pamela could blame her for wanting to avoid the chalet; the sound of Jack's boyhood voice on the videos was enough to drive anyone to ground.

Pamela shifted the bouquet from one arm to the other and proceeded along the arduous, unfamiliar trail, stopping every now and again to catch her breath, wondering how much farther it was to the top and whether she'd be able to make it. Next thing she knew, Stella Mosconi was barrelling downhill straight toward her, no means of escape for either of them. Pamela's discomfort must have been mutual because Stella's face changed when it registered recognition. When she got close enough to speak, she said, "I'm sorry, Pamela. What a terrible thing."

"Yes, well, thank you. I thought a walk might help. I tried to pick a quiet time to come up."

"I won't keep you then," Stella said. She paused. "Just so you know – Sergeant McKean is up at the viewpoint."

"Oh." Pamela was in a quandary now. She didn't want to face McKean again, nor did she want to walk back down with Stella. She looked around helplessly.

Stella seemed to grasp her dilemma. "Have you ever taken the cut-off near the top of the trail?" she said. "It's signposted on the switchback after next. You could find a place to sit and rest until you hear Sergeant McKean pass on the main trail. I'm sure he'll take the direct route down."

Decent of her, but even as a girl Stella had always impressed her as a straight arrow. "Sounds like a plan," Pamela said. "Thanks." Despite the stab at lightness, her voice must have betrayed her. Stella touched her arm before she continued down the path. For a moment Pamela wondered what life would have looked like if Jack had ended up with someone like Stella.

* * *

It was bedtime for Stella's young sons. In their cramped, wood-panelled room, she cleared the floor of jeans and T-shirts and sorted a jumble on the dresser, discovering unseen school notices and one overdue library book. Then she squeezed in beside Nicky on the lower bunk to tell the eight-year-old a story about bears, his all-time favourite subject. Above them, his brother Matt read a library book about space travel, chipping in the occasional remark about bears. When Joe came in to say goodnight, Stella hugged and kissed each boy and let their dad take over.

Now she sank into an easy chair, turned on her laptop, and opened the folder she'd named EMD for Elephant Mountain Disaster. Into it she dumped her preliminary report on Ballard's death and sat back. The piece had made it to the top of the Most Read list on the paper's website and garnered a couple of hundred "Likes" on their Facebook page. The story of Jack Ballard's demise wasn't about to go away.

The boys' bedroom door clicked shut and Joe joined her in the front room. "I ran into Ben McKean today," she said. "You told me he was up at Pulpit on Saturday. He mentioned seeing you there too."

"Guy's a jerk," Joe said. His SAR backpack was still where he'd dropped it by the front door and now he dumped out the contents and sat on the floor to sort his gear.

"I guess it was pretty tense up there," Stella said. "He was semi-apologetic about hassling you. I told him you could probably handle it, being a teacher and all."

"That was nice of you," he said, frowning as he came across his wet rain pants.

Stella looked over at her husband. "Why are you in such a foul mood?"

"Who says I'm in a foul mood?" He emptied the upper compartment of the pack and cursed – a tube of sunscreen had split open, leaking all over his altimeter and compass.

Stella moved her computer to the kitchen table and made some notes on her final conversation with Jack Ballard. She highlighted: *Kieran Corcoran back in town; nature of connection with Ballard?* She also noted her chance meeting that day with Ben McKean. Alone with him up on Pulpit Rock, she'd felt that old familiar tingle, not that she documented the fact – or allowed herself to think about it for more than a minute or two. It had felt good to talk about the case together though. She sensed Ben didn't think Ballard had simply fallen either. That left suicide or homicide, both chilling possibilities.

"Well, I'm turning in," Joe said. He shoved his reorganized pack into the front closet and forced the door closed.

"Goodnight," she called to his back. "Hey, Joe, wait a sec. Are you okay? We haven't really talked about how all this has affected you."

He stopped but didn't turn to face her. "I'm okay. Thanks."

She got up and went to him, and he let her pull him into a hug. The muscles of his shoulders and back felt like concrete, but she hung on until he broke off to move toward the bedroom. Times like this he seemed so cold it frightened her. But he typically closed down under pressure, and his first SAR call-out would have been stressful enough without having to come to terms with the death of a friend. Joe didn't have a lot of close friends in Nelson. Jack had been important to him – an insider who might have boosted his sense of belonging.

She probably shouldn't have mentioned Ben; that was a red flag for Joe. But it wasn't like she had anything to hide. If she was lucky enough to get in on this case, she would do her best to keep relations with Ben strictly professional. He surely felt the same way, having as much to lose as she did if they ever crossed that line again.

Later Stella woke from a dream with a painful ache in her groin. It had been years since that had happened; she and Joe had been college students at the time, not yet living together. She'd called him in the middle of the night, only hours before she had to write a mid-term exam, and he'd cycled from Burnaby to East Vancouver to have sex with her. Now he was lying right next to her and she didn't consider waking him up. She stumbled into the bathroom to relieve the pressure, feeling old and jaded and infinitely lonely.

It seemed the dream had been about Jack Ballard, although Stella couldn't have said how either of them had figured in it. She lay awake for a long time after.

* * *

"Look at me, Daddy. Look." The interminable videos of Jack projected on the oversize TV screen were wearing Pamela down. She kept trying to coax Richard out of his chair. Why not go for a walk, she'd say, or take a drive up the lake?

"*Daddyyy – look!*" Jack's voice at six or seven was surprisingly high-pitched. Pamela couldn't remember a time when he had sounded shrill. In her mind, Jack always spoke in his slow, rambling baritone. She wondered if his voice had already changed at fifteen when she'd moved in with Richard. Was that even possible? Jack had seemed uncannily mature for his age. Happy for his father and inclined to treat her the way any man treats an attractive woman. It had occurred to her then that Jack might have a little crush and she'd gone out of her way to discourage any unwholesome thoughts.

The door opened and Danielle shuffled in wearing a scruffy terry robe, her platinum hair scraped back, exposing dark roots. "I'm out of Perrier," she stated, in a tone that implied neglect on Pamela's part. Richard seemed oblivious to the intrusion.

"Richard," Pamela said, evenly. "Danielle is out of Perrier. Be a dear and get her a case from the garage."

"Oh, Danielle," Richard looked up, brightening a little. "Didn't hear you come in. Let me find my shoes." He got up and drew her into a lingering embrace.

"Poor daddy," Danielle muttered into his chest.

Daddy? Good God.

"Poor birdy," Richard murmured into Danielle's hair.

Birdy: Jack's term of endearment for the girl.

"Okay you two," Pamela said. "We need to get out of this house. Danielle, why don't you get dressed? We'll take you for a nice dinner at a hotel up the lake. How about it, Richard? It will do us all good to get out. We also should get cracking on a memorial service for Jack. People are stopping me on the street to ask about it."

Two pair of eyes turned her way, each seemingly reflecting the other's horror. Pamela Ballard, aka *Cruella de Vil*.

"I can't," Danielle said, limply.

"I understand," Richard said. "Believe me."

Danielle held onto his arm as if to steady herself. "I should get back to the studio. Rory is coming by. Do you think you could get the Perrier now? And maybe a couple beers for Rory?"

Rory again. Well, he'd been Jack's best friend; the three of them had been inseparable. Pamela said, "I guess I'd better do it myself then. Set the wheels in motion for a service."

"Would you?" Richard said, shambling off toward the garage. "There's a good girl. I don't think I have it in me."

In the background, little Jack ran squealing back and forth through a lawn sprinkler.

9

ONE WEEK AFTER JACK Ballard's death, his funeral took place at the Hume Hotel in downtown Nelson. Stepping into the newly updated lobby, Stella was hurtled back to her girlhood. Even after massive renovations, the historic old building still retained a homey, woodsy smell that brought back memories of enchanting Christmas markets and rare family meals out, of the wedding reception of a friend's older brother during which Stella danced under a chandelier and tasted her first champagne. Today servers circulated with trays of hors d'oeuvres while two bartenders mixed cocktails and kept the beer and wine flowing. On a large screen on the back wall, Jack crashed down precipitous trails on his mountain bike. The film played in a continuous loop, the soundtrack apparently mined from his favourite playlists. Stella recognized songs by the Canadian indie rock band Dusted, others by Arcade Fire and Three Days Grace.

Chairs had been arranged around cloth-draped tables topped with stacks of three-hole punched card stock. Kayla from Ballard's Cycles circulated with jars of coloured Sharpies, encouraging guests to record stories about Jack, all artistic efforts to be included in a memory book on display at the store. Stella let Nicky and Matt draw two pictures each of Jack on his bicycle. When an hour passed and the family of the deceased still hadn't turned up, she let the boys knock themselves out. They went through every piece of cardboard in the stack but Stella drew the line at letting them collect more from other tables.

Across the room Cassidy Pickering sat in a circle of friends, including a few Stella recognized from the group she'd photographed up at the viewpoint. She caught Cassidy's eye and waved. The girl nodded forlornly. One friend held Cassidy's hand while another stroked her hair and cried. Cassidy's mother and grandparents sat opposite, visibly uncomfortable with the whole tableau.

The guests were talking amongst themselves when Pamela Ballard entered the room in her trademark Eileen Fisher, today layered in muted grey and black, her shoulder-length ash blond hair pulled back with a narrow ribbon. Richard Ballard followed with Jack's fiancée Danielle, both in dark glasses. It was hard to say who was holding up whom.

An older man Stella didn't recognize introduced himself as the master of ceremonies and started in on a tribute to Ballard that ended with the sentiment – incongruous on more than one level – that Jack had died doing what he loved. A microphone was then passed from table to table and twenty or so people stood up to share remembrances. That seemed to be the extent of the program. When there were no further takers at the open mic, the MC urged everyone to stay and party as Jack would have wanted.

Joe excused himself to speak to another teacher seated at a nearby table and the boys followed. Ben McKean came by, a beer in hand, and pulled up a chair next to Stella's "Guess that was that," he said.

"I wonder if there'll be a receiving line," she said.

"Better be soon or people will start to leave."

Kayla appeared and snapped a picture of them.

"Yikes," Stella said. "That'll be a keeper. Nothing like a candid shot taken at a funeral."

Stella noticed Pamela standing alone and left Ben to go over to speak to her. They were talking quietly when Danielle appeared. "What's *she* doing here?" Danielle said, giving Stella the fish-eye. "She upset Jack at his own party, the last night of his life."

Stunned into silence, Stella felt heat rise to her face.

Pamela said, "I know you're hurting, Danielle, but it's not fair to take it out on Stella." She turned to Stella with an apologetic expression. "If you'll excuse us, dear, I think I'd better organize the receiving line."

"Forget it, I'm out of here," Danielle said.

Pamela looked at Stella and shook her head.

As the two women moved away, Stella took a moment to compose herself. She wanted to feel sorry for the grieving fiancée, but it was difficult to be that noble. Putting aside thoughts of Danielle, she rounded up Joe and the boys to get in line to pay their respects to the family. But after a brief huddle, Pamela, Richard, and Danielle left the room, along with Jack's old friend Rory and a handful of others who formed a human buffer zone around them. Once the family was gone, Ben McKean slipped out a side door and Karen Pickering could be heard coaxing Cassidy to go home with her.

Joe took Matt and Nicky to the bar for sodas and the three of them blended into a group of kids and adults. Stella collected the boys' jackets and was about to wander over to the bar herself when she recognized the thin woman in black from Ballard's party. Alone now at a vacated table, she was slipping her arms into a fuzzy grey cardigan, her thick black hair falling in jagged layers around a ghostly face contrasted by a lot of eye liner.

"Hi," Stella said, debating whether to mention the birthday party. "I guess none of us expected to be at a funeral today."

"That's for sure," the woman said.

"Did you know Jack for long? I'm Stella Mosconi, by the way. I knew him from high school."

"Same here. I remember you from school. Seen your articles in the paper."

"Oh," Stella said. "Well, thanks for noticing. Good to see you."

The woman laughed, showing yellowish teeth. "You don't remember me huh? It's Angela. Angel, they used to call me. I was in Jack's class."

"Okay, right," Stella said, still unable to place her and hoping it didn't show. "Do you still live in Nelson, Angela? Angel, I mean."

"I go by Angie now. I live in Ymir, work in Salmo."

"Oh, what sort of –"

"School janitor. Real glamorous." She laughed again. It was a scratchy, nervy sort of laugh. "But I like it up in those parts. Ymir is too small for people to act snooty like they do here. Present company excluded."

Stella smiled. "Appreciate that. I left town after high school and haven't been back very long. Got to say I find Nelson a bit cliquish too. So, were you and Jack good friends?"

"Guess I knew him better than some. Listen I'm gasping for a smoke. You want to go get a coffee or something?" She fidgeted with her shoulder bag, a large black affair with a fringe that hung down to the top of her tall black boots.

Stella glanced over at her family. Joe had taken off his tie; the boys were jabbing at each other and scuffling with another kid. "I think my crew is about ready to leave, but –"

"Sure." Angie looked away briefly. "Nice talking to you."

"But, hey," Stella said. "I could send those guys packing and catch a bus home later. Why don't we go over to the Dominion? I gather that was Jack's favourite coffee shop."

"Oh, yeah. Jack was a big fan of the Dom, all right." Her tone was hard to read. "See you there."

* * *

The sign on the screen door of the Dominion Café read, "Closed for funeral." Stella probably should have anticipated that – the owner was at the memorial. But she'd never known the place to be closed in the middle of the day. As for Angie the Dark Angel, she wasn't there. Well, maybe she was running a quick errand.

Stella sat at a table in front of the café and scrolled through emails on her phone. How many days had passed since she'd seen Jack Ballard lounging at the same table? A man seemingly at peace with the world.

Twenty-five minutes went by. So, okay, Angie was a no-show. She either saw the sign and took off – or what? Changed her mind? Nice. The bus to the North Shore ran only four times a day and the next one wouldn't leave downtown until 5:30 p.m. Stella made tracks for the Hume, hoping to catch Joe and the boys before they left for home.

She needn't have rushed. At the hotel, Joe was engrossed in a conversation and the boys were lying on the carpet with another kid, staring at an iPad.

Stella waved at Joe and slipped into the restroom.

There on a cubicle wall, just above the toilet paper roll, someone had scribbled a telephone number and the words: *If he touched you, call me.*

10

HOME FROM THE FUNERAL, Pamela peeled off her separates and put on a soft cotton shirt and comfy stretch jeans. Richard opened a fresh bottle of scotch and joined Danielle and Rory in the front room to reminisce about Jack. Pamela didn't like the way Rory always sat close to Danielle and found excuses to touch her, however innocently. When she'd brought up the issue with Richard, he wouldn't hear about it. Accused her of not understanding how young people interact these days. Then he alluded to the special bond he shared with Danielle because of the baby. As if Pamela, with no blood connection to any of them, were an outsider in her own home.

Well, she'd dutifully organized the memorial, gotten Richard and Danielle there and back, and chitchatted mindlessly with legions of people, most of whom she had no interest in now that Jack was gone.

Feeling utterly alone, Pamela excused herself and slipped outside. She'd absentmindedly picked up her car keys from the tray in the foyer but couldn't think of anywhere to go until it occurred to her a walk might help. She pocketed the keys and set out for the reservoir part way down Lucky Jack Road. Years ago, when no one fussed much about permits, Richard had hired a crew to dam up a stream to create the reservoir. He'd bought her a lovely old oak bench and put it under a big cottonwood tree. She often took a break there to enjoy the mallards and herons and other water fowl that stopped by the pond.

Today as she came around the last bend in the road, she was surprised to see a male figure sitting on her bench, a bicycle leaning against the back of it. Hearing her approach, he jumped up and turned, and Pamela had to cover up her surprise. The teenager had on a shirt with the bike shop logo and the type of shorts and shoes Jack had worn.

He seemed taken aback too. He moved the bike away from the bench muttering, "I'm, uh, sorry for your loss."

"Thank you," she said. He continued to stand there awkwardly so she spoke again. "You knew Jack well? If you were at the funeral you'll have to forgive me. I'm afraid the whole thing's a blur at this point."

"Nah, I didn't go." He hesitated. "I thought about going. But, like, with Jack gone I didn't see the point. Know what I'm saying?"

Pamela looked at him sharply. Jack had used that phrase *ad nauseam*. The boy was mimicking him. He didn't seem to notice she'd gone quiet. He was a nice-looking kid, tall and muscular, with longish dark hair that made her want to reach up and push it out of his eyes. He had deep hazel eyes with long thick lashes any girl would have envied.

"The last funeral I went to was my mother's," he added. "After that . . ." He looked down and shook his head.

"Oh, dear. When did you lose your mother?" Pamela said.

"Couple years back, I guess. Yeah, two years now."

"Ah. Well. That's hard." Another motherless boy. Pamela wondered if he was as starved for a woman's attention as Jack had been as a teenager. Jack had nearly devoured her when she'd first moved in with Richard, despite a plucky effort to act grown-up. Still, she didn't have the heart to brush off this kid. "I'm at a disadvantage," she said. "You know who I am, but I don't know your name."

"Kieran Corcoran. At your service." He raised two fingers to his forehead in a mock salute. "Actually, I *am* at your service. I work at the muffler place downtown. Few weeks ago, I changed the oil in your Benz."

"I thought you looked familiar," she lied. "Well, nice to meet you Kieran." She shifted her gaze to the pond, hoping he would take the hint and disappear. Instead he leaned the bike against the Cottonwood and perched on a rock near the bench.

"Yeah, Jack really encouraged me to get my *sh* – act together," he said. "Finish high school online, save up for college. My education got interrupted when my mom was dying back in Toronto." He stood up and stretched. "I had a lot of respect for your son," he continued. "He gave me good advice. He was gonna talk to his bike mechanic and see if I could maybe apprentice with the dude in my spare time."

"Maybe Jack mentioned that to his staff," Pamela said, although she doubted that he had. Jack loved to shoot the breeze, but follow-through hadn't been his strong suit.

"Yeah. Cool. I should drop by and talk to them." Then the boy seemed to catch himself. "Or maybe I should wait until . . . I wouldn't want to be disrespectful."

"Life goes on, Kieran," Pamela said. "You go ahead with what's important to you. But now if you'll excuse me, I'd like to have a few moments alone."

"'Course," he said. "You take care, ma'am," and he was off, barrelling down the road, hair flying, a helmet that had seen better days bouncing precariously on the bike's rattrap.

* * *

Home after a long day in the newsroom, Stella was swamped with housework and laundry but Matt and Nicky wouldn't leave her alone. Joe had stayed in town for another evening meeting and after supper the boys nagged her to go outside and skip stones in the lake.

On the lakeshore Stella kicked off her shoes and waded in, wincing a little at the sharpness of the rocks, the bite of cold water. In no time, both boys were wet up to their thighs and Nicky was getting frustrated in his efforts to skip a stone. He shoved Matt, then Matt pulled him under, and Stella ordered them both inside for their baths.

She was mildly irritated with Joe for not making it home for dinner again. The frequency of his Search and Rescue duties was ramping up, although she didn't have the heart to complain. SAR gave Joe the sense of fitting-in he seemed to crave, and he was desperate to be part of an important rescue, maybe because he hadn't been able to do anything for Jack Ballard.

Once the boys were in bed, she fell into her favourite chair and opened her skimpy file on the incident at Elephant Mountain. She wondered if Ben had found any evidence of foul play in Ballard's death. And not for the first time, she thought about Angie, the mysterious woman at the funeral who'd stood her up at the Dominion Café. Angela, Angel. She should have asked her last name. Too bad she'd thrown out her high school yearbooks. But it struck her that Jack Ballard's personal yearbooks might be even more useful, and his father could likely put his hands on them in two seconds flat. Richard had probably kept all of Jack's memorabilia. It wouldn't have surprised Stella if he still had Jack's class photo from kindergarten.

While she tried to decide whether or not it was too soon to impose on the Ballard family, Pamela called and made it easy for her. She said the Chamber of Commerce wanted to pay tribute to Jack with a memorial dinner; his parents had been asked to say a few words. "Richard will have to do it, of course," she said. "He's balking. But I think I could talk him into it if you were to write the speech. Your stories are always the first ones he looks for in the paper. I know this is a dreadful imposition, Stella. We'd want to compensate you. I don't expect –"

"I'd be happy to help, Pamela," Stella said. "And I wouldn't think of accepting any sort of compensation. Please don't embarrass me by insisting."

"Well, that's more than kind. But it's terribly short notice. The event is less than two weeks away."

"We'd better get started then. Would it be convenient if I came by? Maybe I could look at some early photos, mementos from school – that sort of thing?" Stella assured herself her intentions were honourable. She wouldn't even ask to see Jack's yearbooks.

* * *

The following day Stella worked through lunch so she could get away early to drop in on the Ballards. Once there, she sat down with Richard in the basement of the chalet, boxes everywhere, him leaning back in a worn leather armchair, her on the cracked ottoman at his feet. She wondered if the basement served as a kind of man-cave for Richard. He looked so relaxed in that beat-up old chair, a piece at odds with the elegant furnishings upstairs. Pamela brought down a tray with a carafe of locally roasted coffee and a plate of pastries from the French bakery downtown. "Call me when you get to the high school years," she said merrily, and left them to their task.

Richard was quiet for a moment, then he said, "To be honest, I have mixed feelings about this tribute business, Stella. The family's been so damned depressed we've been no use to each other or anyone else. People want to help, but . . ." He looked away briefly. "It's hard to know what to say to anyone – for Danielle and me especially. But Pammie was over the moon when you suggested dropping by. She threw open the doors to air the place, called in the cleaner, ordered the goodies." He smiled weakly. "Well, let's get to it. I dug out a few old photo albums. Jack's childhood seems the obvious place to start. I think he was on a bicycle as soon as he could walk."

Stella had been nervous about the meet-up too. She had wondered if anything in Jack's history could alter her opinion of him. But images of a lively child just didn't jibe with her memories of him as a teenager. Still, as Richard flipped through the albums, telling cute anecdotes, chuckling over typical boyhood escapades, she couldn't help admiring their evident closeness.

After an hour or so of pouring over the contents of dusty cartons, the effort seemed to be taking a toll on Richard. His hands trembled as he put aside a photo album and Stella said, "I don't want to wear you out, Richard. I could come back another time. Or if you're okay with me taking some of this material along, I could look it over at home and pull out a few more highlights. How about I put together a draft over the weekend and email it to you? We have plenty of time to fine-tune before the tribute evening."

"That sounds fine, Stella. I'll get a dolly from the garage to move the boxes." Stella watched him lumber off, a man in deep mourning for a son who had meant the world to him. She thought of her own dad and their frayed relationship. Twenty-five years now since she'd seen his face. He certainly wouldn't have boxes of mementos from her childhood – she wondered if he had even a snapshot of her.

Richard and Stella were loading cartons into the back of her Pathfinder when the door to the studio above the garage banged open and Danielle Stone thundered down the steps. "What's going on?" she cried. "What are you doing?"

Richard said, "Oh, Danielle, didn't Pammie tell you? Stella's helping me with the speech at the Chamber. She's going to finish the research at home."

Danielle latched onto Richard's arm. "Research – is that what she calls it? She has no right to touch Jack's stuff, Richard. Please take those boxes out of her car *right now*."

"Danielle, honey," Richard said. "No need to get your shirt in a knot. Stella will return it all."

"No, no, it's not right," she said, frantically. "I'm begging you, Richard. Don't let her take Jack's things. *Please.*" She started to hyperventilate.

"There, there, my girl. Take it easy," Richard said. "Sorry, Stella. Do you think you can get by with what we've already discussed?"

"Of course," Stella said. "Don't give it another thought."

Danielle released a few shuddering breaths and brushed invisible tears from her eyes as Stella and Richard put the cartons back onto the dolly and said goodbye to each other.

Stella got into the Pathfinder, started the engine, and turned around in the drive, watching in the rear-view as Jack's father wrapped his arms around Danielle. It was a fitting end to her Oscar-worthy performance.

Within minutes, Stella's phone rang and she pulled over. Pamela Ballard apologized for Danielle's behaviour. "I'm getting tired of making excuses for her," she said. "Richard was almost his old self again today, sitting in that chair, talking about happier times."

"Don't worry about it, Pamela. I have plenty of background. My notes will just be prompts for Richard anyway."

"Well, if there's anything I can do, please ask."

Stella hesitated. "You know," she said, feeling a tad guilty due to her ulterior motive. "I *would* like to take a peek at one of Jack's high school annuals, the one for his grad year, if possible."

"Say no more, Stella. I'll find it and drop it by your office."

11

PAMELA WAS AS GOOD as her word. The day after Stella's visit to the Ballard home, the receptionist at the *Nelson Times* dropped a padded envelope on her desk.

The high school annual for Jack's graduating year was full of scribbles and messages, including the requisite shot of the principal with a tail and horns. Stella found her own photo amongst those of the tenth graders and was surprised to see she'd signed his yearbook. "Good luck in the future!" she'd written, presumably before he'd attacked her at the pond. Someone – Jack? – had doodled curlicues around her picture. Probably best not to read too much into that.

She flipped through the pages and found her old friend Carli, fresh-faced and pretty, then Ben McKean, as dark and serious as ever. She trailed a finger across his closed lips, recalling their shyness with each other, the rare stilted conversations that ensued outside their lockers. Ben's goal in life had been to join the RCMP and see Canada from coast to coast to coast. Hers had been to get out of town, period.

Stella studied the faces of other tenth-grade classmates, many of them long forgotten. She skimmed the eleventh-graders then moved to the grad section where Jack Ballard's photo appeared on the first page, second from the top. Predictably, Jack had been deemed male student most likely to succeed. Hard to believe the boy smiling back at her was dead. When that picture had been taken, he would have been about seven years older than her son Matt was at present, a disturbing thought.

Stella moved on, paging through the rest of Jack's class but she didn't find a girl called Angela or Angel. On her second pass through the grads she noticed a gap in the alphabet. A page was missing between the G's and the L's, and someone had done a tidy job of cutting it out. Stella leaned back in her chair. Angie's picture must have been on that page, in which case the first initial of her maiden name would have fallen between the letters G and L. But who knew what her surname was now, or if it had changed, or why Jack had cut her out of his yearbook.

What the hell. Stella picked up her phone and hit the number from the restroom wall at the Hume; she had entered it under M for Mystery. After five rings, the voicemail kicked in and a husky voice said, "This is Angie. Leave a message."

So okay, Angie *was* the graffiti artist.

Stella hung up without leaving a message. Then, realizing Angie would see the missed call, she pressed the number again. This time Angie picked up. Stella skipped the preliminaries. "Can we talk?" she said. "I don't mean now, over the phone. Any plans to come to Nelson in the near future?"

Angie didn't skip a beat. "Not likely," she said. "I guess you could come up to Ymir. I'd have to think about it though. Talking to you."

"What – you're being choosy? Listen, Angel – Angie, I mean – I got this number off a bathroom wall."

"Yeah, but the message wasn't for you."

"How do you know?" Stella said.

Silence. "Okay, so you want to come here? I don't always have a car."

"You won't stand me up again?"

"Oh, yeah. I mean, no. Let's make it tomorrow before I change my mind. The pub at the hotel okay?"

"I'll be there," Stella said, wondering if the Dark Angel, as she thought of her, would turn up this time. Jack had touched her – that's what the note implied. Had he assaulted her? If so, Angie might have gone to his funeral to find some sort of closure. But why – invited or not – had she turned up at his party?

* * *

At the end of her workday Thursday, Stella got into her car and headed for Ymir, a village some thirty kilometres south of Nelson. She passed a car dealership, a vet's clinic, the place where skiers and boarders hitch a ride to the ski hill in winter, all the time wondering what surprises Angie the Dark Angel would have in store for her.

She arrived at the block-long town centre and parked outside the one-and-only hotel and pub. Inside the quaint building, dozens, maybe hundreds, of original paintings graced the walls, giving her something to look at as the second hand of an old clock juddered around its porcelain face. Stella accepted a coffee and after the first refill, ordered a burger. She was biting into it, sauce dribbling down her chin, when a thin, dark woman stepped through the doorway.

Angie strutted over and plunked herself opposite Stella. She wore faded, skin-tight jeans and a pilled, off-the-shoulder black sweater, heavy make-up that accentuated her angular face and dark eyes. Boho chic – it suited her. "I almost didn't come," she said. "I doubt my little message actually does apply to you. You're probably just being a nosy reporter."

Stella blotted her chin and hands on a paper napkin. "A bit of both, I guess. On a personal level, I can't stop thinking about Jack Ballard's death, even though I didn't like him."

"And you didn't like him because . . ."

Stella paused. "Let's just say he made me uncomfortable." That seemed as good a euphemism as any for her true feelings.

Angie snorted. "I knew this'd be a waste of time," she said, glancing up as the server dropped a beer mat on the table and placed a tall, glistening pint in front of her. A standing order then. She raised the beer and drank thirstily.

"Let's start again," Stella said. "Your message said, 'If he touched you, call me.' Well, he did. Back in high school."

Angie ran a finger across her upper lip, wiping off a trace of foam. "Ya like it?"

"If I liked it," Stella said, "why would I be here?"

Angie gazed over the rim of her glass. "I'm here."

"So why the message?"

Angie shrugged and looked away, waved at a couple seated across the room. They raised their glasses to her. "Why not? I had one of those Sharpies that girl set out for the so-called memory book. What a load of crap. Jack would have puked at the thought." She pounded back the rest of the beer.

Stella waited a moment before trying another tack. "So he touched you?"

"Duh." Angie looked around for the server. "Hey ya, Mags – another one over here." She leaned back and closed her eyes for a moment. "Shit, Jack Ballard. He could've had any girl at school."

"I'm a little confused," Stella said. "Did you *want* Jack to come on to you? I thought maybe he had –"

Angie jumped in. "Like *you* didn't want him to? C'mon."

"I only went out with him a couple of times," Stella said. "When he got rough I broke it off."

Angie snorted again. Mags put another beer in front of her and whisked away the empty glass.

Stella said, "Did he get rough with you?"

Angie leaned back, and looked her in the eye. "Depends what you mean by rough. Jack would do anything for me back then."

"Such as?"

"What are you – one of those voyeurs?"

Stella slipped into reporter mode. "So you and Jack dated back in school?"

"Guess you could call it that. Only place we ever went was under the old footbridge."

Not the pond near his home then. Stella flashed on his hand against her throat and took a moment before she spoke again. "So what grade were you in when you guys hooked up?"

"Twelve, our senior year. The popular girls were all over him. I'd hear them in the toilets, Jack this, Jack that. But I didn't care. I knew none of those airheads were giving him what I was."

"What made you think no one else was, uh, giving him what you were? If you don't mind my asking."

"I do mind. Not your business" Angie said. "Hey, I'm gonna have another brew. Want one?"

"Better not, I'm driving," Stella said, hoping she hadn't sounded too judgemental. She didn't want Angie to close down on her. "I guess you're as curious as I am about Jack's fall. What's your take on what happened?"

Angie's shrug seemed to say nothing surprised her. "He musta jumped."

"Why though?"

"Why does anybody jump? All the bullshit got to be too much."

"Most people would say Jack had the perfect life," Stella said.

"Most people only know what they read on Facebook. Which is stupid. No one tells it like it is on Facebook." She shook her head. "I'm surprised more people don't jump. Or take pills, which makes more sense. Just drift off to sleep, good bye world." Angie tipped back her glass and emptied it. Licked her lips.

The server hovered near their table, holding a coffee pot. "Get you gals anything else?"

"Maybe another half cup," Stella said.

Angie ordered another beer and teased the waitress about the purple streaks in her hair. While they riffed on hairdos, Stella sipped her coffee and thought about Angie's boast. *Jack would do anything for me back then.* This from a woman whose grad photo Ballard had excised from his yearbook. When the server moved on, Stella said, "Getting back to what happened at Pulpit Rock, I can't picture Jack jumping. For one thing, it normally wouldn't be fatal to fall from that elevation. If Jack had wanted to kill himself, I think he would have been smarter about it. And I can't see him simply stumbling over the edge either."

"Yeah," Angie agreed. "That wouldn't be Jack."

"You think someone might have pushed him?" Stella said.

"Ya kidding me? That's crazy." She downed the rest of her beer and started to poke around inside her black fringed bag. "Hey, this has been real but I gotta split."

"Let me get this," Stella said. "But, uh, are you good to drive?" Stupid question. The rake-thin woman had put away multiple beers in a matter of minutes.

"Drive? I live down the friggin' street." Angie laughed as she upped and bolted, weaving her way through the pub, touching backs of chairs, bumping a table and nearly spilling the drinks.

Why the rush to leave? Stella wondered. She still didn't know why Angie had left that message on the restroom wall.

So many questions had been left unanswered. Such as whether anyone besides Stella had called the number – or whether Angie and Ballard had gotten up close and personal more recently than during their high school days. Stella would have paid money to hear her take on Danielle Stone. When Ballard announced his engagement at the party, Angie had *not* looked happy, finally barricading herself in the powder room.

Stella finished her coffee and called for the bill. She was certain she would follow up again with the Dark Angel, a woman whose fraught relationship with Jack Ballard had ended only hours before his death.

But then the same could be said of her, Stella.

Having avoided Ballard while he was alive, she had to ask herself why she was so intent on following his tracks now. Nothing about his death made any sense, but one thing she knew for sure: her need for answers was personal – she couldn't blame it on the job.

12

"THE CORONER RULED THE death accidental. End of story."
As was his habit, the Chief of Police delivered his decree with his
back to McKean, eyes fixed on the view of the lake and mountains
from his office window.

"With all due respect, Chief –" McKean began.

The big man swung around. "Was there ever a more maddening
phrase in the English language?" He settled his generous bulk in a
throne-like armchair. "Accidental death. Full stop. Move on. Plenty
of other duties to keep you busy."

McKean bit back his irritation. "At any rate," he said, "I'm not
entirely convinced the death was accidental. I need more time to
pursue leads. If we find evidence of foul play the coroner will reopen
the file and pass it to us."

"Are you thick, McKean? The poor guy had an aneurysm. A quote-
unquote time bomb that'd been waiting to go off. How would foul
play have come into it?"

"If the impact of the fall caused the rupture, you still have to
ask what made him go over the edge. Signs at the viewpoint warn
hikers of the drop off. You wouldn't expect a former elite athlete to
simply trip or stumble – and I doubt he jumped. He seemed to have
everything to live for. New fiancée, baby on the way, loving parents,
stature in the community."

"What – you think he was pushed? How does a straight-up guy
like Ballard piss off anyone enough to shove him off a cliff?"

"Jealousy? An altercation that went tits up? Financial problems?
An employee I spoke to implied his business was slightly shaky.
Maybe he gambled and got in over his head – people he owed wanted
to give him a good scare or make an example of him. I have a feeling
somebody knows more about what happened up at that viewpoint."

"You have a feeling." The Chief shook his head.

McKean forged on. "I'd like to get access to his health records, for one thing. His body had some curious marks. The pathologist spoke to his GP but the doc is new, took over the practice from a recent retiree. He might not have delved too deeply into the files. And the girl who called 9-1-1 saw a guy in a hoodie on the trail. I want to find him."

"Just make sure the Ballard family is on board before you go poking into his medical records. We don't have a compelling reason to invade their privacy. You can have one more day then let it go. Resume general duties. Are we clear?"

"Yessir." With no time to waste, McKean drove to Lucky Jack Road to seek permission from Ballard's parents to access his medical files. No one was home so he left a message on their landline requesting a return call ASAP. Then he carried on to the Pickering residence for a follow-up interview with Cassidy.

The girl said she didn't want to talk, she was still upset about "Jack's" death. So, she felt more familiar with him now. That happened when well-known people passed. McKean asked her again about the figure in a hoodie she'd seen on the trail that day.

Cassidy shrugged. "He had his hood up. Obviously you don't see much when someone runs past you with his hood up."

"You identified the figure as male though, so you noticed that much. Correct?"

"I guess," she said. Big sigh.

"You said you thought he'd gone all the way to the flagpole because you didn't see him at Pulpit Rock, is that correct?"

"Yeah. Everything was like I already said." She crossed her arms and seemed to curl in on herself.

"I can see this is hard for you, Cassidy, but we need to find this guy. Would you be willing to sit down with a police sketch artist? You might be able to help her come up with a likeness. Your mom could come with you to the station." He glanced encouragingly at Karen Pickering, who was seated next to her daughter.

"I'm sure that'd be a waste of time," Cassidy said, appearing to be on the verge of tears.

"You'd be surprised what a sketch artist can do by asking the right questions," he pressed. "How about it, Cassidy? Can we count on you?"

"I guess so," she said, wearily.

"Great. I'll ask the artist to call and set up a time that works for you, a time convenient for your mom too." He smiled at Ms. Pickering and brought the interview to a close before her daughter had time to change her mind.

* * *

On Friday, Stella's lunchtime errands took her near the hotel where Jack Ballard's funeral had been held. On impulse she slipped in a side door of the Hume and down the hall to the ladies' room. The stall where Angie had scrawled her message was occupied so she fussed with her hair until a woman came out, washed her hands, and left.

The wall had been scrubbed clean of graffiti.

Stella opened her phone and stabbed Angie's number. A husky voice said, "Hi. What can I do for you?" It was like reaching a service where you pay someone to talk dirty.

"Yeah, hi, it's Stella."

Angie made a sound half-way like a laugh. "Like, duh," she said. "Ever hear of call display?" But her tone was friendly.

"They washed it off," Stella said. "Your message on the bathroom wall." Another patron came in and Stella went back out to the street and leaned against the building. A panhandler dressed in shorts and flip-flops, a woolly plaid scarf wrapped around his neck, asked her for change for coffee. Stella fished in her pocket for a two-dollar coin.

"Why'd you go look," Angie said. "Were you thinking about Jack?"

"I guess I was thinking about you. And Jack," Stella said.

"Me and Jack."

"I meant to ask you . . ." Stella said. "Did anyone besides me reply to your message on the bathroom wall?"

"Never mind that. I've been thinking about your story and I don't buy it."

"My story. I assume you mean what I said about Jack and me."

"*I assume.*" She snorted. "You dated Jack a couple times. He got 'a little rough.'" Stella could hear the air quotes. "And you headed for the hills. Maybe what *really* scared you was the way he made you feel."

The barb hit home. Stella paused a moment to regain control. "At this point, it doesn't really matter."

"Lucky you," Angie said.

"So for you, it still hurts," Stella said. "Did you and Jack see each other after high school. By 'see,' I mean. . ."

"There you go again, being a snoopy reporter."

"Sorry, occupational hazard." Stella paused. "I'm curious about Danielle though. I thought she might have noticed your message and called. Did you ever meet her? Before the party, I mean."

After a beat, Angie said, "Seen her around."

Now we're getting somewhere, Stella thought. "From what I know about her, I doubt she would have ignored the message if she saw it."

Angie sighed impatiently. "I thought you called to talk about Jack and me."

Another deflection. "Okay, sure. Maybe you can help me understand him better."

Angie said, "I doubt it. Why should I try?"

Stella countered, "So someone can get to the bottom of what happened?"

"You just can't help yourself, can you? Jack's death is like a big ugly accident on the side of the road – you don't really care but you can't look away. Here's my advice to you, Ms. Ace Reporter, *let it go*." She ended the call.

Let it go. Was that a threat or a warning? For one crazy moment Stella wondered if the Dark Angel could have lured Jack up to Pulpit Rock and killed him. Say when she finally came out of the powder room during the party, they'd argued. She talked him into meeting her at the viewpoint to resolve things but Jack insisted it was over between them. Angie was thin but wiry. Sober, she likely could have made it up to Pulpit, and with the element of surprise on her side, shoved him over the edge. Stella pictured the sylph-like woman taking a run at Ballard, shrieking, "If I can't have you, no one can!" But that scenario seemed too cartoonish to be true and it didn't fit with Angie's skittish temperament.

Danielle Stone, on the other hand, appeared to be tough and strong-willed. Her mood flipped like a switch, but if she took a notion to hike up that trail, she probably could have done it in her sleep, pregnant or not. Maybe she and Jack had words after the party; she *had* seemed uneasy when Richard called attention to the pregnancy. Maybe her drunken fiancé was a big disappointment.

Say she got up early, enticed Jack to walk up to Pulpit, and did the deed. She could have gotten back before anyone had missed her and later told Pamela she'd woken up to find him gone. But why would Stone kill her fiancé? Surely, she had the most to lose with Jack's death, although she wouldn't have been the first person to lash out in the heat of the moment.

Stella returned to the newsroom. She was starting to update the community events page when she picked up on some idle chatter from the adjacent office. Normally she would have gotten up and closed the door, but the conversation was so entertaining she listened in with one ear. One of the sales associates was regaling the others with her take on the film, *Fifty Shades of Grey*, which she'd watched for the second time the previous evening. Then a production assistant weighed in on the book and its sequels, which everyone seemed to agree were superior to the film.

The threesome – all women – began to mock argue about the meaning of BDSM. The production assistant insisted the acronym comprised several overlapping abbreviations. "BD" for bondage and discipline; "DS" for dominance and submission; "SM" for sadism and masochism. Stella interrupted what she was doing to make some notes on her desk calendar.

The production assistant seemed to have more than an academic interest in the topic. She offered the opinion that kinky sex could be equally satisfying for the submissive partner in a relationship. What with today's real-world pressures, she said, it could be liberating to surrender control to your partner, provided everyone played safe and fair. Sexual power plays, she opined, are rarely black and white. Hence all those shades of grey.

At that point, a customer must have come up to the front counter because the discussion came to an abrupt halt. One of the women asked brightly if she could be of assistance. The others presumably returned to their desks.

Now Stella's thoughts shifted back to Angie and their conversation at Ballard's funeral. When Stella suggested meeting at the Dominion Café, Jack's favourite coffee shop, Angie's response had been, "Oh, yeah. Jack was a big fan of the Dom, all right."

She must have spoken off the cuff, but Stella recalled her exact phrasing and ambiguous tone, which seemed significant. If Jack really was "a big fan of the Dom," did that mean he liked to be dominated during sex? It was difficult to picture Jack taking a submissive role in any situation, although Stella could see him being into BDSM, no question. She recalled only too clearly being on the receiving end of his early taste for kink.

Before resuming work on the community events page, Stella tore off the corner of the calendar she'd written on and tucked it into her bag. This BDSM business made her skin crawl, but it definitely warranted a second look with respect to Jack Ballard.

* * *

Days off from the muffler shop were the toughest for Kieran. Without work to distract him, the scene at Elephant Mountain played out in his head in an endless loop. His only escape was to run hard or cycle to exhaustion – that or get ripped on whatever was at hand. He often passed Ballard's Cycles, but he could never bring himself to go in, to speak to Kayla, who had once shown him the grudging respect she showed members of Jack's inner circle, or to nod at Dex the high priest/chief mechanic who'd never so much as glanced his way. Ballard had once dangled the possibility of Dex taking him on as an apprentice, but Kieran didn't delude himself to think that would happen now.

Still, one doable thing Jack Ballard had drilled into him was the importance of a clean bike. So on this particular day off, with nothing better to do, Kieran scrounged a pail, a couple rags, a few basic tools, and set out to de-grease his drivetrain. It was only after he'd removed both wheels and taken a worn toothbrush to the cassette that he realized he was out of food. He was wearing a stained T-shirt and bike shorts so worn his ass showed through in places, but he rubbed the grease off his hands as best he could and jogged down to the mall.

At Save-On Foods, he filled a basket with packets of instant soup, a few apples, and the cheapest energy bars he could find. But a case of Red Bull weighed him down so much he had to stop at the bottom of Hall Street to cadge a ride up the hill.

A half-dozen cars had already whizzed past when a shiny, late model Benz pulled over, Jack's stepmother behind the wheel. Kieran stammered something about his bike, adding he was too filthy to ride in anything other than the back of a pickup.

Mrs. Ballard laughed out loud. "So you were cleaning your bike and you got hungry."

"Exactly!" he said. "I don't suppose you have some paper to put over the seat? Otherwise, I just can't –"

"Get in, Kieran," she said. "Make yourself comfortable."

"Not many mothers would do this," he said, buckling up. Then fearing he'd put his foot in it, he added, "Sorry, that was stupid."

"Don't apologize, Kieran. I guess I am still a mother, even with Jack gone. A step-mother, technically. Anyway, I like to be reminded of Jack."

"I think about him a lot," he said, feeling his face get red. They talked about this and that, and when the car neared a well-kept multi-suite house on a corner, he said, "Well, this is me. Thanks for the ride, Mrs. Ballard."

"My pleasure, Kieran," she said, pulling over. "Anytime."

He got out and watched the Benz carry on up the hill, then hoofed it two blocks east to the dump he lived in, all the time thinking what a fine lady Mrs. B was. Sure, her mansion and fancy car impressed him, but it was something else – some quality she had – that made him want to be around her. He tried out the word "kindness," a phony-sounding, old timey term that seemed to ring true. Yes, Mrs. B was kind and good, not full of herself like most rich people. Kieran wondered if he reminded her a little of Jack. Too bad he had no way to make amends for what had happened to him.

* * *

After school Monday, Cassidy Pickering dragged herself to the police station. Her mom had wanted to tag along, but she had refused to meet with the sketch artist unless she was allowed to see her alone. A friendly receptionist at the NPD led her down a hall to an interview room that looked nothing like the ones on TV. This one had a big window and muted colours, a few fake plants. A coffee machine gurgled beside a tray that held Styrofoam cups, sugar lumps, and a massive jar of whitener. The coffee smelled like it had been made last week.

Cassidy sank into an easy chair, then got up and tried out one with a straight back. She folded her arms across her chest, then unfolded them, checked her watch. She took out her phone and clicked on Snapchat, then jumped when the door opened and a male officer – not McKean – looked in and said, "Sorry – wrong room."

The next time the door opened, it was by a youngish woman who knocked once and stepped in. "You must be Cassidy," she said. "I'm Sam. Sorry to keep you waiting." The sketch artist looked the part. Big glasses, black leggings and slouchy sweater, hennaed hair twisted into a bun held up by chopsticks. She launched into a spiel, likely meant to put Cassidy at ease. Forensic artists don't even try for an identical match, she said. They only aim for an image that gives the "feel" of the person in question.

The second Cassidy could get a word in edgewise, she said, "Sorry, I don't think I can help. As I told Sergeant McKean, this person in a hoodie basically sprinted past me. I barely saw him. It was raining and I was watching my step. Apart from all the mud that day, there's a million roots and rocks on that trail."

"No worries," Sam said. "How about I start with a few questions and we'll see where that takes us? You want a coffee?"

"No thanks."

Sam looked at the coffee fixings and grimaced. "Good decision." She dug into a big green bag and brought out a sketchbook and a zip bag of coloured pencils, opened a laptop computer. "Now you said you barely saw 'him.' What gave you the impression this was a guy?"

"Um, he was running like a guy? It might have been his shoes."

"There you go," Sam said, as if Cassidy had proved her point by making a brilliant observation. "Anything about the shoes stand out? Colour, style, size?"

"Not that I noticed."

"But you noticed his hoodie. That's cool. Any writing or logos on the front or back?"

"I only saw the back and it was plain grey, no logos," Cassidy said. "Darkish grey, I guess."

"Okay. Let's come back to the hoodie later. Pants?"

Cassidy felt like saying, "Yeah, he wore pants," but decided she'd better play it straight. "You want a colour? I don't know, grey or black?"

"Stripe on the side? Stretchy material?" Sam said.

Cassidy shrugged. "Not a clue."

"I wonder if you caught a teensy glimpse of his profile as he passed you?"

"No," Cassidy said. "As I told the officer, I didn't see his face. Just the hood."

Sam leaned back in her chair. "So, you're running along, watching your step, and this guy passes you. Did you hear him coming?"

"Uh, probably not."

Sam frowned slightly. "Did he startle you then?"

"Not really. I must have sensed someone was coming. But runners pass each other all the time. Nobody pays much attention."

"This is a small town though. It would be natural to take a quick look to see if you knew this guy from school or somewhere."

"Never occurred to me."

"A guy typically glances at a girl as he passes her. Which might have given you a quick impression of his face, maybe something about his hair. . ."

Cassidy exhaled impatiently. "That seems kind of sexist. Trail runners aren't looking to pick up. Mostly we're just concentrating on our time."

"O-kay," Sam said, drawing the word out. She sat forward in her chair again. "When you think back, though, does any little detail come to mind? Maybe the way he moved or –"

"I don't *know!*" Cassidy said. "Look, I'm sorry. All I saw was a runner in a dark grey hoodie. I didn't even notice what kind of pants the guy was wearing."

Sam stood up so suddenly Cassidy was thrown off base. The artist thanked her for coming and pulled out a business card. "Call me if you remember anything," she said. "Any detail, however minor."

"I can go then?" Cassidy said.

"Certainly," Sam said. "But don't be surprised if our little talk jogs your memory. If it does, give me a shout. Anytime, day or night."

* * *

Monday afternoon, McKean was downtown on foot patrol while Samantha Tarasoff, a forensic sketch artist from Kelowna, met with Cassidy Pickering in the department's least threatening interview room. Luckily for McKean, since his budget for the investigation was zilch, Sam had a travel day owing her and she'd agreed to delay her departure to Kelowna after a weekend in Nelson. McKean was taking a complaint about a vagrant from a ski-shop owner when his phone rang, Tarasoff on call display. McKean excused himself and slipped outside and around the corner to take the call. "How'd it go?" he said.

"Blood from a stone," said Sam. "That kid would not give an inch. Still, she looked surprised when I pulled the plug. Don't know what she was playing at, but she seemed prepared to hang in as long as it took."

"You think she knew more than she was saying?" McKean said.

"You bet your booties," Sam said. McKean pictured her ensconced in the chintz-covered armchair by the window, one spandex-encased leg crossed over the other, her gravity-defying hairdo held up by chopsticks. "Consider this," Sam continued. "A young girl alone on a trail hears someone behind her. What does she do? She looks back. Any female would –we're conditioned to do that for our own safety. As for the guy in the hoodie, if he sees a girl ahead of him, he'll check her out as he runs by. Human nature. Even if he's gay he'll at least glance at her, giving the girl a quick glimpse of his face and hair."

"But not in this case."

"She deflected the question. Accused me of being sexist."

McKean laughed. "She's hiding something."

"That's my guess," Sam said. "Either she knows the guy and wants to protect him, or she knows him but he intimidates her. And here's another possibility: There was no guy. The guy in the hoodie doesn't exist."

"In which case, she must have had a reason to invent him."

"You got it. I'll let you know if I hear from her. But don't hold your breath."

"I owe you one, Sam."

"Coffee. Next time I'm in town."

"You're on," McKean said, pocketing his phone and returning to the ski shop. He was no further ahead in finding the guy in the hoodie, but at least Mr. and Mrs. Ballard had signed a release that would give him access to their son's medical records.

13

DANIELLE WAS STRESSED TO the max. She'd come back from having her roots touched up to find Pamela and Richard wringing their hands. The cop had called and talked them into signing a release that would allow the Nelson Police to pry into Jack's medical records. How the hell was his medical history any business of the police?

She didn't waste any time with Mr. and Mrs. Mope but went straight up to the studio to call the Chief of Police. The receptionist tried to palm off Ben McKean on her. "I need to talk to the Chief," Danielle said, firmly. "I have a problem with the way Sergeant McKean is conducting the investigation into my late fiancé's death."

Click. In about two seconds the head honcho picked up his phone. "Ms. Stone," he said. "My condolences. How may I help?"

Danielle sank a little deeper into her beanbag chair and sniffled once. "Thank you so much for taking my call, Chief –" *Shit.* She'd forgotten to look up his name. Without skipping a beat, she reached for her laptop, clicked on her browser, and brought up the NPD website. "I'm at my wits' end," she continued. "Sergeant McKean might mean well, but he's making life a living hell for my fiancé's parents and myself. It feels like every last shred of privacy has been stripped away from our family since Jack's horrible accident. And now Sergeant McKean wants access to Jack's old medical records." Okay, the chief's name was Wise. Skipper Wise. Only in Nelson.

"I'm sorry that's upset you, Ms. Stone. But this sort of enquiry is routine – mostly a matter of dotting i's and crossing t's. We want to do our best for your fiancé by being thorough in our investigation."

"I understand, Chief Wise, but I thought doctor/patient confidentiality was sacred. I'm carrying Jack's child. Among other things, Jack must have talked to his doctor about that." Danielle paused a moment and swallowed hard. "For Sergeant McKean to violate the family's right to privacy at this time is cruel and senseless. Jack had an unfortunate accident. He was young and healthy as an ox. It's not like he was a candidate for a heart attack or something."

There was a brief silence at the end of the line. "Perhaps not." The Chief hesitated again. "But there's, uh, always the chance of finding something that could shed light on what happened to your fiancé. As I said, we're just being prudent. Nothing to worry about."

The Chief's pauses had set alarm bells clanging in Danielle's head. Time to take off the gloves. "Is there something in particular you hoped to find, Chief Wise? Because, I'm sorry, but my fiancé's parents have no authority here. Jack and I lived together for more than two years. Legally, I was his common-law wife when he passed away. And Chief Wise? Out of respect for Jack, I refuse to sign that release."

"Well, that's your prerogative, Ms. Stone," the Chief said, brusquely. The conversation was over. He would make McKean back off, so full marks to her for damage control. But her throwaway remark about heart attacks had made him go silent. Why? Jack's heart must have been strong – he was an athlete, for chrissakes.

Danielle googled heart attacks and couldn't make sense of anything that came up on the Internet. But if there was any suspicion around Jack's death, McKean wouldn't let it go. She would just have to keep on denying access to the medical records. Christ, she was tired. And the bitch reporter was sniffing around too. It was no secret Mosconi had inserted herself into a murder investigation headed up by McKean. The story had been all over the news a few months back. The pair of them were likely sleeping together, pure little Stella and the noble cop. McKean was probably as gaga over her as Jack had once been. Yeah, Mosconi was a threat in her own right, but who knew what she and the cop were capable of together.

In her calmer moments, Danielle doubted the autopsy could have revealed anything that implicated her. But the medical records were a black hole. Jack might have sneaked out to see his doctor any number of times without telling her. Jack could be such a baby when he didn't feel one hundred percent.

* * *

Stella packed a camera and recorder for a quick trip to the recreation centre. The community pool had been closed for renovations and the public was up in arms. The paper was getting letters from disgruntled synchro swimmers, seniors missing their aqua-fit, irate parents of kids on the swim team.

She locked her bike to the rack outside and went downstairs. Even empty, the pool spooked her. The cavernous hall and deep basin, the lingering, nauseating whiff of chlorine. She was snapping photos when she heard the slap of boots on tile.

The contractor in charge of repairs shook his head as he approached. Busy man. "What can I tell you?" he said. "Aside from the obvious fact the repairs had to be done."

He handed her a hardhat and she put it on. "The timing isn't great," Stella said. "Why close when the fall programs are just starting? I gather the swim team is hooped for the season."

Big shrug from the contractor. "What can I say – lot of things came to a head."

She followed him down a makeshift ladder, bracing for the sharp drop-off at the deep end, the cleats on her cycling shoes clicking *tap, tap, tap* on the tiles.

"You a user?" he said.

"You make it sound like a drug."

"Folks depend on it." He stopped and looked at her. "Wait a minute. You're the reporter who nearly drowned awhile back. Yeah, I read about it in the paper."

"No biggie," she said, shaking off the memory of choking and flailing, the darkness sucking her under. "What's happening here?"

They stood over a hole large enough to hold a body.

"Now that was a surprise," the contractor said, rubbing his hands together. "Plumbing issue. But one thing goes, everything goes." Stella turned on her recorder.

When she went upstairs for an aerial shot of the demolition, she heard someone call her name. Cassidy Pickering was pedaling hard on a stationary bicycle. "It's a disaster down there," the girl said, dismounting and joining Stella at the window over the pool. "God, I miss swimming."

"Wish I could say the same," Stella said, "I'm not much of a swimmer."

"D'ya ever think of taking lessons?"

"Oh, I've thought about it." Stella hesitated a moment. "I hate to admit it, but I'm nervous in deep water. More than nervous. Terrified."

"I could teach you," Cassidy said, earnestly. "I could. You can totally trust me in the water. I know how important it is to trust your teacher. I used to be a scaredy-cat swimmer myself when I was little."

"Scaredy-cat. So, there's a technical term for it," Stella said. "Listen I appreciate the offer, and I know you're a terrific instructor, but never mind me. How are *you* doing these days?"

"Okay, I guess. I can't stop thinking about Jack though. Even if I wanted to, the police wouldn't let me. This cop keeps hassling me about a guy in a hoodie I saw on the trail the day Jack died. I wish I hadn't even mentioned it. I had to go to the police station to talk to a sketch artist. How do I know what the guy looked like? I didn't even see his face."

This was new. "A guy in a hoodie?" Stella said, trying not to show much interest. "Where'd you see him?"

Cassidy exhaled impatiently. "Near the start of the trail, then I never saw him again. I hope you're not going to grill me about him too."

Stella backed off. "Well, too bad you felt pressured," she said, "but I guess the police have to follow-up on these things. Anyway, I see you're keeping fit, even with the pool closed."

"So far, but did you see the notice at the front desk? The fitness area is going to be torn apart too. Do you know anything about that new gym – Max's?"

"No, I haven't checked it out," Stella said. Nor did she intend to. She had been close to the owner's late wife and he had been a suspect in her death. She still considered Max Huber a shady ex-con, and having tangled with him in the past, she had no interest in renewing acquaintances.

"I think I'll check the place out," Cassidy said. "Pretty soon I'll have to put my road bike away for the season."

"Tell me about it," Stella said. "I hate when it gets too cold and wet to cycle to work."

"I wish my mom would get into cycling. I actually put down a deposit on a bike for her." Cassidy teared up a little. "Sorry. It's just that Jack helped me pick out the bike – he was going to deliver it himself on her birthday."

"Aw, Cassidy," Stella said. "Another reminder of Jack. Are you still going to buy your mom the bike?"

"I don't see the point anymore and I, like, put down my life savings on it. Two hundred dollars."

"You probably could get your deposit back," Stella said.

"Do you think so? That would be excellent. But I don't think I could handle walking into that shop just now."

"I'll come with you, if you like," Stella said.

Cassidy visibly perked up. "Really? That would be so cool. Seriously."

They made a date for the following afternoon.

* * *

When Stella arrived at Ballard's Cycles, Cassidy was pacing outside the store. "I'm not sure I can go through with this," she said.

"Having second thoughts about the refund?" Stella said. "You said you wanted your mom to get into cycling. Did you hope to ride together?"

"Oh, no, it's not that. I just don't like returning things, having to explain the problem. I get all flustered," Cassidy said. "I hadn't really thought about riding with my mom. I don't even know if she'd use a bike. It's too hard to explain."

"Never mind. Let's get this over with. I'll take the lead with the salesperson."

Inside, Stella introduced Cassidy to Kayla, who seemed to be in charge now. "Cassidy wants to talk to you about a refund on a deposit. Jack was holding a bike for her, but her circumstances have changed."

"I wanted to buy it for my mom, see," Cassidy put in. "But she's, uh, not that into cycling? She doesn't even know about the bike, so . . ."

Kayla turned to a computer. "Remember the date of the transaction?"

"It was Jack's birthday," Cassidy blurted, her cheeks reddening.

"Guess none of us can forget *that* day," Kayla said, clicking on her keyboard. "Okay. Pickering, right? Two hundred bucks." She opened the till. "Fifties and twenties okay?"

"Sure, whatever." Cassidy said. "I'm putting it in the bank anyway. Thanks a lot. Sorry for the inconvenience."

"Not a problem," Kayla said, briskly. "Anything else I can do for you ladies?"

Stella said, "You go ahead, Cassidy. I want to talk to Kayla about kids' bikes."

As the door closed behind Cassidy, Stella thanked Kayla for making the refund easy for the girl.

Kayla shrugged. "Jack would have wanted me to."

"I guess he and Cassidy hit it off," Stella said.

"More like he and you hit it off," Kayla said.

"Oh." Stella was taken aback but not keen to pursue the matter. "Listen, Jack recommended a fat-tire bike for my son," she said. "I don't know if he went ahead and put in an order."

Kayla clicked on her keyboard again. "Hmm. No, I don't see an order for you. I could measure your son if you want to bring him in. I can't give you the sale price on a special order though."

"Right. Well, maybe my husband and I should discuss it again before we ask you to order anything."

"Sounds good."

Stella was heading for the door when she turned and said, "Should I read anything into what you said about Jack and me hitting it off?"

Kayla smiled. "I just remember Jack made a big fuss over you last time you were in the store. I could tell Danielle was seething."

"I think she might have been annoyed about something else. Jack and I weren't close."

"All I know is Danielle was über possessive. Hell, the woman made me hand over the pictures I took at his funeral. Look, if *I* caught a vibe between you and Jack, Danielle's spidy sense would have been humming."

Stella thought it best not to protest too much. "Well, that aside, she has my sympathy. It would be bad enough to lose your partner without being pregnant when he died."

"From what I hear she's not coping well. Friend of mine says she doesn't see anyone except Jack's buddy Rory. I'm not sure she even has close friends of her own."

Stella noticed the memory book from the funeral and took the opportunity to change the subject. "It was good of you to put this together," she said, flipping the book open. "Looks like a lot of people wrote in it."

"Your little friend poured her heart out," Kayla said. She reached over and turned to Cassidy's page, where brightly coloured hearts and flowers encircled several hand-written paragraphs. Stella read every effusive word, surprised to see Cassidy had referred to Jack more than once as fatherly. Dear Cassidy. She was just a kid, yet Ballard seemed to have had her charmed. But then Jack Ballard had that effect on a lot of people.

As Stella left the store, her thoughts returned to Danielle Stone. The jealousy theory might explain why Stone had been so rude to her. There was no denying Jack had been especially attentive to Stella near the end of his life. But Jack flirted with everybody. There wouldn't have been enough hours in the day for Stone to go after every female Jack had hit on.

14

MAX STRAIGHTENED THE MAGAZINES in the rack by the cardio equipment, removing an out-of-date copy of the local rag. Jack Ballard smiled from the front page in a shot taken in happier times. Gone but not forgotten, it seemed. Ballard's nose-dive off Pulpit Rock was old news, but folks still speculated about what had happened, most favouring the freak-accident theory. Max had his doubts. Nelson had an underbelly like anywhere else, something the average townie didn't seem to grasp.

Nothing one moron did to another one surprised Max, not after doing a stint in a medium security prison. *Don't ask,* he'd say if pressed for details. That one-and-one-third years had been a dark time, made even darker by his wife's death soon after his release. And yet in his blackest hours, he'd been thrown a lifeline.

At a peal of girlish laughter, Max glanced over to the registration desk where Colette Fenniwick held court. On the shady side of forty, she still gave the young guys an eyeful in her skimpy workout gear. Looks aside, she was sharp as a tack. Long story short, she'd earned herself a share in his gym, no hanky-panky involved.

A crashing thud broke into his thoughts and Max shot a stern look at a trouble-maker name of Kieran. Far as Max was concerned, Kieran had gotten what he deserved when they packed him off to kiddy jail. Now it was obvious the kid had done time: minimal eye contact, speak only when spoken to. "Yo," Max said. "Yeah, I'm talking to you. Read the notice: *Please Do Not Drop the Weights.*"

The kid pulled out one of his ear buds. "You say something?"

"Don't drop the weights."

"You have to set them down hard. They're fucking heavy."

Max shook his head. Back in the slammer, he had vowed to help youngsters like Kieran stay on the straight and narrow through bodybuilding. And this kid clearly had been working out. Maybe his juvie had a decent gym – our tax dollars at work. He wasn't a bad-looking kid if you ignored the man-bun he wore at times. Max had seen him out and about with Jack Ballard. Two peas in a pod.

Kieran sauntered over to the treadmills and Max decided to make nice, try to connect as one ex-con to another. "Too bad about Jack Ballard, ain't it?" he said.

"Yeah, it's a bitch," the boy said, starting his machine without looking sideways.

Now that's cold, thought Max. *Kid has a chip on his shoulder the size of Texas.*

* * *

Saturday afternoon McKean crossed the bridge to visit the scene at Pulpit again. It was a day off but he didn't feel like hanging around the house. He enjoyed being with his little son, but his wife Miranda was another story. If she wasn't on the phone with her mother, she was berating him about their supposed shitty life and his misplaced priorities. Well, the job didn't begin at nine and end at five, goddamn it, and if he had to work outside the lines at times, so be it.

The Ballard investigation was a case in point. Cassidy Pickering was staying mum on the hoodie guy and Danielle Stone had blocked his access to Ballard's medical records. McKean wondered if Miranda would deny access to *his* files if she were in Stone's situation. She might; Miranda was ornery. But it was hard to believe she'd care enough to raise a stink, unless her financial wellbeing was at stake. Maybe that was a factor in Stone's case.

McKean hadn't been able to track down Kieran Corcoran either, despite calling on the kid's uncle on the East Shore, again on his own time. On a previous visit some months ago, the kid was about to be charged for several offenses. Now the uncle couldn't, or wouldn't, provide an address or phone number for the boy. He claimed Kieran was employed, but couldn't recall where. "A garage of some sort?" he'd said, as if taking a stab in the dark. The man appeared to be slightly stoned but there was nothing McKean could do about a person smoking weed in his personal residence; he wasn't breaking any Canadian law.

Kieran's youth probation officer was away on a training course when McKean called, but his office provided an address in uphill Nelson. McKean tried to follow up but no one answered his knock on the door. From the outside, the place looked like a crack house. Graffiti on the faded siding, windows blanked out with flags and cardboard. Used syringes spilled onto the unmown grass from an overfull trash can.

Before the Chief had cut him off at the knees, McKean had enlisted a corporal's help to interview guests from Ballard's birthday party. McKean himself talked to Rory, after he'd admitted to leaving the birthday party with Jack. The pair had crashed at the home of Rory's parents, who were out of town. Rory claimed he'd slept past noon the next day and couldn't say what time Ballard had woken up and left the house.

So far nothing had emerged to cast a shadow on Jack Ballard's sterling reputation. No obvious skeletons in the closet, no record of any offenses or misdemeanours. He was quite possibly the only vehicle owner in Nelson who had never received a parking ticket. The clothes he'd worn to the party and left in his shop the next morning had shown no trace of any common street drug.

McKean parked at the trailhead at the base of Elephant Mountain and proceeded up the path, indulging in a foolish fantasy that Stella Mosconi would be up at the viewpoint with the wind in her hair, just like last time. In his head he'd gone over every detail of that chance meeting a thousand times. But of course Stella wasn't at the top. Nobody was. Still not in a hurry to go home, he stepped under the yellow police tape and clambered down to the place Ballard's body had landed, watching as he descended for signs of its trajectory and mentally reviewing his conversation with the forensic pathologist.

Antoniak seemed to think Ballard had still been alive when he went over the edge. But as McKean made his way to where the body had come to rest, he saw no sign of a desperate man grasping at shrubs and branches. He supposed Ballard might have lost consciousness on the way down.

Now rather than climb back up to Pulpit Rock, McKean cut across the forested slope until he connected with a lower part of the trail. The short-cut probably saved him half an hour, but by the time he got home he was about ninety minutes later than he'd promised to be. He was prepared for Miranda to tear a strip off him, but he didn't expect to find a packed suitcase just inside the kitchen door. The suitcase was his.

McKean did what he could to reason with his wife. "At least wait till we put Aiden to bed," he said. "Then we can talk."

"What's there to talk about?" she said. "I've had it – I'm done here. Ma agrees you should move out till I decide what to do."

It was no surprise Miranda's latest ambush had her mother's backing. They'd been on the phone pounding out a rinky-dink separation agreement that showed less financial acumen than that of the average six-year-old. After several futile rounds with Miranda, McKean was afraid he might explode if he didn't get out of the house. "I'll sleep on the couch when I get back," he told her. "Tomorrow we'll have to come up with a realistic plan. You'll probably need to get a job."

Miranda followed him to the door. "I'm not getting a job, Asshole. Have you forgotten I'm the one that looks after our child? I'll sue you for support if I have to."

McKean escaped into the darkness, afraid if he spent one more second with the crazy woman he might say or do something he'd later regret.

* * *

After a depressing weekend wrangling with Miranda, McKean went back to work and, as per the Chief's orders, resumed general policing duties. It was a welcome diversion when a member of the regional RCMP Forensic Identification Section, FIS, turned up at the station bearing two distinctly different plaster-of-Paris casts taken at Pulpit Rock the day Jack Ballard died. McKean whisked the officer into his office and closed the door.

The member seemed ambivalent about the quality of the imprints. "Dog's breakfast up there – what can you expect?" he said, glumly. But this guy always seemed morose; McKean hoped his pessimism had more to do with his personality than the usefulness of the exhibits.

McKean examined a cast for a right boot, then picked up the second cast and held it up to the light to study the wear pattern from different angles. This one was for a left shoe with a lighter sole than the boot imprint – a running shoe, probably. The casts had been taken at different places near the cliff where dozens of feet had churned up the mud that day. McKean pictured himself enacting a Cinderella-like search of every first responder and SAR volunteer in town. The FIS officer reminded him about the RCMP database of shoes. Even to narrow down a print to a common model could prove useful. "No guarantee, of course," the man added gloomily as he left the office.

McKean was lost in thought when he heard a rap on the frame of his open door. The sketch artist Samantha Tarasoff greeted him with a smile. "Should I take off my shoes, Sergeant?" she said.

"Now that's an offer I don't get every day," he said.

"Thought I'd stop by and say hello," Sam said. "Although I haven't heard from Cassidy Pickering. How's the case going?"

"Slowly. What brings you to Nelson today?"

"Not what – who. My mom lives here. I'm taking her to Harvest Fest tonight. The food bank thing? She's donating a tonne of stuff from her garden so I offered to help fill boxes this afternoon."

"Good on you. Hey, I still owe you a coffee for doing that interview."

"Should be plenty of coffee at Harvest Fest," she said. "Stop by. Anglican Church Hall, six o'clock."

"I'll pop in after I get my son to bed," he said.

"Later then!" and she was gone.

So, it had come to this: Harvest Fest as the highlight of his social life. Well, as long as he turned up in time to put Aiden to bed, he didn't have to answer to Miranda anymore. He'd found a furnished basement suite, which even in broad daylight was dark and bleak with low ceilings and a closet-like kitchen, the only sink a small basin in the bathroom. On the plus side, he could afford the rent, and the owner, a widower in his seventies, seemed inclined to mind his own business.

* * *

At the *Times*, Patrick asked Stella to take on a last-minute assignment. Jade Visser had been felled by a bout of stomach flu and wasn't fit to cover that evening's Harvest Fest, an annual event held in support of the food bank. "I'd go myself," Patrick said, "but my wife is under the weather too. She needs me to take over with the little one."

"I'm on it," Stella said. "I'll just shoot Joe a text to let him know I'll be late."

Joe texted back: *Guess I'll have to make dinner*. In her head, Stella ran through a string of sarcastic responses and settled on no reply at all.

At the Anglican Church Hall, Stella made her way through the crowd, enjoying the earthy, homespun atmosphere. The artfully arranged boxes of fresh veggies were going fast; paintings, pottery, and books from local authors made up a silent auction. Moms nursed babies. One brave couple danced in front of a three-piece band. Stella squeezed through the crush of attendees, snapping photos as she moved along. She was standing on a sturdy chair behind the refreshment table when she spied Ben McKean dressed in civvies. By the time she made her way to his corner of the room, he was talking to an attractive woman with a ginger upsweep held in place by chopsticks. No sign of his raven-haired wife and little son. Stella guessed Aiden, a toddler by now, would be home in the care of his mother.

"Ben, hi," she said.

"Oh, Stella." He flushed a little. "Do you two know each other? Sam is a police sketch artist." He looked at Sam. "Stella's a reporter for the *Nelson Times*."

The women shook hands. "Actually, I'm on the job tonight," Stella said. "So I should go grab one of the organizers." It was a perfect exit line but she didn't turn and walk away. She'd sensed a current between Ben and Sam, not that Ben's private life was any of her business. Still. "Don't want to interrupt," she said to Ben, "but would you mind talking shop for just a second?"

Sam took the cue. "I better go check on my mom. See you in a bit."

So maybe they *were* together. Stella led Ben to a spot outside the flow of traffic.

"How's the case going?" she said.

He shrugged. "Early days."

"I hear you talked to Cassidy Pickering about a guy in a hoodie. At least, I assume you were the officer who questioned her."

"Yeah, I was. Do you know Cassidy?"

"She's the boys' swim teacher, and she filled in for our regular sitter the night of Ballard's party. I bumped into her shortly after she made that 9-1-1 call."

Ben raised his eyebrows. "You have my attention. Can we set up a time to talk about this? How does tomorrow look for you?"

"Tomorrow's a production day," Stella said, which was true. So why did she feel like she was playing hard to get? "I could come by your office in the late afternoon. Should I text first?"

"Yeah, thanks," Ben said. "Great. See you tomorrow." Stella watched to see if he would scan the crowd for Sam, but he maintained eye contact until she turned and moved along.

15

IT WAS NEAR THE end of a production day in the newsroom, the deadline to get the pages to the printer looming. Patrick Taft groaned as he ended a phone call. "Superintendent of schools has changed her mind about resigning," he told Stella. "We'll have to pull the lead story."

"Can't we just tweak it?" Stella said. "She was going to resign but she changed her mind. The story just got more interesting."

"She wants it pulled. Period."

"Can she do that?" Stella's phone rang. Nelson Police Department. "Maybe I should take this," she said.

"Let it go to voicemail. We have thirty minutes to fill that hole on page one. What have you got?"

"Are you kidding me? I've got a service club on the verge of folding because the youngest member is sixty-eight. I have a guy wants to get a jump on winter and organize a used ski equipment drive. Oh, and the food bank is following up on Harvest Fest with a canning workshop."

"Bingo. Call Mrs. Rizzotti up on Observatory and ask her to email a picture of her tomato crop, or what's left of it. We'll do a share-your-harvest thing, light on content, warm and fuzzy. Better than nothing."

Stella's phone rang. The NPD again. "I'm taking this call. With any luck, somebody just robbed a bank."

"Ms. Mosconi?" said a familiar voice. "Sergeant McKean here."

"Sergeant McKean," Stella said. She knew he was smiling. "I said I'd drop by this afternoon, didn't I? Can you give me thirty minutes?"

"Make it ten." He hung up.

"How about you call Mrs. Rizzotti?" Stella said. "This could be interesting. But if I don't get back to you in five minutes go with the tomatoes."

* * *

At the NPD, Ben met Stella in the foyer. "Minor crisis," he said, in an undertone. He led her to his office, closed the door, and handed over a snapshot of a couple sitting at a table with fancy drinks in front of them. The woman wore a low-cut, sequined dress with spaghetti straps; the man had on a shiny suit, his shirt half-unbuttoned, a heavy gold chain around his neck.

"You and me at the funeral," Stella said. "Photo-shopped up the yin yang."

"The FedEx depot sent a runner about a quarter hour ago. Special delivery for the Chief," Ben said. "I think we can assume a copy was sent to the *Times*."

Stella dropped onto a visitor chair and closed her eyes for a moment. "Kayla Chau snapped that photo at the funeral, but this has Danielle Stone's name written all over it. Apparently, Stone made Kayla turn over all the pictures she took that day. Übër possessive was Kayla's term for her. Übër *disturbed* is more like it. What did your boss say?"

"He wasn't happy, but he accepted my explanation that the photo was a fake. That was the best I could do on the spur of the moment. I was too flabbergasted to even figure out where it had come from. You look good in that dress, by the way."

"Well, compliments to whoever the body belongs to," Stella said. "Was there a note?"

He handed her a piece of paper. In jumbo letters someone had keyed: COP AND REPORTER IN CAHOUTS.

"Proving only that Stone can't spell worth a damn," said Stella. "I better go back to the office and see if a copy has surfaced there. Trouble is there'll be others. Our competition in online news is probably posting it as we speak. Maybe we better give our spouses a heads up."

"Okay if I call you later?" Ben said. "What time do you put your kids to bed?"

"Call me any time after eight," Stella said. She raced back to the old railway station and sprinted up the stairs to the newsroom.

"Get anything good?" Patrick said over his shoulder.

"Where are you with the tomatoes?" she said, breathing hard.

Patrick gave her a quick glance. "Up to my elbows. But Mrs. R is gonna fact check. We'll get it done. What was the big deal at the cop shop?"

Stella collapsed into her chair. "The Chief received a doctored photo of Ben McKean and me, supposedly out partying. It came with a note that cast aspersions on our professional conduct. You'll probably get a call from the publisher any second now."

"Any way we can spin this?"

"That's funny, Patrick. I feel like throwing up."

He swung around in his chair. "Listen as soon as I –"

"I know, I know. You're on deadline. If you and Mrs. R can manage without me, I'll be down the hall." She picked up her laptop.

"Hold on now. Don't go running off –"

"I'm fine. See you later."

In the break room, Stella plugged in the kettle, took several deep breaths, and created a new file called "Mischief." She wondered what Danielle Stone was up to – and how this particular attack related to the investigation into Ballard's death. Chances were she had something to hide so she was falling back on the old saw: The best defence is a good offense.

At a tap on the door, Stella looked up. Patrick stuck his head in. "The publisher is on the warpath. She wants to see us both in ten minutes."

* * *

Danielle checked her watch. Rory was five minutes late picking her up for their getaway to Salmo. He'd gone back to his parents' place to mow the lawn even though they were still out of town and wouldn't even know he'd done it. That was Rory – obedient to a fault, which had its compensations, she supposed. She sent him a text: *You know I hate to be kept waiting.* That would bring him running.

She took a pee and freshened her lipstick. It was nice to get away at times and be anywhere but Nelson. Salmo was smaller and even more boring, but no one knew her there, except possibly that slut Angel, or whatever she called herself. Danielle had seen her get out of a car and enter the Salmo Quick Mart, which suggested she lived nearby. After she'd crashed Jack's party *and* his funeral, Danielle had hoped she'd seen the last of her. Angel would have to be off her head to think she had any claim on Jack just because the pair of them had fumbled around in high school.

A few months back, Danielle had spied Jack's yearbook on a shelf in the big house and they'd flipped through it together just for laughs. She made him tell her who he'd had sex with at school – Jack could never say no to her. She laughed in his face when he admitted to banging skinny, flat-chested Angel, but then he started to defend her, which was so not cool. He said she'd read up on sadomasochism and she was tough and gutsy. Danielle made him cut her picture out of his yearbook and burn it and promise never to get in touch with her.

She wouldn't have noticed the reporter's picture if he hadn't doodled a frame around it. Jack denied having sex with her, not because she was a dog, but because – LOL – she was too "pure." He'd begged Danielle not to make him cut out little Stella Hart's face because on the page directly behind her headshot was the picture of a really good friend, a guy friend who had almost died in a car accident shortly after high school. Danielle had let him keep the page but she had to punish him severely for the crack about the reporter being pure. As her mother always said, men are stupid about women, especially the ones they think are too good to fuck.

* * *

When Stella saw Ben's name on her call display, she breathed a little easier. It was 8:10 p.m. and she'd been pacing the beach in front of her cabin, startling every time a fish jumped on the lake. Her nerves were shot. "Well," Ben said, picking up on their earlier conversation, "did our portrait turn up at the *Times*?"

"It landed on the publisher's desk and she summoned my editor and me to her office." Stella heard the screen door open and looked over to see Joe on the top step of the porch, hands in his pockets. He must have noticed she was on the phone because he went back in.

"You still have a job?" Ben said.

"So far. But before she brought out the photo she raked me over the coals for a story I wrote about panhandling."

"Panhandling? What's that got to do with anything?"

"Well, it's a hot-button topic with City Council. I think she just wanted to throw me off balance. Or pile on extra evidence of my lack of good sense. She asked if I was in the habit of 'encouraging' people to beg on the street by giving them money. I said I was never sure what to do, but if a person seemed needy, I wasn't above handing over a dollar or two. She said my left-wing bent was obvious in my reporting. Once she had me wrong-footed, she placed the picture on the table. Carousing with a police officer. Further proof of my flawed judgment."

"Did she realize the thing had been photo-shopped?" Ben said.

"That little factoid didn't seem to interest her," Stella said. "It's all about optics with her. Basically, I'm to sharpen my objectivity and avoid cozying up to you."

"Funny she used the panhandling issue to get you to toe the line," Ben said "Not an impressive management strategy."

"Effective though. I'm not proud of it, but I sucked up. I can't lose my job."

The line went silent. Typical of Ben to think before he spoke. "Look, I want your input on the Ballard case," he said. "I can do subtle if you can. Guess we shouldn't hit the clubs together, but I doubt your publisher will tap our phones."

"She wouldn't be above seizing work emails though, and we probably should stick to personal phones." Stella felt a frisson of pleasure at Ben's interest in her input. All the better if he was prepared to open up to her a little too.

"Too bad the photo got in the way of us talking about Cassidy," Ben said. "I don't want to come down too hard on the kid, but there's something fishy about her trail runner story. At any rate, let's pack it in for tonight. Go get some rest."

"Will do," Stella said. "But listen, my publisher isn't going to be our only problem. We'll have to watch our backs with Danielle Stone. As I said, I'm sure she's behind the altered photo. She's been on my case since the day I met her."

"She doesn't like me either," Ben said. "Funny isn't? If the photo was meant to scare us off, it's not working."

16

KIERAN CORCORAN LOOKED AROUND Max's Gym with disgust. People were cutting in on each other, fighting over equipment, hogging the best machines. The Rec Centre had closed its fitness room for repairs and the regulars were swarming Max's. Some asshole had been idling on the leg press for about ten minutes, diddling with his phone. Feeling like his lungs would burst if he didn't get some fresh air, Kieran bounded up the stairs to the street level.

He put on the brakes when he spotted Stella Mosconi in the hardware store above the gym. Before she looked his way, he turned and jogged back down the stairway. A girl from the rec centre crowd looked to be on her way out. "D'ya forget something?" she said, all friendly.

"Ah, no," he said, thinking fast. "Just need to check the evening schedule. Might come back later."

"You can get a brochure over where you sign in, if any are left. I picked up one yesterday."

"Thanks," he said, no longer in a rush to get away. "So, you new here?"

"Yeah. Thought I'd give it a try," she said. "The owner seems nice."

"He's okay," Kieran said, thinking, *yeah, old Max must be real nice to a hottie like you.*

"I'm Cassidy, by the way," she said.

"Kieran."

"Nice to meet you. Well, see you around." She gave him a dimpled smile and skipped up the stairs.

Nice ass, he thought as he watched her leave. *The rec centre invasion might have its perks.*

Then it hit him: He'd seen her before. Cassidy was the chick he'd passed on the trail to Pulpit Rock the day Jack Ballard croaked. *Holy shit.* Had she recognized him?

Kieran hung back, giving Stella Mosconi time to finish her business and leave the hardware store. When he slipped upstairs again, there was no sign of her. Outside, he pulled on his hood and jogged up the street, taking the stairs at the end of Baker three at a time. He kept on going, crossing Victoria, then Silica, leaping like a freaking gazelle, never pausing to catch his breath. For someone who'd run laps behind a chain-link fence for a couple months, freedom tasted pretty sweet. But he kept thinking about Cassidy, second-guessing himself as to whether he had the right girl.

At his house he took the outside stairs three at a time and bounded to the top floor. His mind still on Cassidy, he pulled the tab on a Red Bull and dropped a cricket into the terrarium. He'd rescued a pet tarantula from an addict who would have let her starve. Kieran had named the tarantula Hela in honour of his friend from jail who was into Norse legends. The friend, Loki, was only sixteen, but he'd killed a man without even knowing why. At times good people did bad things. That was just a fact of life.

While Hela digested the cricket, Kieran took his drink outside to the fire escape and looked out over the rooftops and across the lake to the place Jack Ballard had taken his last breath. He wondered if Loki ever stopped thinking about the guy he offed.

* * *

Stella was at the hardware store on a break when Cassidy popped upstairs from Max's Gym and stopped to say hello. She seemed upbeat, more like her old self; maybe she was ready to talk about the day Jack fell. Stella hit on an idea for a little one-on-one. "Remember when we talked about putting our bikes away for the season?" she said. "Want to do a longish ride with me before the cold weather sets in?"

"Love to," Cassidy said. "When?"

"Joe's been talking about taking the boys hiking on Sunday. Are you game to ride all the way to Kaslo? That'd be about a hundred forty clicks return for you, a hundred for me. On second thought, that seems ambitious."

"No, let's go for it," Cassidy said.

"You sure?"

"Totally."

They entered the date into their phones.

A few minutes later, unlocking her bike at a stand across the street, Stella looked up to see Kieran Corcoran leave the building she had just exited. He pulled up his hood and jogged up Baker Street in the opposite direction. Only minutes before, Cassidy had passed through the same doorway. *So, they both work out at Max's now*, Stella thought. She wondered if they'd met, and made a mental note to broach the subject with Cassidy when she saw her on the weekend. She shuddered to think of her getting mixed up with a con artist like Kieran.

Later, back at her desk in the newsroom, it struck Stella that Kieran could be the mystery guy in the hoodie. Granted, the odds were slim; a high percentage of teenage boys in Nelson likely owned a hoodie. Still, seeing Kieran had given her pause. She flashed on the image of Ballard ejecting him from his party. Could Kieran have been ticked off enough to lure Ballard up to Pulpit Rock and shove him over the edge? That seemed extreme even for Kieran. The kid had a way of finding trouble but he seemed more of a watcher than a hothead.

She noted her sighting of the boy, then texted Ben: *Kieran Corcoran just left Max's Gym wearing a hoodie. Cassidy's trail runner???*

* * *

Joe Mosconi was only too happy to bolt down his dinner and escape his busy household to attend another training session for Search and Rescue. It was his favourite way to spend an evening. He enjoyed his teaching job and all the outdoors activities Nelson had to offer, but nothing compared to SAR and the possibility of rescuing a fellow human being from a life-threatening situation. Not even if the human being in question had done something foolish to get into the predicament. Even the best of people screwed up at times.

Joe drove to the North Shore Hall on Johnstone Road – images of the recovery of Jack Ballard's body flooding his mind – and pulled into a parking space next to Monique Thibaudeau's car. "Hey, Mosconi," she said, as she got out. "You made it." Rubbing it in because he'd missed the last practice. Well, he deserved the dig.

"Yeah, glad to be here, Mo," he said. "How you doing tonight?" He held open the door for her. "I felt bad about begging off last time.

Wife had a meeting." Stella hadn't explained why she had to work that evening, but it was safe to assume she'd been chasing a story on her own time. "As I explained to Mark," Joe continued, "it won't happen again."

"Well, it better not," Mo said. Was she teasing a little? She walked past him and began to talk to one of the older guys.

Their team leader Mark was laying out ropes and pulleys and other assorted pieces of hardware. When he started to explain how to use the equipment he had Joe's complete attention; the next two hours flew by. At one point, Joe asked a question that Mark couldn't answer and Mo gave him a little nod of approval, which pleased him more than it should have.

Mark announced the date for a day-long helicopter practice. He looked at Joe when he said everyone had to be there. "Far out," Joe said, feeling his face colour. "Wouldn't miss it for anything." Joe wasn't the only new recruit, but he *was* the most recent arrival to Nelson – and it seemed no one ever let him forget it.

He and Mo left the building together and on impulse he suggested a drink. "I'm about ready to put on my jammies," she said. "But if you want to stop by my place, I'll give you a beer before I send you on your way."

Joe asked for directions. "I'm two minutes away in Fairview," she said. "Follow my vehicle."

During the short drive to Mo's place, Joe felt a stab of – what? Not guilt, exactly. But a night-time visit to a single woman's apartment was inappropriate at best, especially with a pub right in the neighbourhood. But Mo would have mocked his hesitation. All the guys treated her like one of the gang. He brushed off his misgivings and parked in front of her building.

Mo's apartment was a shrine to Search and Rescue. Next to the front door was a custom-built stand for her backpack, a check-list tacked to the wall above it. All over the place there were photos of rescues and practices – some framed, others held to the fridge with magnets. A poster of last year's SAR team mounted on foam board had pride of place above the couch. Clearly, Mo had her priorities straight. Apart from the backpack and a tidy shelf full of ropes and carabiners and such, the place was comfortably messy. The bed, which he spied from the hallway, was unmade.

Mo went to the fridge for a couple of IPAs and they sat down in the front room. He asked about some of the photos and when Mo began to describe rescues she'd been in on, he was spellbound. After a while, she got up to throw together a snack, sniffing at a container of salsa, carving a chunk of mold off a block of cheese, riffling boxes of crackers to find one that wasn't empty.

Joe had no sense of time passing and Mo seemed in no rush to "put on her jammies." When she chucked off her bulky sweater and put her feet up on the coffee table, he was surprised to notice what a good body she had. Her leggings and tank top revealed well-muscled legs, shapely shoulders and arms – classic proportions. Yet, her usual clothing didn't show off her figure and he admired her inattention to fashion. Yes, Mo Thibaudeau had her act together, and she had a hell of a lot to teach him about Search and Rescue. Midnight had come and gone before he tore himself away and headed home.

17

IT WAS A QUIET Friday afternoon at the gym, which made it all the sweeter for Max Huber when the girl called Cassidy burst in like a ray of sunshine and handed her pass to his assistant Colette. Colette admired Cassidy's new workout clothes, then the pair of them yakked about exercise gear, bemoaning the sad lack of a Lululemon store in Nelson.

But Cassidy had no sooner put away her punch pass than she was swarmed by three lunkheads wearing T-shirts emblazoned with the Nelson swim team logo. Kieran glanced over from his position on the leg press, continuing to do his reps but keeping a protective eye on the young lady. Max had seen them talking together. *She better watch her step with him too,* he thought. *A stint in custody hardens a guy.*

Two of the goons drifted over to the step machines but the tallest, best-looking one commenced to chat up Cassidy. "Hey, my brother's coming from the Coast for the weekend," he said. "He's gonna drive us to the pool in Castlegar tomorrow. You gotta come – it'll be a blast."

"I'll think about it, Galen," Cassidy said. Max wondered if she and the lunk had something going on. He looked over at Kieran again. Poker face.

"Think about it?" Galen said. "Shit, just do it. Better than hanging around this hole." Max shot him a dirty look and the prick flashed him the peace sign. "Sorry, dude," he said "No offense." Max was tempted to drag the scumbag outside for a lesson in manners.

"I *would* love to have a swim," Cassidy said with a sigh. "Are the other guys coming?"

"'Course. There's plenty of room in my brother's Civic."

Finally, after confirming there'd be enough seatbelts for everyone, she agreed to go.

111

Max caught Kieran's eye. If he had an opinion on the matter, he wasn't letting it show.

* * *

Saturday morning Cassidy met Galen and the other guys outside Max's gym. She hadn't told her mother about the trip to the neighbouring town in case her mom asked whose parent was driving. Instead, Cassidy told her she was going to a friend's place and arranged to have the friend cover for her.

Galen's brother drove up in a battered grey Honda Civic, one fender rust-coloured. A cigarette hung off his bottom lip, which worried Cassidy. The last time she'd driven with a smoker, the dad of a school friend, her hair had smelled of smoke for days.

All the way to Castlegar the guys talked in riddles, as if they were in on a joke nobody had bothered to tell her. Once they got to the community centre though, everything seemed cool.

Cassidy came out of the change room to find the guys playing a lame game of water polo, mock-fighting and dunking each other. She ignored them and dove into a lap lane. It was awesome to be in a pool again, water sluicing over her arms and legs, the feeling of power as she ran through her drills, executing perfect kick turns at the end of each length. At some point the boys came to the lap lanes to do some serious swimming and Galen pushed his way into her lane, sometimes accidentally-on-purpose bumping or touching her.

When they were done, they all walked across the lot to McDonald's. After a round of burgers and fries, Galen talked her into going back to the car; he wanted her advice on changing electives at the end of term. The other guys ordered sundaes and promised to join them in about two minutes. But once she and Galen were in the car, she realized she'd been missing the plot. His brother had parked the Civic in an isolated space and the other guys were nowhere to be seen. Galen started coming onto her like never before. "You are so hot," he groaned, forcing his gross tongue into her mouth, grabbing at her breasts and crotch.

"Galen, stop," she said. "I don't like this. I'm getting out."

"C'mon, Cassidy," he said, his hands all over her. "I think about you all the time."

Cassidy grappled for the door handle. Laughing, he leaned over and clicked the lock. "C'mon, don't be a tease. Just relax and enjoy it."

Cassidy pushed his face hard with the flat of her hand. When he yelped and clutched at his nose, she unclicked the lock and scrambled out of the car, reaching back to drag her gym bag behind her. He grabbed for the bag. She wrenched it out of his hands and sprinted across the parking lot and into the community centre.

On a conspicuous bench opposite the registration counter, she waited for her heartbeat to settle down then took out her phone. When her mom answered, she said, "Hi. I made a mistake. I'm at the pool in Castlegar and I need you to come get me."

Her mom said, "Sit tight. I'll be right there."

Safe in the family car less than an hour later, Cassidy cried a little and briefly explained what had happened. Her mom didn't press her for details. Later they ordered pizza and settled in to binge-watch a new series on Netflix.

Her mother waited till bedtime to get down to business. "So. Galen," she said, gently. "Are you attracted to him?"

"*No, God*, I hate him," Cassidy said. "He's a total jerk – I wish I never had to see him again."

Her mom smiled. "You didn't answer my question."

"I'm totally *not* attracted to him, okay? I'm not attracted to anybody, much less an idiot from swim club I've known since I was five. I can't believe he tried that on me. I've never shown the slightest interest in him."

"Okay, okay. I didn't mean to upset you. But when *I* was your age I had a fairly serious crush on a guy, and I just thought, well . . ."

Cassidy's heart almost stopped. This was it. Her mom was going to confide in her about Jack. She sat up straight. "Uh, was that BJ?" she said.

Her mother looked surprised. "How did you know about BJ?" she said, but she didn't sound mad.

"Your scrapbook. I found it at Grandma's house. Sorry for being such a snoop."

"The scrapbook, gee – I didn't know that still existed," her mother said. "Well, I don't mind you reading it. All those soppy poems. Anyway, the whole thing with BJ is history now."

"Did you really love him?" Cassidy asked, shyly. She could hardly believe they were finally having this conversation. After all this time, her mom was going to open up about her feelings for Jack.

Her mom looked kind of misty eyed. "Yeah, I really loved him. When our parents made us split up, it broke my heart for a while. But it was probably for the best."

"How's your heart now?" Cassidy said, feeling extremely mature. "I mean, how do you get over something like that?"

"Oh, honey. For a while I thought we were Romeo and Juliet. Breaking up felt like the end of the world. But time passes and you get over it."

"Do you think you *are* over it, though? I mean with the accident and all?"

"Accident?" she said. "What accident? The Jasmails just moved away to the Coast where there's a big South Asian community."

What?

"Wait – the Jasmails?" Cassidy said. "Who are they?"

"Nice family that used to live here. They ran one of the Indian restaurants on Baker Street – they were the original owners, I think. Anyway, after the move to Vancouver, Bhav and I wrote long, desperate letters. Phoning long distance was so expensive we hardly ever talked. No FaceTime and social media back then." She smiled. "We kept trying to dream up ways we could get together, but we never had the chance. In the end his family moved back to India. I doubt the decision had anything to do with us, but once he was living on the other side of the world we completely lost touch."

Cassidy felt dizzy, like she might faint. Her pulse pounded in her ears.

Her mom said, "What's the matter, honey?"

Cassidy found it difficult to speak. "I don't get this," she said. "Your boyfriend's name was 'Bov'?"

"Bhav. B.h.a.v. Bhav Jasmail. Everyone called him BJ. He was a sweet guy. And drop-dead gorgeous." She grinned.

"How come I never heard about this Bhav?" Cassidy said, her mind reeling. "When did my father come into the picture?"

"Well." Her mom looked off in the distance for a second. "You know his folks and mine were friends and they all hoped your dad and I would marry someday. It started as a joke when we were little, and at some point, it stopped being a joke. They'd say, 'When Karen and Brian get married, houses in Nelson will cost a fortune so we'll have to help them out.' That sort of thing. When I started to date Bhav, my parents told everyone we were just friends. They were polite to the Jasmails. I don't think they were racist, although I thought so at the time. When they realized we were getting serious they had a fit, and Bhav's parents didn't like it either. All four of them were dead set against intermarriage. When I think about it, I'm surprised they took our relationship so seriously. I mean, I was fifteen and Bhav was only a year older."

"It's sad they made you break up," Cassidy said. "Tragic, actually."

Karen put an arm around her daughter. "It *was* kind of sad, honey. But tragic? I don't think so. It was just a sign of the times. I'd like to think that if you were to fall in love with a boy of a different race, I'd support you."

Cassidy stood up to go to her room, but she didn't see how she could make it through the night if she didn't speak up about Jack. She looked at her mom. "You know, I always thought you had a thing for Jack Ballard."

"*Jack?*" Her mom almost laughed. "Whatever gave you that idea? I mean, we were friends. I knew him all his life. But, no, I never had a thing for Jack Ballard."

"Really?" Cassidy said. "I mean, he was a very cool guy – and I think he really liked you."

"Jack was a serious flirt, Cass. He probably made every woman he knew think he was interested in them. But for Jack and me, the operative word was friends, okay?"

"But the way he looked at you in your birthday pictures. . ." Cassidy said. "You never had even a *tiny* fling with him?"

"Not even a tiny one," her mom said, and now she sounded serious. "I'd forgotten Jack came to that party. He must have been home from college or taking a break from competition. But to be honest, I grew a little wary of him as we got older. Not to speak ill of the dead, as they say, but even in high school his reputation was sketchy."

"You mean he was a perv?" Cassidy said.

"God, Cassidy, Jack wasn't a *pervert*, but I think it's fair to say he was a womanizer. That's the term I'd use."

Cassidy felt all twisted up inside as she headed off to bed. Not about Galen, who she would never speak to again and didn't care who knew it. She was sad for her mom, because she probably *hadn't* gotten over Bhav, not completely. But it was what her mom had said about Jack that really shook her world. Her mother's carefully chosen words implied something ugly and offensive to a feminist like Cassidy. And clearly, Jack Ballard had not been her biological father. That was the hardest truth of all. Sadly, incredibly, she had not inherited her long legs and skill at sports from Jack Ballard. Apart from the incident up on Elephant Mountain, she had no real connection with him. He was nothing to her but a big sexist jerk, now dead and gone.

18

SUNDAY MORNING AT THE Mosconi cabin, Joe rallied the boys for an adventure on Elephant Mountain. "Kind of morbid, isn't it?" Stella said, privately to her husband. "An outing to see where Jack fell off a cliff? They've been itching to go hiking with you, but why Pulpit Rock?"

"Kids have a natural curiosity," Joe said in his teacher voice. "With all the talk, it's no surprise they want to see where he went over the edge. In any case, Pulpit will be a side trip. By the time I get these guys all the way up to the flagpole and back they'll have their perspectives back. Hundred percent guaranteed."

"Could I have that in writing?" she said. "By the way, are you up for cooking tonight? I'll be half dead by the time I get home. I must have been crazy to suggest a bike ride to Kaslo with a fifteen-year-old athlete."

Outside, the boys waited for Joe. Stella knew when Cassidy arrived because her bicycle bell began to ding incessantly. She opened the front door and poked her head out. "Hey, you made good time," she said to Cassidy. "And Nick – give that bell a rest."

Once the guys were on their way, Stella and Cassidy pushed their bikes up a path to the highway and headed off in the direction of Kaslo. The village on the west shore of Kootenay Lake was one of Stella's favourite destinations, a jewel nestled within a circle of jagged granite peaks. She told Cassidy to set the pace and suggested she stop and wait at the nearby marina if she got too far ahead. Which proved prophetic. Cassidy was sitting on the porch of the marina store, looking at her phone when Stella pulled up. "You haven't even broken a sweat," Stella said, reaching for her water bottle.

The girl shrugged modestly. They carried on.

In Balfour, they stopped at the coffee shop on the ferry slip to share a pastry and soak up the sun at an outside table. Stella said, "Not long ago I saw Jack Ballard sitting outside a coffee shop like this. He didn't seem to have a care in the world."

"Not long ago? Really?" Cassidy said. "That's funny, because for me it seems like ages since that accident. Hey, could you excuse me a minute? I need to use the washroom."

Stella watched her cross the parking lot to the restroom building. So, no tears today at the mention of Ballard. Well, if Cassidy was beginning to come to terms with his death, that was a good thing. Still though, she seemed to have had an abrupt change of heart. When the girl took her seat again, Stella said, "Don't feel you have to answer, but are you still troubled by what happened to Jack?"

"Troubled?" Cassidy seemed to ponder the idea. "I wouldn't say so. I mean, it's sad he died, but it's not like I knew him very well. It must be hard on his family though. I know my mom would fall apart if anything like that happened to me."

Stella studied her young friend. Not long ago, Cassidy had said she never stopped thinking about Jack. Her attitude about Ballard seemed to have undergone a sea change in a matter of days. Well, maybe she wasn't too fragile to talk about him some more.

"Cassidy," Stella said carefully. "Awhile back you told me the police were pressing you for information about that day up on Pulpit. Something about a guy in a hoodie."

Cassidy visibly tensed. She put down a chunk of cinnamon bun she had been about to bite into and carefully wiped off her hands with a napkin. "Did I mention that to you? It was nothing really. This guy ran past me and I had zero time to look at him. That cop McKean won't let it go. It's bizarre, really. I wish he'd just accept what I told him and leave me alone. I mean, he wouldn't want me to make something up just to get him off my back, right? Cops aren't supposed to do that. It wouldn't hold up in court."

Wow. How to respond to that little speech? Stella sat up a little straighter too. "So, you never saw this guy in the hoodie again? Funny, isn't it? Nelson being such a small town."

"Don't you believe me?" Cassidy said, warily.

Oops. "Of course, I believe you," Stella said. "Hey, we better hit the road if we're going to make it all the way to Kaslo and back."

Cassidy mounted her bike and Stella followed suit. They slogged up the long hill to Toad Rock where Cassidy waited at the top, then took off again as Stella approached the summit.

At Coffee Creek, where the road makes an indented U, clinging to the cliffs on both sides of the creek, Stella was trailing again. She watched as Cassidy sped down the hill, crossed the bridge over the creek, then stood up on the pedals to impel herself up the steep pitch that followed. Stella coasted downhill, crossed the bridge, then stopped halfway up the hill to catch her breath. Cassidy was out of sight when she proceeded on a particularly steep, windy stretch.

Rounding the corner at the top, Stella met a car head-on.

The car almost ran her off the road as it dodged a flock of wild turkeys. Stella barely missed a turkey herself, braking and skidding, ending up sprawled on the asphalt, her left leg pinned under the bike. The damn bird strutted ostrich-like to the other side of the highway and fixed her with a beady stare. The rest of the flock settled down to graze by the roadside.

Her leg hurt like hell. The car, a nondescript dark grey sedan, hadn't stopped, but Stella had caught a glimpse of a male driver and a female passenger. The passenger was Danielle Stone. For a nanosecond, Stella had locked eyes with her before the sedan peeled away.

A blue hatchback had come up from behind, and now it pulled over to the side of the road and a woman of about eighty jumped out and hurried toward Stella. "Fucking turkeys," she said. "I nearly hit one on my way to church last week. Should I call 9-1-1?"

"That may not be necessary," Stella said. "Appreciate your stopping though. I wonder if you can help me move the bike so I can try to get up? If it's too heavy, don't worry about it. I have a friend up ahead who'll likely double back." The woman looked frail but she didn't hesitate to lift the handlebar and steady the bike as Stella wriggled out from under it. "Did you notice an oncoming dark grey sedan as you approached?" Stella said, lowering herself gingerly onto a flat rock, cradling her ankle. "It swerved toward me but kept on going."

"I saw a car lurch around the corner," the older woman said. "That's why I slowed down."

"Did you notice what make it was – or anything about the people in it?"

"Couldn't tell you," she said. "I just prepared myself for another run-in with those accursed turkeys."

Now Cassidy came racing back, cutting across the road, putting aside her bike. "Oh my God, Stella," she said. "Are you okay?"

The Good Samaritan spoke up. "So, you're the friend," she said. "Okay girls, this is what we're going to do." She pointed to Cassidy. "You drag this banged-up bike across the road and hide it in the bush. Somebody'll have come back for it – not a big deal. Right now we need to get Stella here into my car. Should be a piece of cake for a strapping girl like yourself." There was no arguing with the lady. After Cassidy stashed the bike, she knelt down and placed Stella's arm across her shoulder to help her to stand. Leaning on Cassidy, Stella hopped to the hatchback. Once she was belted into the back seat, her ankle red and swollen and pulsing with pain, she took out her phone and hit Joe's number. The call went straight to voicemail.

Cassidy mounted her bike for the solo ride back to town. Stella opened a window. "Better let your mom know about the change in plans," she said. "I'll call you later."

"Hang on tight," said the lady at the wheel, and the blue hatchback burned a U-ey and careened toward Nelson.

* * *

At Kootenay Lake Hospital the ER was humming, a toddler's wails echoing off the high ceiling. When the child's mother complained about the delay, a nurse said there were cases ahead of the toddler's, one of them life-threatening. "I think it was an overdose," a man informed the motley group in the waiting room. He was holding a tattered copy of *Hello*, the Duchess of Kent beaming from the cover. "An old man took pills," he said. "I'm waiting for my neighbour to get a chunk of wood dug out of his leg. Guy was working on his deck. Nobody home to drive him here."

Eighty minutes passed before Stella was admitted to the inner sanctum of the emergency department where a doctor examined her left ankle and ordered an X-ray. She was back in the common area waiting for the results when she heard Cassidy ask for her. She waved her over. "Poor Stella," the girl said. "Do you think it's broken?"

"Guess I'll know soon," Stella said. "I just had an X-ray. Too bad our outing had to end so abruptly. I'm sorry you had to ride back alone."

"No problem," Cassidy said. "Hey, I hope I wasn't too rude at the coffee shop. When you asked about Jack Ballard? I mean, I know I was very upset at first. But I had a good talk with my mom that kinda helped me deal with the whole thing?"

"Glad to hear it," Stella said. She wasn't inclined to mention the guy in the hoodie again.

Cassidy was still there when the doctor recalled Stella. The ankle wasn't broken, he said, but she had a bad sprain. A nurse bandaged her ankle and gave her a Tylenol 3 for the pain and Stella encouraged Cassidy to go home. "Thanks for keeping me company," she said. "But I've left Joe a couple of messages and I'm sure he'll call any minute now. Once he and the boys get off the trail they'll be here in no time."

The nurse let Stella stretch out on a gurney to rest and whipped a circle of orange curtains around her for privacy. Crutches were produced, a loan to tide her over until she could rent a pair on Monday. Stella tried Joe's phone again and left another message. Then, after staring at the ceiling for a while, she wrote a text message to Ben McKean to tell him she'd spoken to Cassidy. He texted back: *Where are you now?*

Stella replied: *ER. Sprained ankle – long story.*

The codeine in the pain medication must have put her to sleep because the next thing she knew Ben McKean was standing at the end of the gurney looking less like a cop than usual in jeans and a faded brown T-shirt. His dark hair was attractively mussed and he hadn't shaved for a couple of days. To wake her up he'd tweaked the toes of her good foot, which had seemed incredibly sexy. Stella propped herself up on an elbow and lowered her voice "You were right," she said. "The person in question seems to be hiding something."

"Appreciate the intel," he said. "Sorry you had to risk your neck to get it."

"Line of duty." Stella smiled, pulling herself to a sitting position. "Actually, I didn't risk it voluntarily. I had a freak fall off my bike that involved wild turkeys, and I'll just leave it at that. I'm waiting for Joe to come get me. I don't know what's keeping him."

"Can I give you a lift?" Ben said.

"Sure, if you don't mind. That would make it easier to talk."

"I'll bring my car up to the entrance."

Stella texted Joe while Ben went off to get his car. Then she struggled out to meet him on the crutches.

Once they were on their way, she said, "Let's start with our friend Danielle – I think she was a passenger in a car that nearly hit me while I was dodging the turkeys. I'm pretty certain it was her. The car was a dark grey sedan. I didn't get a good look at the driver but I'm guessing it was Rory. I need to find out what he drives."

"You think they *tried* to hit you?"

"I don't know. They were dodging turkeys too and the driver didn't stop. An older lady stopped and was kind enough to bring me to the hospital. She saw the other car veer around the corner but didn't notice any details."

"I'll find out what make of cars Stone and Rory drive," he said. "Getting back to 'the person in question' – that was Cassidy?"

"Yup, and just so you know, I don't feel good about talking behind her back," Stella said. "But when I asked her about Jack Ballard, she acted like she hardly knew him. It was a complete about-face compared to a week or so ago. I might have chalked it up to her simply moving on if she hadn't been so evasive. Later at the hospital she apologized for being rude. But earlier, when I mentioned the guy in the hoodie, she closed right down."

"The sketch artist got a similar impression," Ben said. "I want to find this guy, but how do you set up surveillance on a fifteen-year-old? At any rate, I'll drop by Max's Gym tomorrow and follow up on your tip about Corcoran. Be nice and tidy if he turned out to be the trail runner."

"It would," Stella said. "Although I really hate to think of Cassidy getting involved with Kieran."

They were nearing the turn-off to her cabin when her phone rang, Joe on the call display. "Got your messages," he said. "You home yet?"

"Almost," she said. "Where are you?"

"On our way," he said. "Be there soon."

Ben took her arm to help her hop up the porch steps and get through the front door. They said an awkward goodbye. Had he been anyone else, she might have asked him in, or at least given him a hug when she thanked him for the ride home.

Stella was lying on the couch with her ankle elevated when Joe and the boys got back, Nicky bubbling with excitement. "Mo gave us pop, two cans each," he said. "And she had this snack called Cheezies? And me and Matt were allowed to eat all we wanted – Dad didn't even notice. Can I try out your crutches?"

"I'm not really hungry for dinner," Matt said. "Can we watch a movie?"

"Mo?" Stella said.

"Sorry, babe," Joe said. "My phone was off and all your messages came at once. Mo Thibaudeau. One of the Search and Rescue gang. We bumped into her on the trail and stopped at her place on the way back. I didn't open my phone until we were about to drive home. What the hell happened on your ride? How'd you get home from the hospital?"

"I'll fill you in later," she said. "Feeling a bit dozy from a painkiller."

"Hungry?"

"Yeah. Want to heat up the leftover lasagna?"

"Coming right up!" he said.

It was nice to see Joe relaxed and happy for a change. Stella lay back and closed her eyes, wishing she'd had more time to talk to Ben. She hadn't even told him about Angie yet.

19

PAMELA BALLARD'S NIGHTS HAD become a torment. For years menopause had been chipping away at her sleep and now grief had been thrown into the mix, that plus the fact her bereft husband didn't touch her anymore. Her doctor's advice about sleep hadn't helped. She'd taken to leaving Richard snoring his head off in their king-size bed while she slipped down to the kitchen to nuke a cup of milk. The milk didn't put her to sleep, but it gave her something to do other than look at the ceiling.

This particular night as she waited for the timer on the microwave to go off, she saw a light on in the studio. No surprise Danielle was awake too – the girl was a wreck. Pamela stirred the milk and took a tentative sip. Danielle was moving erratically behind the window shades. Surely, she wasn't exercising – night-time activity is more likely to rev you up than put you to sleep. Or so said Pamela's GP in her lecture on sleep hygiene.

Now it looked as if there was more than one person behind the window shades. *Don't tell me Rory is still hanging around,* she thought. But then Jack and Danielle had always been up at all hours, Rory with them. Still, something seemed not quite right. Pamela turned off the kitchen light, threw a sweater over her shoulders, and carried her cup of milk out to the deck. Rory's car wasn't in its usual spot so maybe she was imagining things. Except there definitely were two bodies behind the shades, and muted sounds spilled through an open window. Feeling like a spy on her own property, Pamela crept across the deck until she was directly opposite the window. She sat down on a lounge chair and sipped the milk. The night sky was ablaze with stars; she tried to focus on the natural beauty up there beyond the lights of town, to breathe and relax to make herself sleepy, to try to ignore what was going on in the studio.

But the sounds continued. Sounds Pamela associated with boisterous, unapologetic sex.

After a time, the studio door opened and a figure emerged. Rory didn't even glance toward the deck where Pamela still sat, too stunned to move. He trotted down the stairs and around the corner to wherever he must have left his car.

A stake-out the following night left no doubt that Danielle and Rory were having sex. Pamela was outraged on behalf of Jack and bursting to tell Richard, but something held her back. There was no way to know how he'd react, and she didn't want to add to his misery. And despite her rightful indignation, a faint inner voice urged her to be charitable. The girl had lost her fiancé, the boy, his best friend. Primitive instincts kick in at times like this. She and Richard should have fallen sobbing into each other's arms instead of letting Jack's death drive a massive wedge between them.

The next day Pamela threw herself into housework then walked to the pond, but she couldn't stop thinking about Jack's pregnant fiancée carrying on with his best friend. Danielle hadn't begun to show, so maybe the baby didn't seem real to her yet – that in itself was troublesome. But regardless of what she was up to, Jack's child was going to need a fit mother, and supporting Danielle was probably the best thing Pamela could do for him. She wondered if setting up a nursery might kickstart the girl's maternal instinct. Bring her to her senses. It was worth a try – and decorating was right up Pamela's alley.

With this in mind, Pamela felt quite positive as she returned home from the pond. She found Richard and the prospective mother at the kitchen table, a pad of paper in front of them. "You're back," Richard said. "We were just talking about things the baby will need. I told Danielle to order whatever she wants and I'll foot the bill. Actually, why don't I just write a cheque for you, Danny."

Left out as usual, Pamela got herself a glass of water and scanned the fridge for inspiration for the evening meal. She asked Danielle if she had plans for dinner. "Don't worry about me," she said dismissively, smugly folding Richard's cheque and tucking it into her cleavage.

And now Pamela was struck by an ugly thought. What if Danielle and Rory had been carrying on for some time? If she'd cheated on Jack while he was alive, the baby might not even be his.

Pamela wondered whether a paternity test was possible when the alleged father was dead. Plucking her tablet off the counter, she retired to her bedroom, and within minutes found listings for online businesses that perform post-mortem paternity testing. First, she would need to get a viable DNA sample from her late stepson, which would likely prove more difficult than the detective shows on television lead one to believe.

Jack had been cremated, so there was no body to exhume, and DNA doesn't survive cremation, as Pamela learned from the Internet. Tissue and blood samples would have been collected during the autopsy, but the chemicals used to preserve the samples also destroy DNA. Another strike against her. She thought she might be able to find something of Jack's though – a messy old hairbrush, for example. She read that DNA from hair is found in the roots – not the shafts – and the roots contain such minuscule amounts of DNA, quite a lot of hair is needed to do an analysis. Well, nothing ventured, nothing gained.

She would wait for Danielle to go out, then sneak into the studio. Not sneak in – she and Richard owned the place, damn it. She would enter her own property and look for something personal of Jack's. If not a hairbrush, a toothbrush or a sweat-stained cap. Getting Danielle to provide a maternal blood sample would be another obstacle, but she would cross that bridge when she came to it.

The following morning, Pamela offered Danielle the gift of a facial and mani-pedi at her favourite spa. The girl resignedly accepted. "Why not go today?" Pamela said, casually. "What's a good time for you? I'll call and make the appointment."

It was too easy. An hour later she watched Danielle exit the studio and heard the engine of her Mini Cooper start up behind the garage. Pamela crossed the yard and climbed the steps to the studio.

No surprise to her, the place was a mess, the small cooking area a jumble of pots and dishes and lipstick-stained glasses. But if Danielle hadn't bothered to clean up since Jack died, the chances of finding a personal item of his should be that much better.

A large pair of sneakers peeked out from under the bed but they weren't Jack's. Rory's, presumably. A grungy black T-shirt, also Rory's, lay balled up on the floor. A perfectly clean feather duster poked out from under the bed – so much for good intentions. Next to the bed sat a skookum-looking wooden box, a "Tickle Trunk" according to the hand-printed label. The lid was fastened with a large padlock, overkill for what was probably a box full of junk from Danielle's childhood.

Amidst the general squalor were several pieces of white rope, some tied in intricate patterns, not unlike the macramé hangers Pamela had crafted for her dorm room back in the day. She looked up, and sure enough, sturdy hooks strong enough to support planters protruded from the ceiling. Trust Danielle to start a hobby then abandon it. Well, to be fair, Jack's death would have put the kibosh on any nesting activities.

Prepared for the worst, Pamela approached the bathroom. The door was blocked and she gave it a shove. And there stood Rory, fully clothed yet holding a hand towel in front of himself as if to protect his modesty.

"God, Rory," Pamela said, mildly, "you nearly gave me a heart attack. Sorry to intrude, but why didn't you speak up when you heard the outside door open?"

"Uh, I was in the shower? I mean, I was going to take a shower. Just got here a couple seconds ago." The man was not a good liar. "Danielle said I could stay and wash up while she went out. There's this, uh, plumbing issue at my parents' place? They're down in Palm Springs."

"I see," Pamela said. "Have you called someone to fix the problem?"

"Might try to fix it myself."

"That's ambitious." Pamela felt no compunction to make an excuse for being there. "Well, be sure to lock up when you leave."

She strode back to the chalet, more than annoyed that she hadn't been able to unearth anything useful.

* * *

Back from the spa, Danielle found Rory in a panic. Perspiration leaked from her armpits as he described the Queen creeping around the studio while he hid in the bathroom.

So, first the reporter and the cop, now the evil stepmother. *What the fuck? Had they teamed up to go after her?* Mosconi was the common thread – chummy with both McKean and Pamela. Too bad Rory hadn't finished her off on the way home from the hot springs Sunday. He'd freaked when he nearly ran her down on her bike, swerving to avoid the stupid turkeys. When she yelled, "It's Mosconi – take her out," he'd gotten all huffy. Said she shouldn't say things like that – what if he'd followed her order without thinking? Rory could be such a wuss. She'd only meant it as a joke; Jack used to crack-up when she fooled around like that.

Now she sent Rory packing and sat down in a chair with a view of the chalet. Before long, Pamela came out with a bundle of cloth grocery bags under her arm and disappeared into the garage. The Benz purred like a panther as it reversed onto the drive, swung around, and advanced down the road. Now was her chance. Danielle marched over to the chalet and tapped on the front door.

Richard was slow to respond. "Danielle," he said. "Why are you knocking on the door?"

"Well, it's your house, Richard. Yours and Pamela's. I should really stop barging in all the time."

"My God, girl. What are you talking about? You're family. Come in, come in. I can see you have something on your mind."

"Oh, Richard." She swallowed hard and dabbed at her eyes with a twisted-up Kleenex. "You know me better than I know myself. But the truth is I'm not family. I'm nothing without Jack."

Richard put out his arms and she stepped into a cuddly bear hug. "Silly birdy," he said. " You're just feeling down. You look lovely, by the way. Pamela said you'd gone to the spa."

"It was her treat, which was very sweet of her. But – I don't know how to say this – Pamela searched the studio while I was out. Rory surprised her when she went into the bathroom. I was letting him use the shower because his is broken."

"Strange," Richard said. "Well, Pamela must have had a good reason to go over there. I'll speak to her about it."

"You know what?" Danielle said. "I'm sure she had a perfectly good reason – please don't mention it to her. It's probably time I got my own place anyway. I'd rent something but the vacancy rate is zip. I wonder if I could afford a single-wide trailer?" She was thinking out loud. She assumed all Jack's assets would go to her, but she didn't know how much she was worth yet; the bank manager was acting cagey. Unfortunately, Jack hadn't taken out an insurance policy, but surely a guy his age would have socked away a fair chunk of change.

"A single-wide for you and the baby?" Richard said. "I don't think so, honey. No. Selfishly, I'd like you to stay where you are, but I can see you're ready to be independent. We'll find you a nice little bungalow with a yard for the child. Somewhere close by so we can give you all the help you need."

Richard was a sweetheart, but being loaded tended to mess with his grip on reality. "Do you know what a bungalow in Nelson costs?" she said. "That's just not an option. I wouldn't even know how to get a mortgage – I probably wouldn't qualify anyway."

"I almost said 'leave it to me,' but we're going to do this together, Danny. I'll call a realtor and we'll start from there. And don't worry about money, for goodness' sakes. Worrying is not good for you or the baby. The house will be our gift to you."

What? "No, that's crazy, Richard."

"Nonsense. It's what Jack would have wanted."

Danielle dropped onto the sofa. "I'm just. . . blown away . . . I don't know what to say."

Richard sat down beside her and took her hand. "Just say yes," he said.

"It's not that simple and we both know it," she said, picturing Pamela going berserk. "Of course, it would be amazing for the baby. But . . ."

"Say yes, Danny," he repeated.

"Okay, *yes!*" And now the tears were real.

"Good girl. Let's get cracking then."

Danielle pulled herself together and held up her hand. "This is going to sound awful, but could this be our little secret, just for a while? I don't want to hurt Pamela and she'll feel bad if she thinks I had a problem with her coming into the studio. I mean, she had every right to."

"Pamela has your interests at heart, Danny. But we don't have to spring this on her right away if you'd prefer not to. As I say, I'll make some enquiries and we'll have a look at what's out there. When we find something you like, we'll made an occasion of the announcement. Go to a nice restaurant. You know Pammie – she loves that sort of thing."

20

ANGIE HAD THE DAY off. The teachers at the school were having a "non-instructional day," which meant they got paid to do whatever the hell they pleased while the custodians had their wages docked. It would have been nice to sleep in at least, but her mother was hell bent on going to Nelson to shop and too hungover to drive.

Angie considered dropping the old lady at the mall and seeing if The Great Moscooni had time for a coffee. Although, truth be told, she wasn't sure she wanted to see the smarty-pants reporter. She was a bit hurt that Stella had stopped calling. Plus she couldn't stop thinking about Stella and Jack dating back in school, and the very real possibility that she, Angie, had caught him on the rebound. He probably never would have given her the time of day if sweet Stella hadn't dumped him. God, she was depressed.

She left her mother outside Walmart and drove around for a while, finally pulling over to send Stella a text: *Hey, you. Forgotten me already?*

Stella texted right back: *Sprained ankle. Don't get out much anymore.*

So maybe that's why she hadn't called. Angie perked up a little. *I'm in Nelson. Buy you a java?*

Stella replied: *Sure. Coffee wagon in Railtown?*

Why not? Angie steered the old Ford Escort to the visitor's lot by the railway station and waited. Five minutes later, the door to the *Nelson Times* swung open and Stella hopped out on crutches. She looked like hell. Crooked pony tail, baggy old jeans. Angie got out of the car and walked toward her. "Oh, hey," Stella said, dusting off the back of her pants. "Don't mind my new fashion statement. No elevator in the building so I have to bump down the stairs on my ass."

Angie felt a twinge of pity – and enjoyed the feeling. She told Stella to go sit on a bench by the coffee wagon while she grabbed them both coffees. She had planned to play it cool, but couldn't resist blurting her big news the minute she sat down. "I saw that cow Danielle at the Salmo pub last night," she said. "I guess she likes to go slumming where nobody knows she's preggers and shouldn't be boozing it up."

"Huh," Stella said. Angie was disappointed; she'd expected more of a reaction. Stella took a sip of coffee before she spoke again. "You could see what she was drinking?"

"I didn't have to," Angie said, exasperated with the question. "I could tell she was into the sauce by the way she acted." Danielle's drink *had* looked like a Coke, but it must have been spiked with vodka or rum. Nobody drives from Nelson to Salmo for an effing soft drink.

"I still wonder if she saw your message on the wall at the Hume," Stella said. "If she did, I think she would have called just to see who answered the phone. She's not shy, and she was extremely possessive of Jack."

"Do you ever give up?" Angie said. "I gotta hand it to you, you're some pushy broad, you know that? You must piss off a lot of people."

"Well, I piss off Danielle. She never misses a chance to harass me."

Angie found that funny. "And that pisses *you* off."

"Hey, I'm human."

"Just for the record I hate her guts. And yeah, she called, and she said some mean shit. I was, like, consider the source." And now that she'd gotten started, Angie couldn't shut up. "Her boozing makes me sick, if you want to know the truth. If I had Jack's baby inside me, swear to God, I'd live like a friggin' saint. But that ain't gonna happen, not even in my dreams. I waited years for Jack to come back to me after he ran off to the States. He would have too, if that skank hadn't followed him here. I wasn't even invited to the big birthday party, FYI. I crashed it when I realized it was his fortieth. I've raised a glass to him every fucking year since we were eighteen."

"Oh, Angie," Stella said. "I'm sorry."

"Wah, wah, wah. What does it matter now?" Angie gulped down the rest of her coffee and tossed the paper cup into the trash. She was mad at herself for running off at the mouth and madder still at Stella for letting her. Of course that bitch Danielle had reacted to the message on the bathroom wall; Angie had written it just to torment her. Danielle deserved that and more for trapping Jack into proposing. But even talking about Danielle had made Angie's heart thump like a drum, she was sweating all over. *Enough already,* she told herself, *calm the fuck down.* She told Stella she had to go, adding, "Guess you do too. Now that you're a gimp it must take forever to get anywheres."

Once she was back in the car, Angie felt a bit mean for mocking Stella, kicking her when she was down. But she couldn't help thinking: *Welcome to my world.*

* * *

McKean dropped by Max's Gym around the time Stella had reported Kieran Corcoran exiting the building a few days back. He lucked out. Not only was Kieran at the gym working out, but Cassidy Pickering was too.

The owner Max Huber didn't welcome him with open arms, but then last time they'd spoken, McKean had questioned him in connection with the death of his late wife. Today he nodded at the man and walked up behind Corcoran, who was doing seated bicep curls in front of a mirror. Mid-curl, the kid noticed McKean's reflection and softly groaned. "Hi Kieran," he said. "I'd like a word. Let's step over there by the water fountain."

Kieran slowly rose to his feet, slotted the dumbbell into a rack of weights, and took his time joining him. McKean made himself comfortable on an upholstered bench and flipped open a notebook. "Nice to see you back in town," he said. The boy's eyelid flickered. "I have some questions about Jack Ballard. Did you know him?"

Kieran remained standing and focused on a spot in the middle distance. "Yeah, I knew him. He helped me fix up my bike. I was sorry to hear he passed."

"When was the last time you spoke to Mr. Ballard?"

"I, uh, stopped by at his birthday party? I only stayed a couple minutes."

"Oh?" McKean said. "Why was that?"

"Not my scene, I guess."

"Are you a trail runner, Kieran?" McKean said.

"Yeah, I run trails, roads, whatever."

"Did you go for a run up Elephant Mountain the morning after Jack Ballard's party?"

Kieran scratched the back of his neck. "That would have been the day he fell, right? No. Don't think I went up that day. Weather was pretty fierce."

"Do you own a grey hoodie, Kieran?" McKean said.

"Who doesn't?"

"A male wearing a grey hoodie was seen running up to Pulpit that day. You say you don't *think* you went up. Try again to remember. I want to talk to anyone who saw Ballard on the mountain that day, however briefly."

"Well, I didn't go up so I guess I can't help you." He looked McKean in the eye. "We done then?"

"We're done," McKean said. "For now. Take care."

"Yeah, thanks." The boy went back to the weights stand and hefted a thirty-five pounder.

McKean glanced over at Cassidy; she was running on a treadmill and didn't look his way. Before leaving, he nodded again to Max Huber, who made a show of studying a sheaf of papers at the registration desk. Back in his car, he texted Stella: *Struck out with KC.*

* * *

Cassidy had dreaded running into Galen again after he'd attacked her in Castlegar. But seeing Kieran at the gym made her feel brave. Besides, Galen looked sullen – not his usual smart-ass, in-your-face self. She walked past him as if he were invisible.

There was a subtle buzz when Sergeant McKean came in, smiling and nodding as if it were perfectly normal for a cop in uniform to drop by the gym. Within minutes he'd cornered Kieran and begun to grill him like a common criminal. At least, that was what seemed to be happening over by the water fountain.

So, okay, he must have found out Kieran was the trail runner she'd been careless enough to mention. Well, whoop de doo. At the time, she honestly had not known who had passed her on the trail that awful day. But she'd recognized him immediately when she saw him at Max's. His body, the way he moved. When he jogged up the stairs ahead of her the other day, there'd been no doubt in her mind that he was the guy.

Kieran had appeared to keep his cool the whole time McKean questioned him. Cassidy felt like cheering when the cop left and Kieran went back to doing bicep curls as if nothing had happened. She suspected McKean had left the gym none the wiser.

Kieran was hot, but that wasn't what attracted Cassidy. Well, not the only thing. He had this quiet way, as if he were above the petty stuff other people bitch about. Now he was walking toward the entrance to change into his outdoor runners and Cassidy drifted over there too.

He looked up at her and flashed a big smile. "Hey," he said.

"Hey," she said back. "I saw you talking to that cop, McKean. He's been hassling me too – about being on the mountain that day?"

"No shit," he said, looking surprised. God, he had the deepest brown eyes.

"No shit," she agreed.

"How'd he know you were up there?" Kieran said.

"I discovered Jack's body and called 9-1-1."

He seemed to think about that. "Wonder how he knew about me?"

She gave a big shrug. "Cops – they have their ways."

"You want to go for coffee?" he said.

"Sure. I have nothing else to do," she said, which made him laugh. They crossed the street to Sidewinders and she grabbed a couple of stools in a quiet place by the window while Kieran ordered their coffees. It felt right, as if going for coffee with Kieran was part of her normal routine.

He let his arm brush against hers when he climbed onto the stool. "So, you saw me on the trail that day," he said. "I saw you too."

She giggled like an idiot, but he didn't seem to mind. "Where'd you see me?" she said, boldly.

"Near the start of the trail, right?"

"Guess so. I never pay much attention to where I am up there." She raised her coffee cup.

"Same here," he said. "You kind of zone out, especially on the steep parts."

"I know what you mean," Cassidy said. "Anyway, too bad about Jack."

"Yeah." He blew on his coffee before he took a sip. "Did you know him?"

"My mom knew him his whole life. I was going to buy her a bike from him but it didn't work out."

"I got a bike from him," Kieran said. "I didn't know him all that well, but yeah, it was too bad about the accident."

Cassidy asked him about school and he said he was doing courses online. "Oh, wow," she said. "I never thought of doing that. I guess you can avoid a lot of bullshit that way."

"You got it," he said. They talked until she had to go. She knew her mom would be looking at the clock, working out how long it usually took her to get back from the gym.

As they left the coffee shop, Kieran said, "See you tomorrow at Max's?"

She said, "For sure." She knew he was watching her as she walked away.

* * *

Joe felt bad about going on a Search and Rescue overnighter when Stella was laid up with a sprained ankle. He'd apologized profusely. But it was a key part of his Ground SAR training and had been scheduled for weeks. It was essential for a new volunteer to experience a night in the mountains with minimal equipment – bivy sac, tarp, water, basic rations. The idea was to simulate getting caught out in an emergency. Naturally Joe was stoked having never spent a night in the wilderness without a tent or any of the usual trappings of a campout.

Stella, to her credit, insisted he carry on with his plans. "The boys aren't babies," she'd said. "Matt and Nicky can help me. It'll be good for them to take more responsibility around here. And it's only for one night. It won't be all that different from you being at an evening meeting."

Tonight was the night and he headed up to Kootenay Pass to meet the others. Reilly, the GSAR team leader, would be in charge. And as an experienced volunteer, Mo would be there too, to support and advise the new recruits.

Everyone was on time, and now they huddled around Reilly for a briefing. The forecast indicated snow at higher elevations, a fresh skiff on top of what remained from the previous season. The weather was already beginning to close in as the group reconnoitred in a shelter by the parking lot. Scattered storms were visible over nearby peaks, a predictable situation at that elevation in late September.

Mo passed out instructions to each of the four newbies and they poured over their orders.

Reilly called for questions, and hearing none, wished them all a good night.

Joe reread his notes and hefted his pack. He felt strong and happy, fully in his element. As he forged up a trail he saw an occasional strike of lightning in the distance but the rain was holding off. By the time he reached the snowline, he couldn't hear any voices. He stopped to admire the mountain views and thought about Stella and the boys. He thought maybe he'd bring them all up there camping the following summer; the guys would be old enough to carry their share of the gear. It would be a blast.

After about an hour's time, with darkness closing in on him, Joe started to look for a good spot to bed down. He found a protected ledge, covered in moss. Nowhere to hang the tarp though. He looked around and found a couple of dead branches suitable for supporting the tarp and spread his bivy sack under it. He drank some water, rationing it to last through the night. Then he brushed a dusting of snow off a rock and sat down to eat his first power bar.

When he heard a twig snap he jumped to his feet and did a one-eighty, but it was only Mo coming by to check up on him. "Pull up a rock," he said, sitting down again.

She dropped her pack on the ground. "You look comfy."

"Nowhere I'd rather be," Joe said.

"Same." Mo sat down and pulled out her water bottle.

"You come up here every year?" Joe said.

"I usually come on the newbie overnighter, if that's what you mean. It's not always at the pass."

"Well, nice of you to give Reilly a hand."

"Happy to do it."

Joe turned to face the view again. Mo sipped some water and put away her bottle. She didn't seem inclined to move on. Joe said, "So you've been doing these overnighters for a while. Any incidents that stand out in particular?"

"Oh, you want a bedtime story?"

"You bet."

Mo surprised him; he hadn't expected her to stop and chat at a training session. She launched into a tale about a winter rescue, her first as a new SAR volunteer. Joe was mesmerized. She spoke without a break for about thirty minutes, detailing how a couple experienced in the backcountry had become disoriented on their skis. Realizing they were lost, they'd built a snow cave for refuge. Joe had lots of questions, and darkness soon closed in on them. Mo found a place of her own to sleep. They wished each other a good night.

Joe had slipped off to relieve himself and give Mo some privacy when an ear-splitting roar almost stopped his heart. The roar morphed into a deafening bugling, so close he could almost feel the animal's breath on his neck. Heart hammering, he thrashed through the brush to get back to Mo.

She was sitting up, flossing her teeth. "Bull elk," she said. "Rutting season."

"I knew that," Joe said.

They collapsed in laughter.

Later Joe couldn't remember who had moved first to close the distance between them. Their mouths slammed into each other, hands ripping at clothing, a noisy, clumsy coupling like nothing he'd ever known. At first, they slept apart. Then, half asleep, they crawled together as the sky lightened and grappled again. Afterward, Mo methodically, unselfconsciously put on her clothes. She didn't bother to say good-bye when she headed off in the direction she'd come from.

21

MAX HUBER SIDLED UP close to Kieran Corcoran to catch his attention. When he figured no one else was looking, he made a V with two fingers, pointed at his own eyes, then at Kieran – a signal that said, *I'm watching you, buddy.*

Kieran gave him a cold stare.

Having been around the block a time or two, Max didn't like what was going on right under his nose. The kid had homed in on sweet Cassidy Pickering, and if Max had to put money on who was more dangerous – the swim club goon called Galen or Kieran – there was no frigging contest. Galen was full of himself but it was all hot air. Kieran, on the other hand, must have seen some ugly things go down in juvie, the sort of things that make a guy reckless and apt to take liberties with the ladies. He obviously had no solid family to take him in and smarten him up, otherwise the powers-that-be wouldn't have put him away for minor crimes. Max had an idea of how these things work.

Kieran must have known he was onto him, but he seemed too enamored to care. Cassidy was smitten too, prancing around like a woman does when she knows someone's looking. Miss Cassidy was a fine athlete, steady and light on her feet, but Kieran seemed to think she needed pointers from him.

Max kept an eye on them. If there was one thing he knew, it was how to lift. One day he'd given the young lady a tip or two himself and earned a nice big smile. He knew he was a sucker, but that'd pretty much made his day.

He glanced at the clock. After their workouts the duo had taken to skipping off to the coffee shop across the street. Today as they changed their shoes to leave the premises, his assistant Colette caught his eye. She winked and said, "Young love in bloom."

Max grunted. "Guess you could call it that."

* * *

Saturday morning Stella was in the supermarket obsessing over cheesecakes when Pamela Ballard came up beside her. "I should get a dessert too, with Thanksgiving coming," she said. "I don't have it in me to bake a pumpkin pie. Sorry – that sounded pitiful. It's just that Jack was the one with a sweet tooth."

"How *are* you, Pamela?" Stella said.

"How are *you*?" Pamela said. "What's with the crutches?"

"Fell off my bike and sprained my ankle. It's a pain getting around – I'm hoping the experience will be character building."

"You have plenty of character already, Stella. But to answer your question, I'm fine. I've been going for walks, although to be honest, I haven't felt much like socializing. In fact, I usually pick a quieter time to shop."

"When you're ready, send me a text and we'll get together for a cup of something."

"I'll do that, Stella. I'll look forward to it." Pamela put a plain cheesecake into her basket and moved along.

Stella settled on a cake with strawberry swirls and looked for a check-out with a short line. She had about half an hour to get home and put on a pot of coffee before her long-lost father turned up on the doorstep. He'd called out of the blue and asked if he could stop by for a visit. Decades had passed since he'd walked out on Stella and her mom – and now he wanted to reconnect. He'd come by once before when no one was home and left a note, but that had been months ago. The usual wave of nausea hit as Stella recalled finding the note and agonizing over whether to call the number scrawled on the bottom. When she finally broke down and called, he'd made excuses about coming to Nelson again. Now that he was following through, she was the one having second thoughts. She told herself to grow up; she was an adult with kids of her own and her dad was just another guy who'd baled on his family.

When she got home, the cabin was a mess. Lego and miniature model cars everywhere, the boys at each other's throats, Joe threatening loss of television privileges if they didn't straighten up on the count of three. Naturally Robert Hart chose that moment to arrive.

For starters she didn't know how to address him, having not had an occasion to call him "Dad" for about twenty-five years. Her mom used to call him Robbie, which seemed too intimate a name for Stella to use.

Mercifully, Joe joined her at the door to introduce himself. Her dad latched onto Joe's hand like a drowning man grasping a lifeline. "Bob Hart," he said, then turned to open his arms to Stella. She opted to shake hands too. "Oh my," he said, noting the crutches. "What happened to you?"

"Sprained ankle. No big deal," she said. "But hey, welcome. This is Matt and that's Nicky."

Of course she'd forgotten to brief the boys, and Nicky said, "Should we call you Nonno?" Joe's parents were Nonno and Nonna; Stella's mother and her latest husband were Grandma and Herb.

Pulling both boys into a shared hug, Bob said, "Call me anything, but don't call me late for dinner." The boys dissolved in laughter at the old chestnut, just as Stella would have done at their ages. To cover up the catch in her throat she bustled around fixing the refreshments.

Bob complimented Joe on the red canoe overturned on the beach out front. "We had one just like it when Stella was little," he said. "Remember that, darlin'?"

"Except it was yellow," she said from the kitchen.

"Nope. It was red. Older than this one though, lots of scrapes on the thing. We didn't keep it very long, of course." He sighed and turned to Joe. "I don't know if you've heard the story."

"Why didn't you keep it very long?" Matt asked.

No one answered the question and Stella jumped in to fill the gap. "I remember it as yellow. There's a photo of me at age three leaning against a yellow canoe. The snapshot's faded but the canoe is clearly yellow, a little orange-ish, maybe. Definitely not red."

"I know the shot," said her dad. "I took it myself. You were wearing a little ruffled bathing suit and a white cap with a chin strap. Cute as a button. But that picture wasn't taken in Nelson. The yellow canoe was a rental we used one season up in Sechelt."

"What? No. That picture was taken at Lakeside Park. I remember posing for it. It's one of my earliest memories."

"Sorry, darlin' – take another look. Salt chuck in the background, not Kootenay Lake." He smiled. "We had some good times up in Sechelt."

Stella let it go, although his mistaking the colour of the family canoe infuriated her. Well, he'd left, so predictably he'd forgotten much of their early life together. She hacked the cake into pieces and called the boys to the kitchen table to eat theirs. Even as she served the coffee, she found herself hoping Bob Hart wouldn't stay much longer. Really it didn't matter what anyone called the man, she didn't plan to make a habit of inviting him to their home. For once she was thankful the cabin was too cramped to accommodate overnight guests.

Bob asked Stella about her mother but she had little to report. "I guess you know she lives in Florida now, and she's remarried."

"What's this one – number four?"

"Three," Stella said. "His name is Herb. We haven't met him yet."

After an hour or so of small talk, Bob made noises about leaving and Stella didn't coax him to stay. That was when he told the boys he'd brought them a gift; it was out in the car. *Buying off my kids*, Stella thought, as Bob slipped outside. The boys giggled and covered their eyes with their hands, which tugged at her heart. She hoped he wouldn't let them down. Not ever. Not even with something as trivial as a disappointing gift.

Bob came back in carrying something wriggly, wrapped in a coat.

Then he placed a small brown Labrador puppy on the floor.

The boys whooped and cheered and hugged their new grandpa, and even Joe – the traitor – acted pleased. The puppy peed on the floor.

Stella found her voice. "Just a sec, guys," she said. "It's nice of Bob to want to give you a dog, but this is something your dad and I need to talk about." She found a rag to wipe up the pee. Joe offered Bob a beer.

The boys were allowed to take the pup outside while the adults assembled on the front porch to talk. "This is a generous gift," Stella said. "But I wish you'd spoken to us first. A puppy is a big responsibility. And there are costs to consider too."

"Sorry, darlin' – I just couldn't think of anything two little boys would want more."

"It might be good for them, Stella," Joe said. "As long as they do their part to look after the little guy."

Stella could have throttled him. "So I guess I'll have to be the hammer." She paused. "Regardless of the boys' good intentions, it would fall to you and me to train the dog and take him to the vet for his shots. You don't have a lot of spare time as it is, Joe." The last sentence spoken pointedly.

"I have to meet my obligations to SAR, if that's what you mean, but I'd be happy to pitch in."

"So you're a Search and Rescue volunteer," Bob said. "Gosh, I have a lot of admiration for you folks. I'll bet you have some good stories. Be nice to talk about your adventures sometime."

"I'd like that," Joe said. "Anytime."

"I don't know how you do it all," Bob continued. "The training, the rescues. And I hear you're a teacher too."

"You just do what you can," Joe said, modestly.

Stella brought the conversation back to the dog and asked Bob to explain the numerous responsibilities of puppy care to the boys. Matt and Nicky fervently promised to feed the dog and take him for walks, cross their hearts and hope to die. "We're calling him, Snickers," Nicky announced.

Matt jabbed his arm and hissed, "You weren't supposed to tell yet."

Stella looked around the circle of hopeful faces. "I guess it's settled then," she said.

* * *

Thanksgiving Monday, McKean got up and walked the few blocks from his rental suite to the family home to spend the day with his son. There wouldn't be a special dinner this year, but at least he had Aiden to himself for a while and the weather was pleasantly warm, a light breeze off Kootenay Lake rustling the leaves on the shade trees that lined the streets. His throat tightened as he approached his real home with its well-aged shingle siding and kitschy window shutters, the covered front porch that featured a pair of old blue rockers no one ever sat in. He'd expected to live in that house forever, maybe even pay off the mortgage someday. At least Miranda hadn't asked for his keys. When he opened the front door, his little son came running, one shoe on, one shoe off, a circle of raspberry jam around his mouth making him look like a loveable little clown.

Miranda finally took off after telling him how to take care of his own son. He got down on the floor with Aiden and made towers from wooden blocks, which Aiden knocked down, then he read aloud from a bunch of board books and the little guy chattered along in a language all his own. After the toddler had his nap and ate his lunch, McKean popped him into his stroller for a walk down to Lakeside Park.

Even before they reached the playground, McKean saw Stella Mosconi, crutches and all, laughing as a brown Labrador pup ran circles around her, tangling her up in its leash. Nearby her sons dangled from the monkey bars. McKean opened his phone and sent her a text: *New member of the family?*

He watched as she reached into her pocket for her phone and read the text, looked around until she saw him and smiled. She tapped out a reply: *Gift from my long-lost dad. Think our bosses have us under surveillance?*

He wrote: *You never know.*

Stella crutched over with the dog, smiling all the way, and bent toward the stroller. "Hi Aiden," she said. "Do you like the doggy?" Yes, Aiden liked the doggy – he went a little nuts. McKean undid his straps and lifted him out of the stroller and together he and Stella let him pet the dog without getting nipped.

"Think your publisher would consider this reckless?" McKean said, "Us meeting like this?"

"What the hell," Stella said. "We're both off duty." Her sons ran over and the younger one, Nicky, took Aiden's hand and led him to a baby swing. The older boy lifted Aiden in, and to his obvious delight, the big boys took turns pushing him. McKean and Stella sat down on a bench. He wondered briefly if he and Stella, along with the three boys and one mutt, looked like a family to anyone who didn't know better.

Stella didn't have much to say about her "long-lost" dad. She seemed more interested in the scoop on Kieran Corcoran.

"He denied being on Elephant Mountain the day Ballard died," McKean said. "No surprise that. Thing is, we don't know whether

Cassidy's trail runner – if he even exists – is relevant to the case. I have the unpleasant feeling there *is* no case, to be honest. Maybe no one's to blame other than the guy who slipped and fell. We're still checking boot prints against a couple of casts taken at the site, but it's slow going. Chief says it's a waste of resources. He's finding other ways to keep me busy. Oh, I looked up the makes of those cars. Stone owns an older red and white Mini Cooper, her sidekick drives a dark grey Camry, also about ten years old."

"The Camry fits," Stella said. "Not that anyone other than Stone saw Rory almost run me down. He'd only blame the turkeys if I confronted him. I know I sound paranoid, but Ballard used to make me anxious and Stone seems to have taken over where he left off. She's the only connection between me and Rory. I can't see why he'd go after me unless she told him too."

McKean hesitated. "I'm talking out of school, but after his party, Ballard went for a nightcap with Rory and they ended up at his parents' place. I questioned Rory and he claimed he was still asleep when Ballard woke up the following morning and left the house."

Stella sat up a little straighter. "Are you thinking what I'm thinking? The fiancée and the best friend – if there was something going on between them, that might have been a motive to get rid of Ballard."

"Seems like a leap," McKean said. He should have changed the subject but it was too easy to talk to Stella. "I tried to get access Ballard's medical files, by the way, but Stone went over my head and the Chief nixed it."

"What were you looking for in the medical records?"

He made a face. "I gotta shut up, Stella."

"If I guess, will you give me a sign? A nod? Thumbs up or thumbs down?"

He laughed. "Give it your best shot."

"Okay, but first I should tell you about Angie," Stella said. "She turned up at both Ballard's party and his funeral. An old flame of Jack's known as Angel in high school. Do you remember her?"

"Don't place the name," he said.

"I bluffed because she seemed to know who I was. I've met with her a couple of times, mostly out of curiosity." McKean was listening but he was fighting an urge to brush a small smudge off her cheek with his thumb. Stella continued: "I'm going out on a limb because of something Angie hinted at. Seems she and Jack experimented with BDSM back in the day. I figure if Jack was into kink with Danielle, his body might have shown signs of mild trauma, especially if he was the submissive one in the relationship." She paused. "That last bit might sound dubious, but hear me out – I've been reading up on this stuff. If Ballard was into sadomasochism, you'd think he would have been the dominant partner, right? There's this stereotype of the Dom as a good-looking, highly successful male – athletic too. But apparently some strong men like to take the submissive role. It has something to do with lack of inhibitions in people with power, both men and women. Why not let someone else take charge for a change, provided everyone plays by the rules." Stella stopped talking and waited a second. "So. How am I doing? Feel free to scoff if this doesn't ring true."

"Uh, what was I supposed to do? Nod?" he said. "I think you're onto something."

Aiden screamed and they both jumped to their feet. The big boys had gotten carried away and the toddler needed a rescue.

"Well, that's the end of that," Stella said, as all three kids clamoured for attention.

"Too bad," McKean said, soothing Aiden and strapping him into his stroller. "I want to hear more about this Angie."

"Call me," Stella said. "I should go home to baste the turkey anyway. Is your wife sweating over a hot stove this afternoon?"

"Not really," McKean said, vaguely, regretting that his one-on-one with Stella was over. Not that he stopped thinking about her and what she'd said about BDSM as he wheeled his boy out of the park and up the hill. He wondered if the woman called Angie might be a suspect – and if Stella was putting herself in danger by talking to her. He'd have warn her about that.

At the house, Miranda was waiting to scoop up Aiden and take him to the neighbours' place for dinner. He returned to his grungy suite, popped a turkey TV dinner in the oven, and tried to lose himself in a cop show full of outrageously good-looking people and crazy coincidences.

When he couldn't handle another car chase, he turned off the TV, feeling at loose ends. He supposed the neighbours would have included him in the dinner invitation if he and Miranda hadn't split, not that he cared. It was Stella he wanted to be with. At any rate, what she'd told him that afternoon had reignited his interest in the investigation. Kinky sex could explain some of the bruises on Ballard's body, the ones he got prior to his fall. McKean had been itching to tell Stella about the aneurysm – he trusted her completely – but he knew a leak of that significance could amount to professional suicide.

22

PAMELA HAD BEEN UPSET about Danielle carrying on with Rory, and worried sick about the paternity of the baby, but she'd never imagined the girl would go this far. Manipulating Richard to buy her a house! Pamela couldn't decide what was worse: Danielle using him, or Richard allowing her to, then keeping it secret.

A realtor's wife Pamela barely knew had come up to her at the bank and inadvertently spilled the beans. The woman couldn't be blamed; she'd only wanted to say how good it was to see Richard with a project again, and how generous they both were to look after Jack's fiancée. Pamela had rushed right back to the chalet to do battle, but Richard wasn't home. He'd left a note: *Out on an errand with Danielle. Back soon, R.* Yesterday he'd taken Danielle on an "errand" too. What had he been thinking, and when did he plan to tell his wife what was going on?

Pamela needed a friend and ally, and who better to turn to than Stella Mosconi? She was sensible and smart, she knew the family, and there wasn't much love lost between her and Danielle. She texted Stella: *Would love to talk. When's a good time for you?* Ten minutes passed with no reply, which was to be expected: Stella would be at work and might not get back to her before evening. Not wanting to be around when Richard and Danielle came back, chummy and self-satisfied, Pamela left for a walk. She headed down Lucky Jack Road, passed the pond, and continued into the upper reaches of the town, reminding herself to breathe, to notice the trees. The foliage was already taking on the colours of autumn; the cottonwoods turning yellow, the maples becoming a deeper scarlet. Vegetable gardens were morphing into that musky, wanton jumble of produce past its prime. Her phone pinged with a text from Stella: *At the Capitol Theatre. Tea shop on Victoria St in 20 minutes?*

I'll be there, Pamela replied and picked up the pace. She was clammy with sweat when she reached the tea shop.

Stella was smiling as she approached on her crutches. "I saw Richard and Danielle drive by not thirty minutes ago," she said.

"Tell me about it." Pamela made no attempt to hide her bitterness. "What were you doing at the Capitol?"

"Interviewing a couple of actors mounting a two-man play. Father and son thing."

Inside, they chose a small antique table by the window. Pamela feigned interest in the upcoming play, but Stella obviously saw right through her. "You seem kind of fragile today," she said. "Don't feel you have to pretend with me."

Within seconds, Pamela was blubbering into a fistful of napkins, beyond caring how she looked to anyone in the shop. Stella sat very still and let her cry, not even glancing at her phone when it rang. Finally, Pamela pulled herself together and came clean. "It's Danielle. It sounds ridiculous but I'm almost afraid of her. She has Richard so enchanted he wants to buy her a house."

"That sounds excessive," Stella said. "Although I guess I shouldn't judge."

"Yes, well, that's diplomatic of you, Stella. I haven't forgotten how she treated you when you came to the house, or how rude she was at the funeral. I hope she hasn't bothered you again."

Stella hesitated. "Nothing worth mentioning."

"Oh, no, what's she done now?"

Stella waved her hand dismissively. "Let's talk about you."

Pamela wiped her eyes. She was done crying. "I could go on and on about Danielle, but there's no escape from her. Unfortunately she's pregnant, ostensibly with Jack's baby. And yes, she has given me reason to question the child's paternity." Suddenly Pamela looked horrified. "Good God, who's that?"

Stella looked around to see the panhandler with the woolly scarf peering through the window, his hands in fingerless gloves framing his face, nose flattened against the glass. "Oh, him. Sadly I don't even know his name." Stella gave him a little wave. "I hand him a dollar or two every now and then. But what's this about the child's paternity?"

Pamela made a shooing gesture and the panhandler loped away. "I've been spying on them. Danielle and Rory. There I've said it."

She picked up her cup and took a sip of tea. "From my deck I can hear them having sex in the studio. And, no, I'm not talking about a one-off. It happens nightly. I was trying to show them a little compassion until it occurred to me the affair might have started before Jack died. If she cheated on him with Rory, the baby might be his, perish the thought."

Stella paused. "Does Rory spend a lot of time at the studio?"

"He practically lives there," Pamela said. "Which is nothing new. He was always following Jack around, only now he's secretive. Hides his car when he's over at night. To continue with the true confessions, I slipped into the studio yesterday to have a look around. I'd read up on post-mortem paternity testing and hoped to find something with Jack's DNA on it. If I hadn't been interrupted I might have – the place was a pigsty. I don't think she's tidied up since he died. A feather duster under the bed was so clean I doubt it's ever been used. But, as I said, my sleuthing was interrupted. I surprised Rory in the bathroom, if you can believe it."

"Pamela – wait, back up a minute," Stella said. "This is going to sound strange, but humour me. How would you describe the bed and the space around it?"

"The bed? Well, it wasn't made but there was nothing remarkable about it. Except for the macramé lying around. All these bits of white cord tied in fancy knots, some of them unfinished. Hard to picture Danielle doing crafts, isn't it? There were hooks in the ceiling but no plants hanging from them. Oh, and she has a big box labelled 'Tickle Trunk.' Odds and sods from her childhood, I assume. The thing is secured with a massive padlock as if anyone would care what's in it. Such a drama queen, that girl."

"Pamela," Stella said, carefully. "Have you read *Fifty Shades of Grey*?"

It took a second or two for her to catch on. "Good God," she said.

"Indeed. You just described several items, including the feather duster, that could be props for kinky sex. That macramé sounds like the woven cord used in Japanese rope bondage. Does Richard know what's going on?"

"I haven't shared my suspicions. It would kill Richard if the baby wasn't Jack's. Still, surely he would want to know."

"I feel for both of you." Stella said.

"Well, thanks for listening," Pamela said. "I better let you get back to work."

Stella stood up and gave her a hug. "I'll keep in touch," she said.

* * *

Outside the tea shop, the guy in the woolly scarf was waiting for Stella. She couldn't ignore him: they were the only two people on that stretch of sidewalk. She reached into her pocket for a toonie and he thanked her warmly. The poor guy served as a reminder that part two of her panhandling article was coming due, as well as the blurb for the upcoming play. She told herself to get a move on.

But first she texted Ben to tell him Pamela's suspicions about Danielle and Rory. She still struggled to get her head around the notion of them as a couple, never mind the parents of a child. But the relationship had implications she hesitated to bring up with Pamela. If Danielle and Rory *had* been carrying on before Jack's death, they might have wanted him out of the picture. Particularly if Rory was the father of Danielle's baby.

Stella crutched toward Railtown, her mind humming. She wondered if Rory could be the elusive trail runner, although it was hard to picture Rory as *any* kind of runner. But then it was equally hard to see him as a match for Danielle. Thing was though, if he had gone up to the viewpoint with Ballard, he could easily have done the crime. Jack would have followed him to the edge like a lamb to slaughter. No weapons needed, no excessive force. Stone's part might have been to hunker down in the studio and perform the grieving-widow routine, then work on Richard to buy them a house.

Stella crossed the four-way stop to Railtown, carried on another block to the station, and slowly made her way upstairs to the newsroom. Jade Visser was at her desk, the publisher's Bichon Frise snuggled up on her lap. She was wearing earphones, presumably transcribing notes as she clucked over the dog.

Stella tuned her out and resumed work on the panhandling feature, first searching for a stock photo to avoid invading the personal space of any of Nelson's homeless. But she was so preoccupied with Pamela's dilemma, she found herself having to check and double-check every single detail of her story. In her humble opinion, multi-tasking was highly over-rated.

* * *

Joe had mixed feelings as he stood in his empty classroom, anticipating the SAR meeting scheduled for that evening. The purpose was to debrief from the overnighter at Kootenay Pass and he would have to face Mo. He wasn't worried about her getting emotional or making any demands on him – that wasn't Mo. But it was more and more difficult to hold it together in front of Stella. He'd never cheated on her before and had taken some pride in resisting temptation. It wasn't as if other women had never come onto him and, being human, he'd been mildly tempted to stray on occasion. That seemed natural given how long he and Stella had been married. Too many years had slipped by since they couldn't keep their hands off each other.

He knew none of that was an excuse for being unfaithful. Stella was a good wife and a wonderful mother. The dishonesty of what had happened up at the pass bothered him as much as anything. He and Stella didn't have secrets – nothing this big, anyway.

Just as well he would have to face Mo that evening and work at dialing back his attraction. They were colleagues with a common interest, pure and simple. He hoped to God he'd be able to look her in the eye without thinking of her naked. *Shit.* Now his head flooded with images of them going at it, leaves and needles and dirt stuck to hot flesh, the air cold enough to see their breaths as they puffed and groaned. Alone in his classroom, Joe adjusted his pants to ease the pressure of an erection and tried to kill his ardor by picturing horrific situations like being maimed by a hideous disease, or forced to raise his kids in a war-torn country.

Later at home, he put the potatoes on for dinner and yelled at Matt and Nicky to clean up their toys and set the table. Stella was late. When she finally shuffled through the front door on her crutches he went silent and started shutting cupboards with more force than necessary.

"I haven't forgotten you have SAR tonight," she said. "I'll quickly make a salad while you fry the chops. You can just eat and leave. I'll clean-up."

"I thought that was the boys' job," he said. "How are they going to learn if you take over all the time?"

Stella stopped and looked at him. "Am I missing something here?"

"Sorry," he said. "Guess I'm overtired."

"Somebody needs a hug," Stella said.

"Watch out – boiling water," he said, lifting the pot of potatoes before she could get close enough to touch him.

* * *

Stella cleaned up after dinner and nudged the boys to get ready for bed. After Joe had stormed out for SAR training, everyone seemed out of sorts. Nicky said, "Why is Dad always yelling? He's never fun anymore."

Matt had been furtively teasing the dog with a chew toy. "He yells 'cause you're a pain," he said. "You make him mad."

Stella said, "That's not true, Matt. Apologize to your brother. And if I hear you talk that way to him again you're going to lose a privilege."

Joe *had* changed, though, and it was no surprise the boys had noticed. He'd swing from cheery to angry in the blink of an eye, the rare upswings usually associated with Search and Rescue. It was frightening to think SAR might be the only thing that made him happy, the only thing that made living with him bearable. Nicky was making a habit of crawling out of bed at night for an extra cuddle and Stella had taken to faking her reassurances.

The boys were already tucked into bed when the dog whined to be let out. Stella opened the door and followed him down the porch steps, carrying her crutches. When she saw headlights, she thought for a second it was Joe racing back because he'd forgotten something. But no, it was an unfamiliar car, a beat-up old Chevy, the right front bumper held on with duct tape. Out jumped a man, ripe with body odour and stale smoke, claiming to look for an address. Doing her best not to recoil, Stella checked the number scrawled on his cigarette packet. "You still have a way to go. This address is out near Balfour," she said, referring to a community farther up the lake. She could see through the windshield food wrappers and bedding strewn around the interior of the Chev, signs that he lived in his car.

"No, no," he said, sniffling, his eyes darting here and there. "I been to the place before. I 'member it's real close to here." He wiped his nose on the sleeve of a filthy jacket, the other hand jiggling something metallic in his pocket.

"If the address is correct, the house is farther up the road, maybe a fifteen-minute drive from here," Stella said firmly, glancing at his plate number and committing it to memory. Snickers meanwhile growled and yipped and ran around in circles and the stranger began to dance around the dog, laughing and clicking his tongue. High on something, obviously. Stella planned her move: Hop up the porch steps, call Snickers, and hope for once he would obey. But the cabin door swung open and Nicky came out onto the porch.

"Oh, I thought I heard Dad's car," he said.

"He'll be here any minute, Nicky," Stella said. "Go back to bed."

"You said he wasn't coming till late."

"In you go, Nick."

"Oh, ho," said the stranger. "Dad's out chasing tail and not coming home till *real* late."

"In, Nick," Stella said. "I'll be right there." Nick hesitated a moment then wandered back inside. "And close the door," she called after him.

"Hey, I know you," said the weirdo. "I seen you on the street tossing a coin to Robo. Guy wears that weird scarf? A bit touched, ol' Robo, but he wouldn't hurt a fly. Listen, do ya think ya could help me out a little? Ain't had much to eat today and this here ol' buggy's about to run outta gas. Don't think it would get as far as Balfour."

"Sorry," Stella said. "Have to go tend to my son." She crutched toward the stairs, whistling and coaxing the whining dog.

"C'mon lady, spare me a couple bucks," he said, the smell of him engulfing her as he followed too close behind. She didn't look back as she hopped up the stairs. On the porch she dropped the crutches, scooped up the dog, and limped inside, Snickers peeing all over her as she slid the deadbolt. She watched through the peephole as the stranger paced and muttered, finally returning to his jalopy and gunning it up the drive with a spray of gravel.

Later, after stripping off the pee-soaked clothing and taking a long hot shower, she heard her phone and make a dash for it, hoping it was Ben. But it was Angie and she sounded drunk. She sobbed and carried on about Danielle on the theme that she'd effed up Jack's life and was now destroying his unborn child with her drinking. Much as Stella disliked Danielle Stone, she was skeptical of Angie's theory about her alcohol intake. When she'd pressed her, Angie hadn't seemed sure of her facts. Now as Stella listened to the rant, tossing in the odd word of solace, she kept one eye on the driveway, ever vigilant for the amped-up addict to return to murder her and her children.

23

THE NEWSROOM WAS EMPTY when Stella got to work the following morning. The publisher had sent Patrick and Jade to a forum of local charities and she relished the peace and quiet as she reflected on the unwelcome home visit from the creep in the Chevy. She thought about Ben too, and their conversation at the park on Thanksgiving. She was sure he'd been about to tell her something important about the case when all three children needed attention. He hadn't followed up, then last night while Angie raved over the phone about Danielle, he'd sent a text: *Complications at home. Talk soon.*

Stella wondered if home was ever uncomplicated.

At the patter of little dog feet, she looked up to see the publisher's Bichon Frise padding toward her, followed by the boss herself. The dog sniffed at Jade's desk and hopped up onto her chair. "I'm sorry, Stella," the publisher said, getting straight to her purpose, "but I'm going to have to give you notice. I can't see any way around it."

Stunned into silence, Stella struggled to collect her thoughts. Should she offer the woman a seat in her own newsroom? It seemed more appropriate to stand up and face her.

The paper had been struggling to support two full-time reporters for some time, the publisher explained, a situation that had put Stella in a precarious position even before the incident with the photo. Stella had more experience than Jade overall, she conceded, but Jade had been on staff longer and she was a good fit for the *Times*. She knew the town, understood the culture, had the right instincts.

Stella stammered and stuttered, hating herself for being pathetic, grateful that Patrick and Jade weren't there to witness the sorry spectacle. But the publisher held out a faint hope. Stella's employment was not to be terminated forthwith; she would be suspended with pay for a period of two weeks. The intent was to demonstrate to the public that reporters at the *Times* were held to a higher standard, i.e. no lily-livered, left-wing editorializing was tolerated. Budget permitting, Stella would be reinstated after the suspension and put on probation for the subsequent six months.

"So, this suspension . . ." Stella began, steadying her voice, standing tall on her crutches.

"Effective immediately," said the publisher. She whistled for her dog and turned on her heel.

Stella assumed Patrick had been given a heads-up. She sent him a text to say she was going home to lick her wounds, then turned off her computer, cleared her desk, and hobbled down to her car. Her next move was to drop off the crutches at the rental place. The crutches had turned her into a snivelling baby and she was done with them. Worst-case scenario, she'd limp for a while.

As for the suspension, she told herself not to overreact. She had not been fired, she was still on the payroll. Why not look at the situation as two weeks of flex time? If she kept under the publisher's radar, she could work on the investigation. She texted Ben, then slipped her phone into the in-car holder to await his reply.

Ben still hadn't gotten back to her by the time she got to the cabin and she wondered again about those "complications at home." Being a man of few words, Ben was unlikely to elaborate, although he never seemed aloof or distracted with her. Quite the opposite, really. She hoped she wasn't projecting.

She let Snickers out and sat down on the porch steps to decide what to do next. It felt strange to suddenly have time on her hands, almost like being a kid again, school cancelled due to snow. Maybe it was the childhood memories that brought her dad to mind, but she dialled his number with nothing much to say. She thought she might tell him a few stories about Snickers – the good, the bad, and the ugly – just to hear him laugh.

A woman answered.

"Oh," Stella said. "Hi. I was calling for Bob? This is his daughter."

"Uh, he's not here."

"Could you tell him Stella called? Will he be available later?"

"No. I mean, yes, I'll tell him you called if I get a chance. But I doubt he'll be able to get back to you today. Not sure when he will."

"Okay," Stella said. "Well, whenever it's convenient. Thanks."

"Yeah, bye," the woman said.

Stella disconnected. So, okay, she'd reached a home phone rather than his mobile. Had that been his wife – did he have a wife? The woman could have been anybody, a cleaner, for example, not certain when she'd connect with Bob again. If she *was* Bob's partner though, why hadn't he mentioned her, or brought her along to meet the family? But it seemed reasonable to want to check the lay of the land before introducing a stepmother. Stella decided to give it a few days; if he didn't call, she'd try again.

She went inside and rooted around the linen closet for the photo albums and boxes of loose snapshots, hoping to find the picture her dad had taken of her at age three, leaning against a yellow canoe. The photo was slightly smooshed with one bent corner. But there she was in her little bathing suit and cap, and the canoe was clearly yellow. Not much of a background, but if you looked closely you could see a faint landform.

Wait a minute.

The view was of a distant island, not the houses and forest directly across the lake from the local park. Sechelt, rather than Nelson then. The yellow canoe must have been a rental on a family holiday on the Sunshine Coast. Her dad had remembered correctly, which she supposed counted for something.

What now? She thought of Pamela and picked up her phone again.

Pamela answered on the first ring. "This is a pleasant surprise," she said. "I assume you're at work."

"As it happens, I'm not," Stella said. "I don't suppose you'd like to drive out to my place for coffee."

"I'm walking toward the front door, picking up my car keys," Pamela said. "Tell me where to turn off for your drive."

* * *

Pamela had crossed the big orange bridge to the North Shore and followed the lakeshore for about ten kilometres when she sensed something wrong with the car: first a strange vibration – the steering felt off – then the tell-tale flapping of a flat tire. *Damn, damn, damn.* She pulled to the side of the road and looked up the number for BCAA. The BC Automobile Association assured her that roadside assistance was on the way, possibly within the hour – two hours at most. She called Stella to report the delay.

She was pacing the side of the road, telling herself to be patient, idly watching a white sailboat tack back and forth on the lake, when a cyclist pulled over and greeted her as Mrs. B. Without further ado, Kieran Corcoran pulled off his sunglasses and knelt by the flat tire. He seemed personally affronted that a car serviced at his place of employment could get a flat.

"Never mind, Kieran," she said. "I've called BCAA. They'll be here in an hour or so."

"I can have you on the road again in fifteen minutes if you have a spare," he said.

"Oh, I have a spare and a jack too – Richard insisted on it. It's ridiculous how many cars are sold without a spare these days."

"Right on," Kieran said, moving to the trunk.

Pamela cancelled the service call.

Kieran was wearing his helmet today, along with a torn, no-name T-shirt and baggy shorts. One well-muscled calf was streaked with bike grease and she caught a whiff of manly perspiration as he pulled the spare out of the trunk. He had the car jacked up in minutes. "So, how're you doing today, ma'am," he said, as he loosened the bolts on the flat tire and set it aside.

"I'm fine thanks, Kieran," she said. "I sure appreciate your help."

He shrugged as he pulled off the tire. "I been thinking about what you said the other day about Jack. It can't be easy," he said.

She hadn't expected that. "No, you're right. It's not easy. But things are okay. How about you? Did you ever drop by the bike shop to see about that apprenticeship?"

"Nah," Kieran said. "With Jack gone. . ." He left it at that.

He worked quietly, positioning and bolting the spare, putting away the tools, then he straightened up and said, "I hope things'll, you know, get better. . . If there's anything I can do. . ."

"That's good of you, Kieran," she said. Gosh, he was a likeable kid. He seemed to truly understand her grief, but then he'd lost his mother. When she thanked him, she was tempted to give him a hug, but reined herself in and simply patted his shoulder. He beamed with pleasure.

Once he'd taken off on his bicycle, Pamela rang Stella. "Am I too late for that cup of coffee?"

"Are you kidding?" she said. "Come right over. I'll throw in a sandwich.

Pamela found the cabin after only one wrong turn, and Stella limped out to greet her. "No crutches," Pamela observed. "I see you're limping though. Is that why you're off work?"

"My ankle's on the mend," Stella said. "No, I'm off work because I've been suspended for a couple of weeks. I'll fill you in later. Good to see BCAA got you on your way again so quickly."

"It was no credit to the roadside assistance service," Pamela said. "A young fellow I know came to the rescue. Do you know Kieran Corcoran? He was a friend of Jack's."

"Kieran?" Stella said. She seemed surprised. "Yes, I've met him," she said. Her tone was wary. "What was his connection with Jack?"

"A kind of protégé, I gather. I don't think they knew each other for long, but he seems awfully nice. I keep bumping into him."

"Huh," Stella said, a small frown knitting her brow. "Interesting. Come in and have a bite of lunch." Pamela didn't press her, but something about Kieran seemed to make Stella uneasy. Well, that might be a topic for another day.

Picking up from where they'd left off at the tea shop, they soon got to talking about Danielle. Pamela said what she'd read about sadomasochism on the Internet had disturbed her. "It's upsetting to think of Danielle as a dominatrix," she told Stella. "Particularly if she forced Jack to go along with her depravity. Still, the lot of them – Jack included – certainly qualified as consenting adults. The pregnancy is the most troubling part."

Stella said, "Do you think that was planned?"

"I'm sure it wasn't," Pamela said. "I don't believe Jack would have proposed if she hadn't fallen pregnant. He was a nervous wreck when he came to tell Richard and me. Clearly, his back was against the wall. Later on, out of Richard's earshot, I took him aside and asked him if he was sure about it – if he was certain Danielle was 'the one.'"

"What did he say?" Even calm, rationale Stella appeared to be on the edge of her seat.

Pamela recalled every nuanced word and quoted him precisely. "He said, 'With a baby on the way, I'd better fucking be sure.' Then he apologized for the language, as he always did – a remnant of his teen years." Pamela's voice had almost failed her when she'd quoted

Jack. He may have had his faults, but he'd been a good boy, a good man. Too good for that self-serving bitch who followed him across a continent to sink her claws into him. Fortunately, she had kept that last unseemly bit to herself. She'd been too choked up to let rip with the full extent of her rage.

Stella asked if she'd found out anything about the child's paternity. "Nothing beyond speculation," Pamela said, "although I'm thoroughly convinced the father is Rory, aka Johnny on the Spot. But regardless who the biological father is, the child will have to be cared for and I'm prepared to help financially. But I draw the line at buying Danielle a house, particularly if the baby isn't Jack's. Richard will agree once he realizes he's been duped."

Together they tried to think of a way to stall Richard from inking a deal on a house. Stella kept saying, "You have to speak up, Pamela. Tell Richard everything before it's too late."

But Pamela insisted the time wasn't right. "I need conclusive proof that Danielle cheated on Jack before I upset Richard," she said. She didn't want to admit she was afraid to speak up. Afraid that if she was wrong about the baby, Richard would never forgive her.

* * *

"Two weeks of *free time*?" Joe said. "You're a hair's breadth away from losing your job and you're looking at the suspension as a paid holiday?"

"Keep your voice down or you'll wake the kids," Stella said. "Do you think I enjoyed being raked over the coals by the publisher? I was terrified she'd fire me. I'm just trying to be positive and make the best of the situation."

"Oh, well, by all means, let's be positive. I hope the bank will be positive if we can't make our mortgage payments. For Christ's sake, Stella. You always have to get up on your high horse. Why can't you just cooperate and do your job instead of trying to be a hero? Do you think I don't know you're running around trying to 'solve' the big mystery as to why Ballard fell off the cliff? He was tired and wasted and he stumbled over the edge. Accidents happen every day."

"As do crimes that get covered up as accidents."

"Fuck." He opened the fridge door and slammed it shut again. "I'm going to the marina to pick up some beer."

"Wait a sec, okay? Let's not fight. I know you've been unhappy lately. It's been a tense time for all of us. But when you and I don't get along, it affects the boys."

"How will it affect the boys if you lose your job? Have you thought about that?"

"Of course I have. Look, I do good work at the *Times* and I'll do my best to cooperate and hold onto my job. But let's not fight. How about I make a pot of tea?"

"Sure, do that. I'm going out for a six-pack." He slammed the door.

Stella made the tea and sat down to wait for it to steep, assuming Joe would be back within fifteen minutes, possibly contrite. Then she'd pour him a beer and they'd take their drinks outside to look at the stars together. Meanwhile, her mind wandered back to the conversation she'd had that day with Pamela. Stella was troubled about Pamela's predicament with Danielle, but almost as disturbed about her connection with Kieran. Bad enough he might be hanging around Cassidy – but ingratiating himself to Pamela? That seemed especially worrisome. She would have to find a way to talk to Pamela about Kieran without unduly worrying her.

A quarter hour went by and Joe hadn't returned. An hour passed and he still wasn't back. Stella tried his cell and the call went to voicemail. When he finally crept into bed, she kept her back to him and pretended to be asleep.

24

CASSIDY AND KIERAN SAT side-by-side at the coffee shop across from the gym. "That's cool," she said, referring to a small amulet on a chain around his neck. "Is it new?" She reached over to touch the silver charm, letting her fingers linger on the hollow of his throat.

He squeezed her thigh. "Got it from a friend," he said. "Guy I met last summer at a camp in Vancouver. He's seriously into Norse mythology." The pendant had come in the mail from Loki's girlfriend, who must have needed some quick cash. She said the money was "to make Loki more comfortable on the inside." *Yeah, sure.* Kieran wasn't allowed to communicate with Loki, or any other inmate at the youth custody centre, but his loser girlfriend had obviously gone back to hustling after her release. She said the lucky Thor's Hammer amulet was worth two hundred fifty bucks wholesale, but Kieran had seen it on Amazon for less than twenty.

"A camp in Vancouver," Cassidy said. "Far out. How'd you swing that?"

"It was my mom's dying wish," he said. "This rich uncle sent her there as a kid? The tuition ate up the bit of cash she left me, but what the hell. It would have meant a lot to her to know I went."

"That's so incredibly sweet. I'm sad about your mom though." Cassidy rested her hand on his leg and stayed quiet a minute. "So what sort of thing did you do at this fancy camp?"

He shrugged. "Oh, you know, worked out. There was a good gym. Little more upscale than Max's."

Cassidy laughed. "I guess *so.*"

"Mostly I just hung with Loki. I miss the guy. Now he's on some big cruise on the family yacht and I can't even talk to him. His folks are loaded but they're not into cell phones and social media and such.

Like to keep themselves to themselves and Loki goes along with it. I guess he's a bit of a loner too."

"It's nice he had you to hang out with at the camp," Cassidy said. "God, I wish I could go somewhere like that, meet interesting people."

"Hope I'm not boring you."

She laughed again. "*You* are very interesting, but you know what I mean. This town is so boring." She sighed. "You working tonight?"

"Yeah, but I got all day tomorrow off. Want to go for a bike ride? I guess you have school."

"I can't cut school without my mom finding out. If she grounded me, I wouldn't be able to leave the house, never mind go cycling. What about the weekend? Do you have to work the whole time?"

"I'm off Sunday," he said. "We could meet at Max's around ten."

"Perfect," she said. He leaned over and gave her a quick kiss and her face turned bright red. How could anyone who looked so hot be so. . . what? Naïve, innocent? He doubted that asshole Galen had gotten to first base with her.

After they kissed again (no tongues) he jogged home. He fed the tarantula and looked around his shabby room trying to picture Cassidy there. Nope. Before that could happen, he'd need to make some upgrades starting with new sheets. He thought about her all the time now.

They never talked about Jack Ballard and he wondered if she had a reason to avoid the subject, which put him on edge. He watched Hela poke around her terrarium and refilled her water dish, then pawed through a box in the closet to find his stash and rolled a joint. Man, what he would have given to talk to Loki.

* * *

Stella saw the boys off on the school bus and wandered back to the cabin. Another day with time on her hands and still no word from Ben since she'd received his terse message about complications at home. She looked online for some exercises to strengthen her ankle. Snickers was all over her as she put herself through the paces, dutifully raising the throbbing ankle to trace the alphabet in the air with her big toe. It didn't take long for that to get old.

She figured she could handle her bike if she supported herself on the handlebar as she pushed it up the steep path to the highway. The route into town was reasonably level; one hill might be a problem, but she could always get off and walk, or limp.

Assuming she'd make it to town eventually, she planned her day. She needed a few groceries so she grabbed a panier for the bike. She texted Cassidy to see if she was up for an after-school coffee, but the girl declined, saying she was training hard to be ready for future swim meets when the pool renos were done. *Well, good for her,* Stella thought. Still, she couldn't help worrying about her. So much had been left hanging after that aborted bike ride to Kaslo. Maybe it wouldn't hurt to touch base with Cassidy's mother. Karen picked up on the second ring.

"I just wondered how Cassidy was doing," Stella said. "Last time I saw her, she seemed to have put Jack Ballard's death behind her. But I wondered if I was hearing a touch of denial."

"She never talks about Jack or the accident anymore," Karen said. "I don't know if I'd use the word 'denial,' though. I think it's more a matter of getting on with her life. Her latest preoccupation is working out every day. There seems to be a boy involved but she's tight-lipped about him. I suggested having him over to the house but she said he was nobody special."

"Well, glad to hear she's doing okay," Stella said, although if Kieran Corcoran was the boy in question, she didn't like it. She wished Karen a good day and added a few notes to her file on Corcoran, fervently hoping Cassidy hadn't stepped into something she couldn't handle.

Next, she tried Ben's cell, but when his voicemail kicked in she decided to proceed to town and follow up later. Once she'd shoved her bike up to the highway, the straight stretch was a cinch. It was wonderful to be riding again, pushing through the cool autumn air, smelling the lake and the occasional bonfire. Now that the fall rains had reduced the threat of forest fires, homeowners were burning their garden clippings.

Stella carried on along the lakeshore, dodging the odd patch of gravel and a few fallen branches, making way for the slackers who passed her on their electric bikes, one of them barely pedalling. But the big hill proved even tougher than anticipated and her ankle started to hurt like hell. She found a place for the bike and sat down to rest on a grassy verge, pulled out her water bottle. A patrol car passed going in the opposite direction, flashed its lights, and didn't stop. Her phone rang and Ben McKean asked if she was okay.

"Just dandy," she said. "Where you off to?"

"Checking on a home invasion out your way."

"Hey, there was a sketchy guy snooping around my place the other evening. I caught his plate number." She rhymed it off.

"Excellent, thanks. Good to see you out with the bike. Aren't you working today?"

Stella recounted the sad tale of her suspension

"That stinks. Guess I should watch my step at the station too," he said. "Can you appeal the suspension?"

"I doubt it. Meantime, I'm using the break to follow up with some people close to Jack Ballard." Stella told him about Angie's message on the restroom wall, a detail she hadn't brought up last time they spoke. She also mentioned Angie's animosity toward Danielle Stone.

"Do you think this Angie could have been involved in Ballard's death?"

"It's crossed my mind, although it seems pretty far-fetched. At first, I wondered if the message meant Ballard had assaulted her. I thought she might be trying to rally other women he'd molested to mount some sort of posthumous #MeToo movement of her own. But now that I've gotten to know her better, I think she honestly loved Ballard and never really got over their high school romance. She seems more bitter than vengeful."

"I'd be wary of her," Ben said. "People with nothing to lose can be dangerous. Listen, I need to sign off. Can I get back to you later?"

"Anytime." She got back on her bike and slogged up the hill, and now her thoughts turned to Pamela and her troubles with Danielle Stone. Pamela's budding friendship with Kieran Corcoran also niggled, particularly in light of the fraught relationship he'd had with Jack Ballard – Pamela probably had no idea of that. And again Stella worried about Corcoran getting close to Cassidy. He'd proved himself dodgy in the past and she couldn't see any reason to trust him now.

By mid-day, having cycled twenty clicks to town and run several errands, Stella realized her ankle wasn't up for the long ride home. Fortunately, the North Shore shuttle was outfitted with a rack for bicycles and she pushed her bike to the bus stop. With forty-five-minutes to kill, she found a place to sit and cast her mind to the numerous links between Jack Ballard and people she knew. When she needed a break, she tried her dad's number again. Last time, a woman had answered, sounding vague and noncommittal, and her dad hadn't returned the call. Now after six rings the woman picked up again. "Hi, it's Stella," she said. "I called a few days ago to talk to Bob?"

"Oh, yeah. Sorry."

"That's okay. Um, who am I speaking to, if you don't mind my asking?"

"It's Linda." There was a pause. "Like I say, I'm sorry, but he's gone."

"Gone?" Stella said, her mouth suddenly dry. "You don't mean . . ."

"He left."

Stella went still. "Are you my dad's partner, Linda?" she said.

"Yeah. Was. Well, I guess I'm still his wife. Look, I don't feel much like talking."

"Gosh, I'm sorry," Stella said. "Look, I hate to bother you at such a difficult time, but do you have a number where I could reach him? I guess you know I haven't seen much of him since I was a kid. I didn't even know he had remarried."

The line seemed to have gone dead.

"Linda?" Stella said. "Sorry, that was really thoughtless."

"You got a pencil?"

Stella entered the number Linda gave her into her phone and pressed it.

"Sorry, darlin'," her father said. "Should have called before."

"Be nice to keep in touch," Stella said. "So you broke up with your new wife?"

"Not so new," Bob said. "We were together fourteen years. Same as with your mom – I don't know what that means."

"I suppose it means you're good for fourteen years."

"Okay. I deserved that."

"Not from me though. Where are you?"

"Cranbrook," Bob said. "Thinking of relocating here. Got an interview at the Honda dealership, so we'll see."

Cranbrook. Well, that would bring him a few hours closer to Nelson, close enough for weekend trips. As if.

Later that evening, Stella was icing her swollen ankle when her cell rang and the Ymir Hotel came up on call display. It was Mags, the server at the pub. "Is this the Stella from the newspaper?" she said. "Angie's friend?"

"Hi, yes, that's me," Stella said.

"Better get here pronto. Ange is across the road down by the river, drunk or high, and it doesn't look good."

Exhausted from her ride to town, Stella wished she had gone to bed and turned off her phone. She considered calling Ben but it seemed simpler just to go to Ymir. "I'm on my way," she told Mags. "I live on the North Shore so it'll take me a good three-quarters of an hour to get there."

"Sooner the better," Mags said, and hung up.

Stella looked across the room at Joe. "I have to go out," she said. "It's an emergency."

Joe sighed. "It always is with you."

She didn't have the time or energy to counter his snide remark. She looked in on the boys and hit the road, leaving Joe to sulk. Traffic was light on the lakeshore highway but she checked her speed when she saw an oncoming patrol car. The cruiser wasn't Ben's, but she considered what he'd said about Angie having nothing to lose. She slowed again to get through Nelson – two traffic lights and a four-way stop – then it was clear sailing until she was on the approach to Ymir where a light fog had settled over the road.

Mags the server was hovering under a dim light at the entrance to the pub. "I didn't know who else to call," she said. "Her mother's usually blotto this time of night." She gestured toward the fogged-in darkness across the street. "Ange is out there somewhere."

"Has she been drinking?" Stella said.

"Oh, yeah. Might have chased the beer with a line or two of coke, who knows? She's down by the river, crying and carrying on. Or she was last time I checked. Sounds quiet now though, doesn't it? Shoot, that's not good."

"Why didn't you call the police or 9-1-1?" Stella said.

"If I called the cops every time Ange was off her tits threatening to do something stupid, they'd be here every week," said Mags. "This time seems a little different though. I called you 'cause you seem to be her only friend, the only sensible one anyway."

Stella got a flashlight from the car and crossed the street, passing two or three picnic tables and a ghostly outhouse as she felt her way toward the river, conscious of every step. Mags's reference to cocaine worried her; the drug fit too well with the Dark Angel's paranoia about Danielle, as well as her general edginess. Stella stumbled over a root and reminded herself to pay attention. The flashlight's feeble beam wasn't much help. The only sound was the burble of the river, occasionally punctuated by the faint hoot of an owl in the distance. With no knowledge of the river's depth along that stretch, Stella forced herself to take baby steps as she neared the water, straining to hear a human voice. The bank sloped, suggesting a sharp drop-off, the grass and mud squishy under her canvas shoes. Slippery too. The old familiar fear of water made her pulse thud in her ears. She stopped and aimed the flashlight down at her feet, trying to gauge how close she was to the river's edge. "Angie," she called. "You out here?" Afraid to retreat, afraid to advance, she strained to see her but couldn't make out a thing.

She jumped when a voice rose out of the darkness. "I'm here," Angie said. "What – did ya think I was gonna throw myself in the effing river?"

Stella swung the flashlight until she located the black-clothed figure a couple of metres to her left, squatting or sitting on a low stump or rock. "Mags was worried enough to call me," Stella said. "I didn't ask how she got my name and number." She inched toward the figure, trying to make sure one foot was on solid ground before she lifted the other one.

"I guess I musta told her," Angie said, quietly. "I *was* thinking about jumping into the river, but shit, it's fucking cold." She gave a short, shrill laugh then went quiet again. Stella couldn't see her face clearly enough to tell if she was crying, but her shoulders appeared to be shaking. Picking her way gingerly along the muddy bank, Stella reached out a hand to pull Angie to her feet. But the Dark Angel threw her off balance. Stella stumbled into the water and cried out, letting go of Angie's hand as she splashed onto her knees and struggled to regain her footing.

"Hey, it's only a couple feet deep here," Angie said, her breath reeking of beer. "Never thought The Great Moscooni would be afraid of getting her feet wet."

Stella stepped onto the bank but she didn't reach out to the Dark Angel again. "Shut up and follow me back," she said. "We could both use a coffee." She inched forward until she saw the hotel lights and felt safe again.

Mags was waiting for them in the doorway. Angie said, "Can't a girl go for a walk in this town without some joker pushing the panic button? That scream came from her, by the way."

Once they were seated, Stella said, "Okay, Angie. What's going on?"

"Nothing's going on," she said. "That's the fucking problem. Jack is gone and that bitch Danielle is killing all that's left of him with her partying. For all we know, she killed him too so she could run off with his best friend."

"Angie, listen to me," Stella said. "You have no control over what Danielle Stone does. You can only control yourself, okay? That's all any of us can do. Now I want you to drink up that coffee and go home. And I'm going to get in my car and do the same."

"I'll just have a beer and chill a while. Hey, Mags, a cold one over here."

"You don't need another beer, my friend. It would only make you sadder. Drink your coffee. Want me to wait and drop you off at home?"

"*Silly*," Angie said. "I told you I just live up the street."

"Goodnight, Angie," Stella said, dropping a bill on the table, not looking back as she strode out to her car. She started the engine and boosted the heat because she was shaking like a goddamn leaf. Maybe Joe was right about her wanting to be a hero – The Great Moscooni. Yet, all in all, the night's efforts had been a colossal waste of time.

25

ANOTHER FRIDAY IN NELSON and finding the perfect house had not been the slam dunk Danielle had thought it would be. Some places were such tips she and Richard didn't walk through the front door. Or if the agent knew the owners, they whipped around fast, just to be polite. That was the thing about Nelson, or maybe the whole country. In Cincinnati, nobody would worry about hurting the feelings of a real estate agent. If a place was a shithole, they wouldn't mince words.

Richard was picky, which was okay because who wants a place that needs fixing up? But the "project," as he called it, had gotten old fast. She suspected Richard wasn't in a hurry to settle on a house; he liked to be with her and show off his smarts. Yeah, Richard was in his glory driving from one house to another but not her.

If only she could sleep. It amazed her she was even able to function on the few hours of rest she got. Her mother would have said, "guilty conscience," but then her mother wasn't one to talk. Danielle rolled over and studied herself in the mirror – the sex mirror – on the wall by the bed. Jack had vetoed putting one on the ceiling and she'd given in. She'd done that at times, let him have his way to make him feel "valued" as her old shrink would have said.

Jack had loved having sex with her and he'd always obeyed – almost always. On the rare occasions when he'd passed out for a second or two or maybe coughed for a couple days, he would get all uppity about what he would or would not do in bed. Jack knew it was his job to speak up if he wanted to put a halt to an agreed-upon limit. But that was the trouble with a jock being a Sub. A jock never wants to say no to his coach.

Danielle turned this way and that, running her hands the length of her torso. Jack had worshipped her body. She hated that now there was always someone looking for a baby bump, sneaking a peek at her. She couldn't believe what pregnant women have to put up with. Danielle had never given much thought to having a kid, not that she'd minded when her period didn't come. She was more curious than anything, curious about what she'd look like in the months to come. Her tits would get bigger, but how much bigger? Impossible to imagine them hanging down to meet a big round belly, but anything could happen. Danielle liked surprises. Her period had been ten days late when she teased Jack about it. Just to get a rise out of him, she told him she was going to get fat and gross and it would be all his fault. How did she know the big goof would run and tell Richard and Pamela, then go out and buy the hugest rock in the jewellery store?

Rory was no substitute for Jack. He wasn't smart or rich, or even funny, and he was chicken-shit about bondage. But he was loyal and obedient and there wasn't much he wouldn't do for her. Rory would never be a problem. Unlike Queen Sourpuss. Fortunately, Richard could be counted on to protect her from the Queen. He was so much like Jack it was scary. She'd assumed at first he was attracted to her (she hadn't met many men who weren't). But even when she was alone with Richard, she never picked up on any icky vibes, not even when she teased him a little. Which is not to say his feelings might not change with time.

* * *

Thank God it's Friday, Joe thought. School was out for the week and he'd been tempted to go for a drink with his cronies, but he wanted to change the oil in the Subaru. Hell, he might even wash and polish it. Tomorrow was a big day. He was about to head outside when he caught a call on the landline. "Joe?" the caller said. "Bob Hart."

"Bob," Joe said. "How's it going? You probably want to talk to Stella but she's off grocery shopping."

"Well, it's good to hear your voice. We never did get around to chatting about Search and Rescue. Any action on that front?"

"Nothing much. You might have heard about the recovery of Jack Ballard's body. But that's old news – happened before your visit here. Got some helicopter training tomorrow. I'm pretty stoked about it. Promised the family they can come out and watch."

"The boys will be all over that," Bob said. "How's the pup?"

"Great. The guys are having a ball with him. You coming this way again any time soon?"

"Don't think so, Joe. Got stuff going on. Possibly a move to Cranbook, but that'll depend on the job situation."

"Well, it'd be nice to have you closer."

"Real nice," Bob said. "Tell Stella I called, won't you? I'll give her a shout another time. I have her cell number. Keep up the good work with Search and Rescue."

"Will do, Bob. Cheers."

When Stella got home, he told her about the call from her dad. "That's refreshing," she said. "Him calling me for a change."

"Give the guy a break. We had a nice little talk."

"Well, good. How about a hand with the groceries?"

Joe helped carry in the groceries then went back out to work on the car. Stella's snarky remark about Bob's call bugged him. Seemed high time she let bygones be bygones with her old man. The guy had reached out. Brought the family the best gift he could think of. So he'd made a mistake about a hundred years ago – did that mean he had to pay for the rest of his life?

Joe's cell rang. M. Thibaudeau on the call display. "Hey," he said. "What's up?"

"I talked to Reilly about letting you partner with me for the heli training," she said. "He's cool with it."

"Fantastic," Joe said. That meant he could fully participate in the entry/exit training the following day, a rare opportunity for a volunteer with only a basic level of helicopter training. "Appreciate you sticking your neck out for me."

"I assume you're fully capable, Mosconi. Don't go thinking I'm being soft on you." Mo's tone held only a faint hint of anything personal between them.

"Hey, I won't let you down," Joe said. "I'm jazzed. Counting the hours."

"So, what else are doing, besides counting?" she said.

He laughed. "Changing the oil in my car – how's that for excitement?" Stella came out on the porch and held up a cup of tea. He shook his head.

"Guess it'll have to do," Mo said. He wondered if that constituted flirting. She sounded a little breathless.

Stella came out again and held up a beer. He mouthed "Later."

"What was that?" Mo said.

"Nothing. What are you up to?"

"Walking over to the pub to meet Reilly *et al.*"

Joe felt a pinch of jealousy. "Ah, the gang. I guess you guys all grew up in Nelson."

"Most of 'em did. I'm a Calgary girl, born and bred. Only been here eleven years, but they tolerate me," Mo said. "Oh, shit. Browning nearly got hit by a bus pulling over to pick me up. See you tomorrow. Ciao."

"Yeah, later," Joe said, but she'd already ended the call.

* * *

McKean returned home from traffic duty and popped the cap on a cold beer. Another good old Friday night in Nelson. The Chief was riding him hard but he was getting results. Stella's tip about the sketchy prowler had gotten the bum arrested in a road block set up at the north end of the big orange bridge that evening. The guy's marginally road-worthy Chev Malibu had a trunk full of stolen electronics and a plate number that matched the one Stella had provided. They'd netted two DUIs as well, but the weirdo who'd menaced Stella had been the primary target of the road block and it had felt good to cuff him. Now McKean picked up his phone and pressed Stella's number, but the call went to voicemail. Too bad. He shot her a text about the arrest.

McKean clicked on the TV and found a hockey game. For the first time in years, he was actually looking forward to the weekend. He and Miranda had settled into a routine that entailed him looking after Aiden on Sundays and her taking off for the day, neither of them having to account for themselves. In some ways they got along better than they had before the separation. He missed living at home, but he was starting to enjoy the quiet late evenings in his basement suite. And when he had Saturday off work, he had the whole day to himself. He'd gotten into running again, which felt good.

The sketch artist Sam Tarasoff had emailed earlier to say she was coming to Nelson for the weekend to help put her mother's garden to bed. She'd suggested meeting for coffee, maybe going for a run together if he was into it. She ended her note with a smiley face.

Feeling like a prize jerk, McKean made up a feeble excuse about having to spend time with his son. He liked Sam; she was a warm, good-looking woman who seemed to like him too, and there was no question he was lonely for female company. But the last thing he wanted was to draw her into the morass of his personal life. That plus the fact he couldn't offer her the kind of relationship she deserved.

In a perfect world, he and Stella would have dated back in high school and stayed together forever. But that ship had sailed, and the world wasn't moving any closer to perfection. He was already in bed when his phone pinged with a reply to his earlier text to Stella. *Congrats on the arrest. Can't sleep but not a bad night for star gazing.*

McKean read the message twice. It pained him to think of Stella losing sleep over the case, digging ever deeper in spite of her shaky job situation while he held out on her, playing by the rules. His finger hovered over her number a moment before he pressed it. When she picked up, he took the plunge. "I can't sleep either," he said. A little white lie. "Getting back to that chat we had on Thanksgiving . . . your reference to BDSM hit home. Ballard's body showed bruising that might have occurred prior to the fall."

"Okay," she said. Stella always knew when to keep quiet and wait for more.

Ben continued. "So he might have been into kink. I can't see what his bedroom habits had to do with the fall though, unless his partner pushed him over the cliff. But here's the thing: the fall as such didn't kill him. The official cause of death was a ruptured aortic aneurysm. It probably burst on impact when he landed on the ledge."

Stella didn't respond right away. "What would have caused the aneurysm?"

"Might have been congenital, according to Antoniak. But he said trauma was a more likely cause for an otherwise healthy guy Ballard's age. Be nice to know if he was ever in a serious MVA, but I couldn't take a look at his medical records. At any rate, the guy was a professional mountain biker, no stranger to physical trauma."

"You think the sex might have been rough enough to cause an aneurysm?" Stella said.

"Antoniak didn't speculate on that. The coroner ruled accidental death due to a ruptured aneurysm."

"Well," she said. "I want to find out more about aneurysms. Thanks for letting me in on this, Ben."

He didn't want to end the call. "So, it's a good night for stars, is it? Can't see much of the night sky from my basement window."

"What are you doing in your basement this time of night?" she said. Teasing now.

Here goes. "Living here. Miranda and I split up so I rented a suite near the house."

"Oh, Ben," she said. "I'm so sorry."

"It happens," he said. "Listen, I better let you go."

"Take care, okay?" She was gracious enough to end the call.

26

"THE DAMN DOG HAS taken one of my boots," Joe said, storming around the house like a madman. It was Saturday and for days Stella had been walking on eggshells with him.

"Matt, check outside," she said. "Nicky, look under the beds. Oh, know what? I see it behind the TV cabinet. Yeah, here it is – not too many teeth marks."

Joe grunted and sat down to lace up the boot. He'd gotten up three or four times in the night and Stella couldn't tell whether he was simply excited about the helicopter drill or worried sick about her job situation. But when he finally struck off to meet his Search and Rescue crew, he seemed more like his contented old self.

The boys wanted to watch their dad's helicopter training, but first up was their soccer games and Stella asked them to put Snickers in his kennel for the drive to town. When they reached the fields, she walked the dog on the sidelines while Matt and Nicky warmed up with their teams. After the games, it was off to the concession stand at Lakeside Park for lunch. Stella was talking to another soccer mom when Nicky spilled his chocolate milk and Snickers slurped up every drop, earning them all a mini-lecture on dog nutrition from the soccer mom.

Then it was back into the car. Snickers whimpered for the duration of the drive and the reason for his distress was clear when they got to the training site. The chocolate milk had given him a bad case of diarrhea and he had been so desperate he'd fouled his kennel. Stella found a plastic bag to contain the mess, cleaned him up as best she could, and attached his leash to his collar. "We'll watch the helicopter training for a bit," she told the boys, "but we might have to take Snickers to the vet."

She unpacked the binoculars and let the boys flip a coin to see who'd get to use them first. Matt, who lost the flip, griped that she hadn't parked close enough to the action.

A helicopter was circling the field, occasionally hovering close to the ground so that, one-by-one, the SAR volunteers could practice entering and exiting the noisy machine. "We don't want to distract Dad," Stella said. "But you'll get a chance to use the binocs when his turn comes up." She privately hoped Joe would *get* a turn, and if so, that they hadn't missed the chance to see it. Apparently new volunteers aren't always given an opportunity like this, but Joe seemed to think he had an in with somebody.

An hour passed and it looked like everyone but Joe had had a chance to enter and exit the chopper. Snickers wagged his tail and sniffed around, appearing none the worse for wear. "When's it gonna be Dad's turn," Nicky asked, for the third or fourth time. "Hey, that's Mo."

This would be the person who had fed the boys soft drinks and Cheezies while Stella languished in the ER with a sprained ankle. She raised the binoculars.

Joe was moving to the centre of the field with the woman. Now Mo was pointing and gesturing, apparently giving Joe instructions. They both squatted on the ground, shoulders touching. The machine made an approach and hovered about a metre above the field, the turbulence mussing their hair and billowing their jackets. The door swung open and Mo went first, scurrying in a half-crouch toward the chopper, climbing up onto a skid and pulling herself inside with no wasted moves. Now Joe would have to do that and Stella felt queasy; she hoped he wouldn't slip and either get hurt or embarrass himself, which would be worse for Joe. "Now we'll get to see Dad do it," she said, handing the binoculars to Matt.

Joe moved forward and got up onto a skid. He took a moment to position his hands, then, a little clumsily, pulled himself into the helicopter. Relieved, Stella told Matt to give Nicky the binoculars. The chopper made a circle and came around. Now the pair would have to exit the machine. The door swung open and Joe appeared first; he climbed out onto the skid and sat there a moment before lowering himself to the ground. Stella breathed easy again. Mo exited smoothly, and joined Joe. They both gave the pilot a thumbs up.

The helicopter took off and Joe looked their way and waved. Mo followed as he joined the family. "Hey, guys, was that amazing or what?" he said.

Nicky said, "Why didn't you just jump out, Dad?"

"You have to be careful not to throw the chopper off balance," Joe said, then launched into a technical explanation of what they had just watched.

Mo said, "You're boring them, Mosconi."

"Gosh, no," Stella said. "This is all new to us."

But Joe didn't seem to need defending. He looked at Mo in a way that seemed too familiar. Intimate, almost. Mo responded with a funny face and a jab to his upper arm. Then she turned and walked away, leaving him looking rattled. Joe segued back into lecture mode, but now he seemed off his game. Matt and Nicky started roughhousing, Snickers got excited and barked, and Joe reprimanded all three of them, denying Matt's request to ride home with him. "You guys run along with your mother," he said "I have to touch base with my team before I leave."

The boys complained that the car stunk of dog poo and Snickers yipped and whined. Stella ignored them all, her only thought: *What the hell just happened?*

* * *

Kieran was on his way to the muffler shop Saturday morning when Richard Ballard drove past in his pickup, Danielle Stone in the front seat beside him. He wondered if Mrs. B knew they were out together.

Later, after he'd just come back from his lunch break, Stone brought in her Mini Cooper for a lube and oil change. She chose to wait for it, distracting him out of his gourd. Up till then, he'd managed to avoid her since Ballard's death. Today, this guy called Rory followed her into the customer waiting area, all kissy-kissy. A bit too fucking friendly in Kieran's opinion, considering Stone was basically a widow and pregnant too. She and Rory acted like they were alone, maybe thinking he couldn't hear them with his head under the hood. She started in bitching about the "queen" being a pain in the ass and Rory said, "One thing I'll say for Pamela – she really cares about the baby."

Then Stone said, "Try not to be a dipstick, Rory. It's not a major turn-on."

It almost killed Kieran to hear her trash Mrs. Ballard, and what was up with this Rory dude? Was the fiancée shagging him with Jack barely cold in his grave?

"That Mini Cooper almost done?" Stone was suddenly so close he could smell the heat coming off her body. He nearly cracked his head on the fucking hood as he straightened up to face her.

"Yeah, almost," he said.

She put her hands on her hips. "Let's go then. Chop-chop. I'm, like, growing old here."

That was when he decided to do a little recce up on Lucky Jack Road and try to get to the bottom of what was going on between Stone and kissy-face.

* * *

Pamela was nicely settled on her lounger Saturday night when she saw something move on the roof of the studio. A flash of something shadowy, then it was gone. A large bird? *No, God*, it was a human figure, moving like a cat, leaning over the skylight now, circling it. The figure moved in a low crouch to the edge of the roof over the balcony, then stretched out on its front for a view of the front room. Pamela felt in her pocket for her phone but it wasn't there. She must have left it on the counter by the microwave.

Afraid of drawing attention to herself, she stayed still, barely breathing. The figure resumed its crouch and crept farther along the roof, finally dropping down onto the small balcony. He/it leaned against a wall, then shifted to look into the window again. A Peeping Tom? *Good God.*

A balcony light flashed on – had Danielle heard something? – and the figure ducked back and flattened himself against the wall. The light went out, but before it did, Pamela caught a glimpse of a hooded figure dressed in dark clothing. The light must have been activated by a motion sensor; Danielle might not even be home. In any case, the figure soundlessly slipped down the stairs and around the corner.

If Danielle *was* home, the hooded figure could have seen her lying naked on the bed, but maybe she was out with Rory. The pad where she parked her Mini wasn't visible from the deck, and Pamela had no idea where Rory left his car when he made his clandestine visits.

At least, thankfully, she hadn't heard an engine start up when the figure disappeared around the building. Danielle always left the Mini unlocked with her keys in the cup holder, despite frequent warnings from her and Richard to lock the car.

Pamela waited two or three minutes and crept back into the kitchen. The time was 10:15 p.m. She texted Stella: *Are you awake?*

Within seconds, Stella rang her.

"Do I have a story for you," Pamela said.

Stella laughed. "I'm all ears."

* * *

Kieran was charged when he got back from his mission. He'd scaled the studio above the garage and looked in the windows, all without being seen. He wouldn't have dared approach the big house, but so what? Everyone knew that poor, pitiful Danielle Stone lived in a studio over the garage, alone now with only her unborn child to comfort her. *Yeah, right.*

He pulled up a chair in front of Hela's terrarium to watch her poke around her fake log and thought about his trip up to Lucky Jack Road. After being tossed out of Ballard's party on his ass, it felt more than weird to return to the property now that he was gone. Not that Kieran had cycled up there to thumb his nose at Ballard. He would have given anything to turn back the clock and meet up with him at the pond again, smoke a couple of blunts and chill.

But there was no point in looking back. Tonight he'd gotten up onto the studio roof without making a sound and boldly looked down through the skylight. The studio had been dark but not pitch black – he would have known if anyone had been inside. Even with the Mini on its pad behind the garage, he saw no sign of Danielle Stone or the guy called Rory.

Kieran had been thinking about Loki and reading a lot of interesting shit on the Internet about Norse myths, but he was too restless to go online that night. He was stoked, hopped-up on pure adrenaline. He was also unbearably horny, this being the eve of his bike ride with Cassidy. He went to his closet for his stash and found just enough to take the edge off.

27

SUNDAY KIERAN PULLED UP in front of Max's to wait for Cassidy. Today would be the first time they went anywhere other than the gym or the coffee shop, and he'd thought about this first real date all week. Her mother sounded like a piece of work though. She might have caught wind of the outing and grounded her. But just when he was ready to punch a hole in something, he saw Cassidy riding toward him. When she yanked off her helmet, her hair looked like a halo, wild-like, the morning dampness frizzing up the ends. Kieran wanted to kiss her so bad.

"So," she said. "Where to?"

"Trails or roads?" he said, showing off that he could ride anywhere. He expected her to choose roads on account of the skinny tires on her bike though he didn't care what she chose, he just wanted to make her happy. He wondered if reading all that Norse folklore was making him soft, but Loki wasn't soft. Or if he was, it was in a good way. Loki told him gentleness doesn't make you weak or cowardly. It's anger that saps your strength and screws with your power.

"I guess we could do the rail trail, at least as far as Cottonwood," Cassidy said, choosing the rougher route.

"You're the best," he said, which made her blush. God, she was beautiful.

They rode along Baker to Stanley than geared down for the steep hill, proceeding all the way up to Observatory, where he stopped to check-in with her. "You're one tough little chick," he teased.

"*Little?* – I'm almost as tall as you," she said, pretending to pout, trying it on for size. He liked that she wasn't too innocent to flirt, not that she had anything in common with that hardened bitch Danielle. He forced himself to clear his mind of Danielle Stone. A follower of

Norse mythology wouldn't lower himself to associate with the likes of her; that was one of the Nine Charges he had read about.

At the rail trail, they stopped again, but after a couple minutes, Cassidy was keen to push on. When the trail got steep and rocky – too harsh for her skinny tires – they got off and walked their bikes and talked. Before long, Cassidy tapped her handlebar bag and said she'd packed a lunch. Kieran said, "Hey, beautiful *and* smart." She laughed at the compliment.

The weather was fine, and they both had worked up a sweat when he suggested they stash the bikes and climb up onto a little knoll to eat the food she'd brought. "It's not much," she said, but it was. She'd made deli-type sandwiches on thick slices of dark bread, crammed with meat and cheese and lettuce, oozing with mayo. She'd thrown in pickles and homemade cookies and a couple apples. "You're too good to be true," he said.

"No, *you*," she said, poking him in the chest. "Yeah, you – I'm talkin' to you."

And then they were rolling around, grabbing and tickling, and she was right in there, giving what she got. She was the one to take it to the next level, sitting up and pulling off her top. *Holy crap.* "You're killing me," he said.

"Oh, sorry," she said as if she meant it. Then she unfastened her bra.

It was the best afternoon of his life and they didn't even go all the way. He knew he had to take it a step at a time with Cassidy and felt proud of himself for holding back. They lay in each other's arms for hours, talking about everything – almost everything. He wanted to correct some of the lies he'd told her, half-believing she'd forgive him. But he was afraid to spoil anything – to break the spell. No one mentioned Ballard, and for once he didn't think about the past or what was coming up next. He just held on and breathed.

* * *

The day after Joe's heli training, Stella woke up with a sick feeling in the pit of her stomach. She told herself not to overreact to the spark she'd sensed between Joe and his Search and Rescue friend Mo. The boys found it hilarious that their names rhymed and kept repeating "Joe and Mo," until she told them to knock it off.

The helicopter training had brought home to her the extent of the risks Joe would be exposed to on Search and Rescue operations. The work could be dangerous, and volunteers had to be able to trust each other with their lives, which necessarily entailed a certain degree of intimacy. But while these thoughts soothed her rational mind, the rest of her body sounded an alarm. Damn that fight or flight response.

With exercise her go-to remedy for stress, she turned to her ankle-strengthening routine. She put on an old Tina Turner album, and got down on the floor, blasting *Proud Mary* when that tract came up. Stella had been a school kid when that song was popular and she felt a little weepy recalling her dad singing it around the house, serenading her mom. She wished she could remember how her mother had responded. Marylee Hart was a pretty woman, but brittle. Such a loathsome adjective that.

Later, Stella watched as Joe tinkered with his car, then sat reading a fat novel with his feet up on the porch railing. He didn't seem like a man torn between two women. She wondered if the helicopter training had released something in him. She looked for a sign of the old Joe and thought he saw it. When the family gathered in the kitchen for a pickup lunch of bread and cheese and apples, he seemed relaxed and happy.

After lunch, breathing easier, Stella hunkered down with her case notes. She tried to be subtle about it, having transferred the key points to a small notebook that fit in the back pocket of her jeans. She mostly stared into space, occasionally picking up a pencil to draw a line between Jack Ballard's name and that of anyone connected with him or his family. She was developing her own pool of "persons of interest." Added to the list was the unidentified prowler Pamela had reported in her late-night call.

Interesting that Pamela hadn't been concerned enough about the intruder to call the police. "Don't ask what held me back," she'd said. "I also didn't wake up Richard or try to reach Danielle on her cell. But I was dying to tell *you*. It seemed like the latest instalment in a soap opera."

"Seems creepy though," Stella had replied. "If there's a next time, you might want to call the police."

Later, when the boys were in bed, Stella was folding laundry and pondering another week without a job when Joe said, "I might grab a beer and go sit on the beach."

"Want some company?" she said. They hadn't really talked all day.

"Sure," he said. "Get you a brewski?"

"No, thanks."

They dragged a couple of beach chairs close to the water's edge. A cloud slipped in front of the moon, extinguishing the shimmering reflection on the lake. Stella wrapped her arms around herself.

"Cold?" Joe said.

"Not bad," she said. "Did you enjoy having a day to kick back and relax after all the excitement yesterday?"

"Sure," he said, "although I'd happily have gone out and done it over again. Getting in and out of that chopper was quite the rush."

"Weren't you ever frightened?" she said.

"Oh, maybe a little. But the riskiness is part of the fun."

"Do you think Mo enjoys that too – the riskiness?"

He kept his eyes on the lake. "Who knows? You sure I can't get you a beer?"

"I'm good.," Stella said. "Might turn in pretty soon."

He stood up and tossed a stone into the lake. It skipped three times. "I'll join you in a sec," he said.

28

"I DOUBT SHE'LL USE the bathroom," Kieran said. "She'll only be at my place a couple hours."

It was Monday, the day after Kieran's bike trip with Cassidy, and he was in the linen's aisle at Walmart with a sales associate who had guessed he was sprucing up his room for a girl. She'd asked him a bunch of questions and handed him a lavender sheet set; now she wanted to sell him towels. "Trust me," said the saleslady. "She'll use the bathroom."

"That's gonna be a problem," he said.

By the time he got out of Walmart, he'd spent fifty bucks, and along with the sheet set and one matching towel, the big plastic bag he balanced on his handlebar held a toilet brush, a bottle of bleach, and a giant tub of wet wipes.

At the muffler shop, Kieran stuffed the bag into his locker and changed into his coveralls. He was daydreaming about taking the next step with Cassidy when Mrs. Ballard's voice brought him back to earth. He went over to reception where she was talking to his boss. "Hi, Kieran," she said. "I'm dropping off my car again. I brought it in the other day to get that tire repaired and Harv found a mechanical problem."

"If there's anything I can do, Mrs. B," he said, "just say the word."

She gave him a tired smile that made the lines on her face stand out. He hoped Danielle wasn't giving her too much grief. "Harv says the car has to go to Kelowna," she said. "It's still driveable, but the repair shouldn't be delayed much longer."

The boss broke in. "Andy can deliver the car to Kelowna for you, Mrs. Ballard. He's a good driver, nothing to worry about. We can give you that silver Corolla until the Benz is ready to pick up."

Fucking Andy, thought Kieran. *And a Corolla? Is that the best Harv can do for a lady who drives a Mercedes Benz?*

"That'll be fine, Harv," she said.

Kieran said, "I'll wash that Corolla for you on my break, Mrs. B."

"That's sweet of you, Kieran," she said, then turned again to the boss. "Richard is out front waiting for me, Harv. Will you let Kieran run the car up to the house after he washes it?"

"Not a problem, Mrs. Ballard," said Harv. "It will be our pleasure."

Kieran washed the Corolla on his coffee break and told Harv he'd take the second lunch shift and deliver the car on his own time. The boss had no objection to that. At 1:05 p.m. Kieran picked up the key for the Corolla, enjoying the look of respect on Harv's face when he said, "The Ballard place? Yeah, I've been there."

It felt good to be behind the wheel of a car for longer than the time it took to drive in and out of a repair bay. Kieran was tempted to detour to the highway and put the Corolla through its paces, but he was eager to see Mrs. B again. He'd never known anyone like her – a beautiful, classy older lady who lived in a world so different from his, yet seemed to sincerely care about him. Kieran owed it to Jack Ballard's memory to look out for her. It was the least he could do after the cockup on Elephant Mountain.

He took the curves on Lucky Jack Road like a pro, swung up in front of the chalet, and rapped on the door using a big cast-iron knocker. Mrs. B opened the door herself. "Oh, Kieran. Hello, again." She looked past him to the Corolla. "Thanks for the special delivery – I'll see if Richard is free to take you down the hill."

"No worries, Mrs. B. I'll just run back down to the shop. I need the exercise."

"Nonsense. You get plenty of exercise on your bike." She called over her shoulder, "Richard!" She waited a minute then turned back to Kieran. "I thought he was home but he might have gone out again."

"Seriously, Mrs. B. I can run down there in two minutes. No worries." He backed down the front steps, turned, and bolted past the garage. The Mini Cooper was in its usual spot, which made him wonder what Danielle Stone was up to in her studio apartment.

Kieran was part way down Lucky Jack Road when he heard the engine of a pickup gear down and realized Richard Ballard must be on his way home. Strange that Mrs. B hadn't seemed to know where he was. The truck was getting closer. Kieran slipped off the road and ducked behind a tree, just in case the old man stopped to question him. Kieran never would have missed a chance to talk to Mrs. B, but her husband was a complete unknown. He might be a geezer version of their son and Kieran didn't need the hassle.

The pickup whizzed by with Richard Ballard at the wheel and Danielle Stone in the seat beside him. Before the truck disappeared around the next bend, she reached up and rubbed Mr. Ballard's neck.

Holy shit.

This was not the first time Kieran had seen Stone in Ballard's car, but fondling his freaking neck? Her carrying on with Rory was disgusting enough. But cheating on Jack with his own father – how low could she stoop? And what kind of man would let that happen? Poor Mrs. B. No wonder she looked tired and sad. She'd lost her stepson and now the evil vixen was screwing her husband. Or had it gone that far?

Maybe it wasn't too late to stop her – but how? Loki would have told him to wait and watch, to be clear on his motives before acting. He wanted to drive his fist into the tree trunk but he made himself cool down and clear his head. Danielle was like an evil spirit that spoiled everything in her path. She'd come between him and Jack and now she was coming between Mrs. B and her husband. Nothing was going to bring back Jack Ballard, but there had to be a way to stop that evil bitch from totally destroying his step-mother's life.

* * *

Struck by a sense of déjà vu, Pamela watched Kieran Corcoran lope past the garage on his long, lean legs and recognized the figure who had crawled all over the studio roof and balcony the other night. Well, of course the boy was fit and strong and more than capable of getting up there. But what on earth had provoked his interest in Danielle and/or the studio? He'd appeared to be spying. Perhaps the fuss about washing and delivering the car had been an excuse to come up to the property in broad daylight and snoop some more. Except Kieran seemed too open and honest and fond of her to be up to no good.

But he *had* been nosing around and she wondered if she should confront him, lay her cards on the table and engage him in a heart-to-heart. Then again, perhaps not. She liked to think she was a good judge of character, but she hesitated to put her intuition to the test. She picked up the phone and hit Stella's number.

* * *

Stella was on her way to interview a street artist next to his mural when she saw Cassidy and Kieran come out of Max's Gym and jaywalk across the street to Sidewinders. They looked cozy. Bad enough Kieran had been prowling around Pamela's place – now here was solid evidence he knew Cassidy. It was clearly time to do something before anyone got hurt.

By the following morning Stella had talked herself into approaching Max Huber. Past run-ins with the old ex-con had made her want to avoid him at all costs – and he still creeped her out. But she suspected Huber would be a keen observer of what went on inside his gym.

Now she sat across the desk from him in a combination office/ cleaning supplies cupboard at the back. She'd chosen to drop by at a time the two young people weren't likely to be there. In the makeshift office, she took a chair next to an open door, so as to be visible to the people working out. "I don't think Kieran is a bad kid," she said, once they got down to the purpose of her visit. "It's just I feel protective toward Cassidy. She's a friend of the family."

Max leaned back in his swivel chair and took his time to reply. Stella didn't look away but it cost her something to hold his gaze. "Been watching the kid," he finally said. "He has a coldness about him I don't like. Cassidy's a nice girl, but she's too damn pretty for her own good."

Stella let the sexist remark pass. "I'm curious about how they met," she said. "Do you think they knew each other before Cassidy started working out here?"

Max shrugged. "Hard to say. Doubtless you know McKean came in here to question the kid about something. He split and the little lady made a beeline for our boy. They had a friendly chat and left the premises together."

So Ben's questioning of Kieran had prompted a "friendly chat" with Cassidy. At that point, they both had been interviewed by the police about the incident at Pulpit Rock. "Interesting," Stella said.

"Ain't it," Max said. "Now the pair of them treat this place like the Love Boat."

"Just to be clear," Stella said. "They may have known each other before, but after Sergeant McKean questioned Kieran, things heated up."

"That's the long and short of it," Max said. He put his hands on the desk and pushed himself to his feet. "Any more questions – no? Then if you'll excuse me, I got a gym to run."

Stella got up too. "Appreciate your time." After a flicker of hesitation, she reached out to shake his meaty hand. On her way out, she nodded to Max's assistant Colette and glanced around the gym. It was easy to picture Cassidy and Kieran in the laid-back scene.

She crossed the street to Sidewinders, bought a coffee, and carried it to a stool in front of the window. In her little notebook, she traced with one finger the line she'd drawn between Kieran and Jack Ballard, a line inspired by Ballard having bounced the kid from his party. Now the connection didn't end there: Kieran had been seen prowling around the Ballard property, even after Jack's death.

There was already a link between Cassidy and Jack up on Elephant Mountain. Now Stella could connect Cassidy and Kieran in the same general location. Kieran must have lied to Ben – he had to be Cassidy's hoodie guy. But why had she kept him a secret? Was she covering up for him? If so, why? Maybe she had seen Kieran push Jack over the cliff and was afraid to tell anyone. Even Max Huber seemed leery of Kieran.

But if Cassidy was afraid of Kieran, would she still hang out with him? Possibly. Huber seemed to think the pair was love-struck. Well, girls and women fell for bad boys all the time. Maybe Kieran was responsible for Cassidy's recent change of heart about Jack – she'd shifted allegiances.

But whatever the case, the pair had likely been the only people besides Jack Ballard up at Pulpit Rock in the lead-up to his fall. And of the two of them, it was easy to see who would have presented the greater threat. Stella shivered as she underlined Kieran Corcoran's name, now convinced he was the prime suspect in Jack Ballard's death.

She had to talk to Ben.

29

KIERAN USED HALF THE bottle of bleach and most of the wet wipes to clean the shared toilet down the hall from his room. He'd timed the operation as close as possible to Cassidy's arrival, hoping none of his lowlife housemates would use the bathroom and pollute it again. He made up the bed with the new lavender sheets and draped the single pristine towel over a chair. The finishing touch was a strip of condoms he placed on the window sill by the bed. He had debated putting the condoms in a drawer so as to seem less of a lech, but he figured he might need them in a hurry. He was just about to go downstairs to wait for Cassidy when he noticed the price tag on the towel and yanked it off and stuffed it into his pocket. Then, *oh shit*, he remembered the tarantula and with a silent apology to Hela, shoved the terrarium into the closet.

Cassidy was late getting there, which did a number on his nerves. It turned out that instead of riding her bike, she'd taken the bus and she arrived slightly flushed after running uphill from the bus stop. She wore tight, torn jeans and a pink top that showed the outline of her bra and he wanted to jump her on the spot. He had to dig his fingernails into his hands to slow himself down until they were up in his room and she was ready. She'd brought some chocolates and a short, thick candle that smelled like peppermint candy. She smelled good too. He put his arm around her waist and had to swallow a groan when his fingers touched bare skin between her top and jeans.

Upstairs he kind of held his breath when he opened the door to his room, saying, "Sorry there's nowhere to sit but the bed."

She said, "Nice sheets."

He pulled off his shirt and undid his pants. She did the same and faced him in her bra and ripped jeans. Then she blew his freaking mind by pulling a rubber out of her pocket. "Don't think I'm a dork," she said. "But I want us to be safe. Did you know these are free in the washrooms at the public health centre?" She suggested they put the towel over the sheets in case there was blood and he felt an extra jolt of heat, privately vowing to take it as slow and gentle as he possibly could. He found a saucer for the candle and lit it.

Afterward, when they took a break to eat the chocolate, she called her mom to say she was still at some chick's place and would be home by ten.

Then they did it again.

Lying together later, she asked him to tell her more about the fancy camp in Vancouver. He piled on more lies, feeling like a total shit. It felt better to talk about Loki and his passion for Norse myths, her hanging on every word. It was all perfect till she asked if she could take a shower.

"Fuck," he cried. "I didn't clean the tub." Which sent her into a fit of giggles. He laughed too while she wiggled into her clothes, batting his hands away. He walked her to the stop and when the bus came it nearly killed him to let her go.

* * *

"I'm, like, lit," Cassidy mumbled into the phone. "I try to hide it from my mom so she won't guess what's going on and lock me up." Naked under the covers in her bed, she squirmed as she pictured their love-making the night before.

"I'm lit when I'm with you," Kieran said, his voice husky. "Without you I'm nothing."

"Aww, poor baby," she said. "Are you going to the gym tomorrow? Maybe we could go to your place after instead of Sidewinders."

"Hey, yeah," he said. "We'll be so sweaty we might slide off the freaking bed." She assumed that must be a turn-on for him.

"Just talking to Chloe about the science quiz," she said. "Goodnight!"

"Huh?"

"That was my mom. I gotta go. See you tomorrow."

"Cool," he said.

Cassidy made a smooching sound and ended the call. It was incredible how free she felt with Kieran. Thank God she'd saved herself for him and didn't let that dickwit Galen get anywhere near her little cherry. On fire now, she rolled over and threw off the covers, got up and opened her window. She looked at the moon and wondered if Kieran was looking at it too.

She wished her mother could be as over-the-top happy as she was. But her mom's online match was a dull, homely guy who worked at the credit union. It bothered Cassidy to think she'd settled. Her mother said dating websites gave you a sense of a person's character, before you could get side-tracked by superficial qualities like appearances. But Cassidy remembered her face when she talked about her first love Bhav, and described him as drop-dead gorgeous. She wondered what her mom would think of Kieran but was afraid to find out.

The next day at the gym, just for a laugh, Cassidy and Kieran pretended to be strangers. He said, "Excuse me miss, are you done with the leg press?" And she said, "Why, yes I am. Haven't I seen you here before?" Max gave them a dirty look, which sent them into muffled hysterics. Then without saying a word, they both drifted over to the exit a quarter hour earlier than usual. They left the building holding hands.

As they passed Sidewinders, Cassidy said, "Oh-oh, Stella Mosconi's in there. Keep walking, I don't want her to see us together and tell my mom."

"How do you know Mosconi?"

"She's a friend actually," Cassidy said. "I teach her kids' swim lessons. Do you know her?"

He made a face. "Don't want to slag a friend of yours, but let's just say I can't really respect her on account of her doing the nasty with that cop, McKean."

"What?" Cassidy said. "You sure we're talking about the same person?"

"Oh, baby," Kieran said. "I love how you only see the good in people. Don't let me burst your bubble."

"No, c'mon. Tell me."

"Her and McKean have been getting it on for years."

"No way!" Cassidy could hardly believe what she was hearing, but she knew Kieran would never lie to her.

"Let's talk about something else," he said. "I fucking hate gossip."

"Me too," Cassidy said. "Shit, though. Poor Joe."

"Yeah, he's that teacher, right? He talked to me once, offered to help me with my online courses."

"He's my science teacher. Everybody loves him."

Kieran gave her ass a little slap. "Do you think you could run a little faster?" he said. "We got more important things to do than talk about the Mosconi broad."

* * *

It was Parents' Night at Matt and Nicky's school and Joe begged off to meet up with his SAR buddies. "What gives?" Stella said. "It's not the usual training night. You know Matt's math grades have been slipping. You're the teacher, Joe. I need you to be there to ask the right questions."

"Matt just needs us to ride him a bit harder to finish his homework," Joe said. "I have to be at the debrief on the chopper training."

Stella bundled Matt and Nicky into the Pathfinder and drove to the school, handing over the boys to the sixth graders who were supervising some sort of free-for-all in the gym. In the line-up to speak to Nicky's teacher, she introduced herself to a woman she recognized as the wife of one of the other SAR volunteers. "I see you're alone too," she said. "Is it just me, or do you resent them needing to debrief tonight instead of being here?"

"Hell, yes," the woman said. "Particularly since 'debrief' is code for lolling around the pub in this particular instance."

Stella mulled over that one for the rest of the evening, and later when Joe's car finally rolled down the drive, she was ready for him. He whistled softly as he approached the front porch where Stella was stationed on a wicker chair, ignoring the book open on her lap. "Oh, hi," he said. "How was Parents' Night?"

"Fine," Stella said.

He didn't break his stride. "Good. Think I'll turn in."

"Oh, worn out are you – from the big debrief?"

He stopped in the doorway, her tone apparently not lost on him. "I wouldn't say I was worn out. Just pleasantly tired."

"Kinda late, though. Did you drive anyone home?" she said.

"Well, Mo was on the way."

"You and Mo – I'm not imagining it, am I?" She could hardly believe she was wading into the subject she most wanted to avoid.

She waited for him to ask what she was talking about, almost hoping he'd lie, so things could go on as before.

He sat down in the chair next to hers, leaning forward with his elbows on his knees, hands clasped. "You know I love you, Stella," he said, looking down at his own damn hands. "You and the boys are everything to me."

She started to shiver. "Have you slept with her? Oh, God, not the overnighter, the event that was absolutely critical to your becoming a fully-fledged member of the club."

He faced her. "Look, it won't happen again. It was a stupid, circumstantial thing that meant nothing. Less than nothing. You and the boys –"

Stella bit down to stop her teeth from chattering. "Circumstantial? Like you won't find yourself in similar circumstances ever again? Come on." They sat in their separate worlds for what seemed like a long time.

Finally, Joe said, "I told you – it was nothing. It won't happen again."

Stella couldn't trust her voice yet. She looked up at the dark sky, almost unconsciously putting her hand over her heart. *It's true what they say about broken hearts,* she thought. *The physical pain is real.* "So, to be clear. Are you prepared to give her up?" she said. "Because I don't want to wonder if you're running to her side every bloody time you leave the house. I won't live like that. No, I don't want you to touch me."

"It won't happen again," he said, angrily. "End of story." He paused and when he spoke again he tempered his tone. "I think she and I are mature enough to work together without getting personal. At first, I just wanted to impress her. SAR is her life. She put me down for having other priorities. Then when she started to show me a little respect, I was flattered. But, as I say, it's over."

"You can't even say her name," Stella said. "I assume you're attracted to her. How're you going to handle being thrown together at meetings and rescues? Especially rescues – life or death situations where emotions run wild. I don't see how you could do it."

"Don't ask me to give up SAR," Joe said. "I can't. It's . . . it means too much to me."

"I guess you'll have to make a tough choice then," Stella said.

They both repeated themselves, raising their voices at times, though not loud enough to disturb the boys asleep inside. They both cried, but didn't touch each other. In the end, Joe said he would spend the night at his department head's place. Apparently, the guy's wife was out of town, visiting their son at university. The department head was not the type to gossip or ask a lot of questions, Joe said.

"If you go to her now, it's over," Stella said.

Joe got all bristly. "Give me a *little* credit, will you?" He went inside to pack a toothbrush.

30

THE MORNING AFTER, STELLA concocted a ridiculous, made-up excuse to explain to the boys why their dad wasn't there when they got up. Once she'd sent them off to catch the school bus, she called Pamela, who started in with the usual courtesies, hi, how are you, isn't it a beautiful day, and Stella said, "Joe cheated on me."

"Has he lost his mind?" Pamela said.

"I'm not sure his mind is what's at issue here," Stella said.

"Good. You haven't lost your sense of humour. Should I come over? The Benz is in the shop but I have a courtesy car."

Pamela brought a pumpkin loaf from the French Bakery and offered to make tea. She was a good listener. Stella told her story, alternating between anger and despair, interspersing reportorial logic with spells of crying. Once she was spent, she got up to blow her nose and wash her face. "Every marriage is vulnerable," Pamela said, putting on the kettle for a fresh pot of tea, "I've been holding back on you. I didn't want to admit I was afraid to confront Richard about Danielle and the new house. I didn't want to appear petty and jealous and drive an even bigger wedge between us. My biggest fear is that he's attracted to her, the sexy young mother-to-be. What fun he'd have being a daddy again, moving in with her. Leaving me in the big house, the bitter, wicked step-mother.

"I don't know what to say, Pamela."

"Never mind. I didn't mean to shift the focus to me. Keep your chin up, dear. I know that sounds trite. But I think Joe will come to his senses. He won't want to break up his lovely family. Give him a bit of time to come back wholeheartedly, and when he does, try not to make him feel even guiltier. There'll be an awful temptation to do that."

When Pamela left, Stella turned again to her case notes to keep herself from falling to pieces. Escaping into her work had always been her best antidote to heartache. It might have been instructive to get Pamela's take on Kieran Corcoran. But if Kieran had had anything to do with Jack's death, she couldn't very well talk to Pamela about him. Besides, that was quite rightly under Ben's purview.

Her thoughts were interrupted by a text from Joe. *Okay to come home after work?*

She replied: *Call first to talk about what to tell the boys. I lied to them about last night.*

* * *

Joe claimed to have had a day from hell after losing sleep the previous night. He'd arrived at the cabin before Matt and Nicky got home from school but now the boys could be heard coming down the drive. Stella asked him what he'd decided to do about Mo and SAR.

"I told you I broke it off with her," he said.

"No. You said it wouldn't happen again. Not the same thing. Have you talked to her?"

"I sent her an email to make sure we were on the same page," Joe said. "Can we consider it settled? Please."

He didn't trust himself to talk to her in person, Stella thought. "What about SAR?" she said.

"Look, I can't let my team down," he said. "You're going to have to trust me on that one."

Now the boys spotted them on the porch and Matt yelled, "Yay, you're back."

Nicky said, "Daddy! Are you staying home tonight?"

Joe glanced sideways at Stella. "Hope so, guys. I still have a lot of work to do at the school, but I'll try."

"Guess I should rustle up some dinner," Stella said.

"I'll help," Joe said, following her into the kitchen.

Later they had a hurried conversation down by the lake while Matt and Nicky watched a bonus half-hour of television. Joe kept insisting he could continue business as usual with Search and Rescue and still keep his hands off Mo Thibaudeau. Stella didn't buy it. *I hate this,* she thought. She remembered her mom and dad sniping at each other. Wondered if there had been another woman. Wondered what had made her think she would be immune to a fractured marriage.

In the end, they lied to the kids. Joe drove back into town to "mark papers at the school" and have another "sleepover" at his department head's house. Stella got the boys to bed and sat down to call her dad, she wasn't sure why. She asked him about Linda.

"Not a lot to say about Linda," Bob Hart said. "We kind of drifted apart. Different interests. You know how it goes – or maybe you don't. Joe seems solid. I hope you're happy, Stella. I'm glad you have a nice family. Your mom and me – we didn't set a real good example in the marriage department."

"Well, no sense dwelling on that."

"Exactly," Bob said. "See, that's the whole trouble. People get stuck in the past. What's done is done, right? You can't go back and fix it."

Not what I need to hear, Stella thought. "Did Linda get stuck in the past?" she said.

"I'm not going to dump on Linda," Bob said. "I was no angel, believe you me."

Stella choked out a question she was almost afraid to ask. "Did you have any kids with her?"

"No, we were older when we met. She has kids from another marriage. And I have you." He said that last bit tenderly.

"Are you close to Linda's kids?" Stella said, not able to leave it alone.

"We get along okay," Bob said. "But someone else's kids – it's not the same."

Stella had no response to that.

"So how's it going with Snickers?" he said.

"Snickers is great. The boys love him," Stella said, happy to switch to a less-loaded topic. "Oh, by the way," she added. "I found that photo of me on the beach with the yellow canoe. You were right. It was taken at Sechelt."

"That's a sweet picture. Glad you found it."

"I was so sure that shot had been taken at Lakeside Park. Makes me wonder what else I got wrong from those days. I still think about the canoe accident."

"Aw, darlin.' Like we were saying, best not to get stuck in the past, eh? But hey, I better let you go. We'll talk soon, okay pardner?"

"Sure," Stella said.

"Hi to Joe," Bob added.

Stella ended the call.

* * *

On his second nighttime visit to the studio, Kieran was blown away. He had seen some weird shit online, but the view from the skylight made him want to puke. Danielle Stone, bare-assed in a black leather corset that exposed her big brown nipples, stood over that poor bastard Rory, a high-heeled boot on his butt. Rory down in doggy pose, was naked except for a studded collar and leash, which Danielle tugged on the way some sick fuck might abuse an animal. Kieran hadn't expected to find them curled up playing computer games, but he hadn't imagined anything like this. He crept toward the edge of the roof and lowered himself onto the balcony. At the foot of the stairway, he retrieved his pack and, staying close to the wall, moved to where the Mini Cooper was parked around the corner. He crouched by the front end to collect his thoughts.

Kieran was no stranger to porn, but the scene upstairs had unnerved him. He wondered if Ballard had let her humiliate him like that. He didn't overlook the possibility she'd put a spell on him. And now he was afraid Ballard's old man was about to fall under her spell, if he hadn't done so already, putting an end to Mrs. B's marriage.

Kieran had all the proof he needed that Danielle was evil, but now what? Somebody had to stop her and who else would do it? The thing was, he'd have to get rid of her without harming her child or he'd prove himself as evil as her. Well, he had come prepared.

He reached for his pack and lifted out a cardboard gift box from the Dollar Store and gently took off the lid. Hela appeared to be asleep. Tarantulas can survive months without food and he'd dampened the moss packing to make sure she didn't get thirsty. He closed the box. Then, placing one hand on the building, he summoned up everything he'd read about Norse curses, and improvised: *I curse you, Evil Vixen of this Dwelling, to dream about spiders. And you better believe you have enemies in this town. The next spider you see in real life will be an omen that you're gonna die. To escape this curse, go now! Leave this town and don't come back.* He paused, and thought a moment then added: *Leave the whole country and go back where you belong.*

His heart was pounding in his chest, his pulse almost deafening him, but he couldn't stop now. He couldn't take a chance on Stone laughing off the dream, so he opened the Mini's passenger door and placed the box on the seat, thanking Hela for her sacrifice. If all went as planned, the greedy bitch would climb into her car tomorrow and open the box. And when she saw the tarantula she'd remember the dream and freak out. She'd run back upstairs and start packing, then she'd get the hell out of Dodge – and out of the Ballards' lives forever. And maybe, if his plan worked, Kieran could someday forgive himself for what had happened to Jack.

31

PAMELA WAS PENSIVE OVER breakfast and Richard seemed to pick up on her mood. "What's the matter, love?" he said. He had begun to use little terms of endearment again.

"Just a mild case of the blues, darling," she said. "Nothing to worry about."

"Well, do something special today," he said absently, and took up his iPad.

Pamela was worried about Stella, of course, and more than a little angry at Joe, but she was still anxious about this thing between Richard and Danielle. She hadn't confronted him about the house-hunting, and now that he was acting like a husband again, she hated to risk upsetting the apple cart.

There was also the issue of Kieran prowling around the studio, which still had her baffled. As she had told Stella, Danielle and Rory could look after themselves, but Kieran was only a teenager. Pamela had no way of knowing whether he had appeared on their property again because she'd given up her nightly post on the deck. For the first time since Jack died, Richard had asked her to come to bed early last night. He'd stroked her back and nuzzled her neck and she'd wiggled into position to spoon with him the way they used to. It was a start. Tonight she would wear a lacy little number she'd bought for their last anniversary and see what developed.

It was just past eight in the morning and the radio was tuned to the CBC news. Illegal immigrants were being turned away at the border; the Atlantic coast had been battered by a hurricane. Nothing like a hit of current events to put Pamela's own worries in perspective. Stella would provide perspective too – and Pamela was determined to support her in return. She hoped Joe had smartened up and returned with his tail between his legs. She opened her phone and sent Stella a text, suggesting they meet.

A few minutes later, a reply from Stella popped up: *Great – I'd like to talk too. Lunch at the taco place?*

Pamela smiled. *Taco place it is,* she wrote. *I'll get there just before noon to snag a table for us.*

"I've just arranged to meet Stella for lunch," she told Richard.

"Good," he said. "I'm taking Danny to town to pick up a dresser for the baby. Want to tag along?" His eyes had been glued to his tablet, but now he looked up. "I'd rather you came with us than drive that old Corolla."

"It's fine, darling," Pamela said, happy to hear his concern, pleased to have been invited along on the outing with Danielle. Maybe they really were just picking up a dresser.

But later when she opened the garage door, she noticed the right back tire of the Corolla was soft. *Damn,* another flat tire. And Richard had already taken off. Well, Danielle always left her keys in the Mini, despite frequent warnings to be more security conscious.

Pamela went around the corner to the Mini and found the keys in the cup holder. She adjusted the driver seat and mirrors, and started the engine.

* * *

Stella checked her phone for messages; nothing from Ben. She wanted to update him on the investigation from her end. But in the meantime, a nice lunch with Pamela would be a welcome break.

Stella parked on Kootenay Street, planning a quick side trip to the library to return some books, but as she passed the taco place she noticed a sign in the window: *Sorry - closed! Illness in family.* She texted Pamela to propose switching to the Thai restaurant, but didn't receive the usual immediate reply. She tried phoning, but after a half-dozen rings, the call went to voicemail. Something didn't feel right. Stella returned to her car and proceeded uphill.

She followed the bus route to avoid stop signs, then took alleys to avoid buses. By the time she turned onto Lucky Jack Road, she'd convinced herself she was being silly. What could be amiss? Pamela must have switched off her phone or forgotten it at home. Stella pictured herself reaching the empty chalet, only to turn around and dash back downtown. Pamela would be waiting in front of the Taco place. They'd have a good laugh and walk to the Thai restaurant together.

Still, she kept on going, and after the third bend in the road, came across the Mini Cooper half-submerged in the pond. *What had Danielle gotten herself into now?* Stella slammed on the brakes.

The silence was awful – no other traffic, no birdsong, not a soul around. Stella was petrified to touch the Mini in case it slipped even deeper into the pond. But she'd heard you only have minutes to rescue someone from a car sinking into a body of water. Emergency help might not make it in time. She forced herself to wade in, terrified of slipping, fully expecting to see Danielle slumped over the wheel. She was already reaching for her phone to call for help.

But God, no. Pamela was the one belted into the driver's seat, a look of confused terror on her face. The driver-side window was down just enough for Stella to squeeze her arm through and reach the up-down switch. But it didn't work. She touched Pamela's shoulder, tried to get her attention. "Pamela," she said, loudly, "Can you hear me? Are you okay?"

No response.

"Pamela," she said again. "I have to get help." She fumbled her phone and pressed 9-1-1, screamed her location.

The dispatcher said, "Ma'am? You'll hear sirens soon. Stay on the phone."

Pamela groaned and muttered, not really registering what was going on. Her face was bloodied. Water covered the lower part of her body. Stella shoved her arm through the window again to unbuckle the seat belt but couldn't reach in far enough. She shouted that help was on the way, kept a hand on Pamela's shoulder, stroked her hair – and watched the water level rise another notch on the steering wheel.

She'd read somewhere that when a car is full of water, the pressure inside and out equalizes and you can sometimes get a door open. Stella tossed her phone onto a dry patch of ground, put one foot against the car for leverage and pulled hard on the door handle, falling backward into the waist-deep water, fighting off panic as she sank onto her hands and knees into the mud, gulping, inhaling, blinded by the churned-up water. She felt for the side of the car, got hold of the door handle, and pulled herself up. Coughing and spluttering, tried to talk to Pamela, tried to get her to unbuckle the belt so she could squeeze her arm in again and hold her head above the water. No dice. Pamela was out of it and the water was up to her chest now. Stella could hear sirens as she thrashed through the water to dry land and grabbed a rock, returning to bash at the front edge of the driver-side window, trying to keep as far away as possible from Pamela, now neck-deep in the water.

It felt like a dream when hands pulled her out of the way and a swarm of first responders converged on the car. A man in uniform half-dragged/half-carried her up onto the bank, wrapped her in a blanket, and guided her to the oak bench. And then Ben was there, and she tried to tell him through chattering teeth how she'd found Pamela but she couldn't stop coughing. He put his hand on her shoulder, his eyes reflecting the horror he must have seen in hers.

* * *

Richard had dropped Danielle at the mall and was on his way to the hardware store when a fire truck and ambulance passed him, sirens blaring. Instinctively (he didn't know why) he stepped on the gas and followed the flashing red lights at a distance, incredulous when the emergency vehicles kept on going higher and higher uphill, finally turning onto Lucky Jack Road. As he neared the pond and saw all the chaos – the Mini in the reservoir – he swerved to the side of the road and parked.

Stella was standing alone with a blanket wrapped around her, hair and shoes soaking wet. The look on her face stopped him in his tracks. Shivering and coughing, she told him Pamela was in the car and didn't appear fully conscious.

Which was so out of character for Pammie, he thought. She always had any given situation in hand. Richard had assumed that once emergency personnel arrive at an accident scene, they made things right in short order. But in this case, time seemed to stand still as first responders worked at freeing Pamela. Richard tried to be patient; he had to believe they'd soon have her out of the car and off to the hospital where a cheerful nurse would take charge, reassuring his poor bashed-up sweetheart, while a team of doctors checked for broken bones and such.

The emergency people were still working at getting her out when Danielle phoned to ask where he was and what was keeping him. He told her in a voice he barely recognized as his own she would have to take a taxi back to the house.

"What happened?" she shrieked. "Richard talk to me. For Christ's sake, what's going on?"

"I can't talk now," he told her. "I need to be on the spot when Pamela comes to." At that point a sob bubbled up in his throat so he ended the call. A burly firefighter walked past and Richard said, "They'll soon have her out, won't they?"

"They're doing their best for her, sir," he said, but the man's face was ashen.

Danielle's taxi must have been stopped some distance below the scene. He heard her arguing with the flag person, her voice shrill and insistent. It seemed the flagger wouldn't let her pass. *Just as well,* Richard thought. *I can't deal with her right now.* Perhaps it was unkind, but he found himself thinking how peaceful life had been before Danielle Stone had followed Jack home. But then again, there was the baby to consider. The baby made up for all her mischief.

* * *

Danielle hit Rory's number and shouted into her phone, "Come and pick me up this fucking second. There's been an accident – I can't even get to Richard."

Rory was slow on the uptake. "An accident? Where are you?"

"Part way up bloody Lucky Jack Road. Get your ass over here."

"Uh, I'm getting a hair-cut? It's nearly finished so –"

"Get over here. Now!"

He was still fussing about his hair when she leapt into his car. "Drive," she said. "I'll fill you in on the way. Don't stop till we get to Salmo."

Rory made a U-turn and headed for Highway 6.

Danielle did her best to calm down and collect her thoughts. "The flagger said she drove a Mini off the road. Why would Pamela have taken my car instead of the ugly rental? But I guess I answered my own question. The rental is crap, so the Queen opted for a nicer car."

Rory ran a hand through his half-styled hair and looked in the rear-view. "So, *why* are we going to Salmo? I mean, too bad about Pamela, but it's not your fault she crashed your car."

"Think, Rory," Danielle said, disparagingly. "Pamela is an obsessively careful driver. What would have made her veer off the fucking road into the pond?"

"Uh, distracted driving? She got a call or text and glanced down at her phone?"

"Okay," Danielle said, relaxing a little. "That's possible." Score one point for Rory. Even good drivers make mistakes. She'd been afraid that Pamela was jealous enough to kill herself and bitter enough to use the Mini to do it. But what would have put such a stupid idea into her head? She could hear her mother's voice drone, "Guilty conscience." Seemed no matter how far she ran, she was never free of her tired old mom.

"You still want to drive all the way to Salmo?" Rory said, peevishly.

"Yeah, I want to drive all the way to Salmo. I need to chill. We'll grab some lunch, have a couple drinks."

"Your wish is my command," said the doofus.

Danielle reached over and ruffled his goofy, lop-sided coif. "You got it, babes."

* * *

Kieran had been changing the oil in a van, not paying much attention to the sirens, when the tofu guy came in with Harv's weekly order. He'd just made a delivery at the firehall and heard about an accident up on Lucky Jack Road. Kieran's blood ran cold. Minutes earlier he'd seen Richard Ballard drive by with Danielle beside him, a big piece of furniture in the back of the pickup. Mrs. B would have been home alone. She must have decided to drive to town and crashed the Corolla.

"I need to check up on Mrs. Ballard," he told Harv. "Can I take your truck?" Harv knew the so-called courtesy car was a piece of shit. He didn't hesitate to hand over his keys.

A flagger stopped the truck before Kieran could get to the accident scene. "Older lady drove a Mini Cooper into the pond," the flagger said. "Guess they haven't gotten her out of the car yet. Ambulance hasn't gone by."

Older lady. Mrs. Ballard. In a Mini Cooper. *Shit.* Hela must have gotten out and scared her out of her wits. Kieran parked and ran toward the pond. Mr. Ballard was standing near the partly submerged mini talking to Stella Mosconi. The reporter was wrapped in a blanket, hair dripping down her back. McKean was there too, hovering around Mosconi. Kieran retreated, trying to think straight as he drove back to the muffler place. *His finger prints would be all over the Mini and Hela's box. He had to get out of town. Would Cassidy come with him?*

When he returned Harv's truck, he told him his girlfriend was sick, she'd just texted to tell him. "Doesn't rain but it pours," said Harv. "You need the truck to go get her?"

"No, I'll take my bike and walk her back to my place," Kieran said, shucking off his coveralls. He texted Cassidy: *Emergency – call me.* Then he called his uncle.

"To what do I owe the pleasure?" his uncle said. "You in trouble again?"

"No big deal," Kieran said. "I need a number. Guy you used to do business with in Idaho. Mr. X?"

"Thought you'd gone straight," his uncle said. "What do you want with that prick? I haven't spoken to him since he ripped me off on a deal."

"Friend of a friend needs a favour."

His uncle sighed. "No shit. Okay, hold on."

Back at his flophouse, Kieran threw a sleeping bag and a few clothes into his pack. He took one last look at the lavender sheets then rolled up the blood-stained towel and stuffed it into a trash can on his way out. Got back on his bike.

It nearly killed him to think of Mrs. B injured in a horrendous crash due to his supreme stupidity. *Fuck,* he thought, *what if she dies?* He was such a total screw-up he'd sacrificed the only pet he ever owned and still the evil vixen had outsmarted him. The cops would put it all together and nail him for Ballard too.

His phone rang. Cassidy getting back to him. "Hi," she said in a silky voice. "What's the big emergency – you miss me?"

"Something real bad has happened," he told her. "Do you trust me?"

She had her bike at school, but no extra clothes other than gym strip. He told her to bring what she could carry on her bike and meet him behind the school. He held back on telling her the plan he was formulating even as they spoke, thinking they could ride out to Balfour and hop on the ferry, stopping at Crawford Bay to use the ATM and grab some food, then following the low road to Creston. He'd get hold of Mr. X and find out exactly where to sneak across the border into the States. Drug mules like Mr. X had crossed near Creston thousands of times – it would be completely safe. He and Cassidy could start a new life together where the cops in Canada couldn't touch him. It was way too soon to tell her all this – or about the easy money he'd be able to make peddling dope in Idaho, about later moving on to California, where there were places a million times better than that imaginary camp he'd lied about.

He made his way up to the high school and leaned his bike against a railing, looking out over the town, maybe for the last time. If Cassidy hustled they might even catch the afternoon bus along the North Shore, throw their bikes on the front rack, and get to the ferry even faster. Once they made it to the East Shore, he'd contact Mr. X and get the details on a safe route across the US border. He would have to agree to some crazy-shit demands. He just hoped he could count on his uncle to back him up.

32

CASSIDY DIDN'T LIKE TO cut school, but what the hell. She'd spent her whole life being a good little girl and where had that gotten her? She'd never been happier than she was now. Leaving her mom was going to be a much bigger problem than skipping school though; Cassidy had never gone a day without hearing her voice. She hoped she'd be able to call her mom often, even if she had to keep their location secret. At least her mom was seeing someone; she wouldn't be alone.

For now, Cassidy had the logistics covered. She often stayed at Chloe's on Friday night to go for a run Saturday morning then hang out afterward. She'd text her mom to say she was eating dinner at Chloe's and sleeping over; they'd probably spend the whole weekend together. Chloe's parents were attending some play that night, so there'd be no questions asked at her house.

Cassidy crammed her gym strip into her pack and walked super casually down the empty hall toward the exit closest to the bike racks. Her hand was on the doorlatch when she heard a deep voice say, "Cassidy?"

She froze – and turned to see Stella's husband coming up fast. "Oh, hey, Mr. Mosconi," she said.

"Bell just rang," he said. "Don't you have a class?"

"Yeah, I have French. But, uh, I just need to speak to someone for a minute?" She opened the door enough to slip through the opening.

He swung back the door and stepped outside behind her. "Is that who you want to talk to? I think I've seen him before."

"Yeah, he said you offered to help with his online courses? That was real nice of you, Mr. Mosconi. I know he appreciated it. I'll say hi for you."

Joe hesitated. "Well, make it snappy. Better stop by the office for a late slip before you go to your class."

"I will," Cassidy said, forcing herself not to turn and run toward Kieran. Joe went back inside. Poor guy, she thought. She wondered if he had any idea Stella was cheating on him.

"Ready?" Kieran said, acting jumpy, not even trying to kiss her. She unlocked her bike and followed him down the hill to Nelson Avenue, him riding like a maniac, blasting through busy intersections without even slowing down. They missed the North Shore bus due to her dawdling, and had to cycle about thirty clicks to Balfour. Then they nearly missed the ferry too, careening through the parking lot and down the wharf, screeching the bikes to a stop behind the cars already loaded. He laughed then and they high-fived, and a few passengers watching from the upper deck clapped. Kieran didn't like that though. He said they had to be more discreet. Within hours the cops would be looking for them, he added, which wasn't what she wanted to hear.

They found a fairly deserted place to sit and Kieran held her tight to keep her warm – the wind off the lake was cold – but he seemed to be choking back tears. To cheer him up, she said, "Only one more big hill to Crawford Bay. Then we can get something to eat." He still didn't say much so she kissed him and said, "Hey, it's all good."

"Oh, baby," he said. "It's *so* not all good. I never should have dragged you into this. Something so fucking bad happened. Mrs. Ballard crashed a car – she could be dead for all I know – and it's my fault. It's a long story, but Jack's fiancée has been banging his best friend *and* his father, and I was trying to protect Mrs. B from her. I screwed up though. I screwed up bad." He looked at her with an expression she'd never seen before. "When the ferry gets to the other side, I want you to stay on board and go back home."

"No, un-uh," Cassidy said. "Whatever happens, we're in this together."

"Cassidy," he said. "I was insane to take you away from school. It all happened so fast I wasn't thinking straight. They'll come after us. We can't outrun the cops on our fucking bikes."

"Are you afraid I'll slow you down?" she said. "I mean, I know you can ride faster than me and you have way more street smarts, but –"

"No! Fuck. You're the best. But if anything happened to you – aw, shit."

Cassidy hugged him and stroked his hair and gave him feathery little kisses all over his face. "I love you," she whispered. "Where you go, I go. And that's final, babe." He sank into her arms and closed his eyes. When he fell asleep, she slipped away to the ladies' room and texted her mom.

Later at the grocery store in Crawford Bay, they caught a bulletin on the radio: *Nelson police are investigating a motor vehicle crash that occurred around noon today on Lucky Jack Road. Pamela Ballard, age 62, mother of the late Jack Ballard, is in critical condition at the Trail Regional Hospital. In other news.* . . Cassidy stopped dead in the middle of an aisle and looked at Kieran, but he kept moving, his eyes on the grocery shelves. "Hey, baby," he said, and his voice was just a little shaky. "What kinda granola bars do you like?"

* * *

Stella ushered Richard into her car to drive to the Trail Regional Hospital. He'd begged the paramedics to let him ride in the ambulance with Pamela, but with so many personnel attending her, there wasn't enough space. Before leaving Nelson, Stella asked Richard to hang tight while she stopped at the newspaper office to change out of her wet clothes. She always kept an extra outfit in the bottom drawer of her desk. Fortunately, the publisher and her Bichon Frise were nowhere to be seen. Stella said a quick hi to Patrick – *You don't see me* – and nipped down the hall to the restroom to peel off her wet things and put on dry jeans and a pullover, replacing the sodden canvas shoes with a pair of leather flats.

On the drive to Trail, Stella and Richard talked about Pamela. At the accident scene, she had drifted in and out of consciousness, prompting the paramedics to put a tube down her throat to ventilate her for transport. Richard had broken down then at the sight of his wife, pale and incapacitated, a machine breathing for her.

After an hour-long drive from Nelson, Stella pulled up to the Trail Regional Hospital and dropped Richard at the emergency entrance. When she caught up with him, he'd already spoken to a doctor; the trauma team was assessing Pamela. Stella and Richard sat down to wait. When her phone rang, she excused herself to take the call outside.

Angie didn't bother to say hi. "Yeah, I thought you might want to know that witch Danielle is drinking at the hotel in Salmo again. Her baby is going to be pickled, and I don't mean that in a jokey way. I'm sure the kid's life is already ruined."

Stella briefly closed her eyes. "You know what, Angie? Danielle Stone is way down my list of concerns right now. Pamela Ballard was in a serious car crash a few hours ago. I'm at the hospital in Trail, waiting in the ER with her husband."

"Aw, shit," Angie said. "Is she going to be okay?"

"I don't know. She was driving Danielle's car, by the way. We don't know why. She was coming to town to meet me for lunch when she went off the road. Listen, I should get back to Richard. Can I call you tomorrow?"

"Yeah, sure. Interesting it was Danielle's car though. Funny how when shit happens, she's involved. She doesn't deserve to take up oxygen."

"Well, I don't like her either, but I can't see how we can fault her for this one. I have to go, okay?"

"Yeah, yeah. I gotta run, too." Angie ended the call.

Back in the ER, Richard was on his feet, speaking to a doctor in scrubs. When the doc strode off, Richard said, "They've stabilized her and sent her for a CT angiogram – think that's what he called it. It's a test of some sort to determine internal damage. He thinks they'll have to operate."

"I'll keep you company while you wait, Richard."

"You don't have to do that, Stella," he said.

"Nowhere else I need to be. Listen, can I get you a coffee or juice? Water?"

He looked dazed. "Maybe shoot a text to Danielle," he said.

Stella crafted a short, factual message for Danielle Stone, then called Joe to fill him in on what was happening. He sent his regards to Richard and told her not to rush home. After a couple of nights away, he seemed happy to hold the fort and cook dinner for the boys. She went to the cafeteria and bought sandwiches and fruit juice to take back to the ER.

Time stood still while they waited for the doctor to come back. When he did, he told them a surgical team was preparing to operate on Pamela to repair her spleen. He used the term "trauma laparotomy" and didn't make it sound easy. Pamela likely wouldn't be going anywhere for at least a week, he said. But the doc assured Richard he'd be allowed to visit his wife in the Intensive Care Unit soon after her surgery.

"I'll stay here tonight," Richard told Stella. "Immediate family only in the ICU. Go home to Joe and the boys and I'll keep you posted."

* * *

Angie put away her phone, still smarting after Stella all but hung up on her. You'd think she might have spared a minute of her precious time for a friend who was hurting, and for an unselfish reason too. Sure it was awful that Pamela Ballard had been in a serious accident, but she was fairly old and she'd had a good life. It was tragic that Danielle was destroying Jack's unborn baby and Stella didn't seem all that fussed about it.

Angie was disappointed in her. But put a person on a pedestal and she's bound to fall off. Life sucked, and anyone who said otherwise just hadn't thought it through. That's the way things were these days. A feeling that couldn't be summed up in a Tweet wasn't worth shit.

Angie had just gotten off work and would have enjoyed trundling down the road to raise a cold one at her local in Ymir, but someone had to keep an eye on Danielle. Well, Angie was no stranger to the bar in the Salmo Hotel either – this was the town she worked in. Angie went back to her table in the section where Danielle and her boyfriend were yukking it up over drinks. How fair was that? Jack's stepmother was at death's door and his so-called fiancée was out partying. Weird that Mrs. Ballard had been driving Danielle's car when she crashed. Angie wondered if Danielle had messed with it, set the whole thing up to get rid of Mrs. Ballard so she could take over as lady of the house. Wicked was the only word for Stone. Now she was pawing at her new boyfriend like a bitch in heat. If he actually *was* a new boyfriend. Maybe they'd been fooling around for years. The baby probably wasn't even Jack's.

God, she felt down. Being depressed was normal for Angie, but today she felt shittier than usual. Her janitorial job stunk; the students were slobs and the teachers were snots. She had no real friends other than drinking buddies, no money. Why couldn't Stella have said, "Screw that sleazebag Danielle. I'll stop by on my way home from Trail and we'll have a couple of laughs." But no. She'd been mistaken to think Stella was any kind of a friend.

Angie had already put away a beer or two, but she ordered another one to justify being there. Danielle waved at the server. "Yoo-hoo," she said. "Bring him another pilsner. I'll switch to rum and coke."

Never one to keep her mouth shut, Angie said, "I have half a mind to call the health department and put a stop to this. You're destroying that baby inside you."

"Part of what you say is true," Danielle said. "You have half a mind." The boyfriend forced a chuckle. Angie just snorted and drank her beer. The server seemed to take his time looking after Danielle. At least someone was paying attention.

Angie decided to wait them out. She had nowhere to go. The three of them sat there exchanging insults for the rest of the evening. It was late when the boyfriend got up to take a leak and said he was going to book a room for the night. Danielle left the table too – probably to make sure the room was good enough for the likes of her. Anyhoo, while they were both gone, Angie made her move.

Honestly? She didn't much care if she saw another day. And she didn't mind taking the woman who had ruined Jack's life with her. It would be a kindness to save an innocent child from a lifetime of disability and misery.

Angie was prepared, and had been for some time. Other than doing the odd line of coke, she wasn't that much into drugs, but she had a reliable dealer and she'd grown partial to fentanyl of late. With all the fentanyl-related deaths in this country, nobody would bat an eye over a couple more. Angie pulled out her little packet and doctored Danielle's rum and coke. Then she fixed up what would be her last beer.

She got restless waiting for the star-crossed lovers to return, and the server was slack about clearing the used glasses. But Danielle wouldn't bother with dregs. She'd reach for her fresh rum and coke and suck it back.

Angie staggered a little when she went to the lobby and stretched out on a couch to think about Jack. She wanted her last thoughts to be of those days long past, down by the footbridge, her calling the shots based on that tattered old sex manual her dad had hidden in the garage and forgotten about. She'd always been able to make Jack laugh, whether by imitating a popular girl or making fun of a teacher, and he loved to tell her all about his hopes and dreams for making it big. She always egged him on, stroked his ego.

Angie rolled over onto her front, as she'd done so many times before, and conjured up the sensation of her and Jack's young, hard bodies pressed together, her on top, telling him whatever came into her head. That had been the best time of her life, and no one could take it away from her . . .

* * *

Danielle was on the can when her phone pinged with a text from Richard. She hadn't bothered to reply to the note Stella had sent earlier "on Richard's request." Now she finished her business and washed her hands before opening Richard's new message. He was still in Trail, waiting for Pamela to come out of surgery. The text was long and confusing; Danielle had to read it twice to take it all in. The message didn't exactly sober her up but it smartened her up. She clicked on the reply box and wrote: *Dear, sweet Richard, my thoughts and prayers are with Pamela.* She considered amending it to "with you and Pamela," but Richard would want to keep the focus on the Queen at a time like this. If Pamela survived, life at the big house would return to normal. If she didn't, well, anything could happen.

On her way back to the table, she saw Angie lying face down on a couch in the lobby. A grumpy-looking guy at the front desk sneered and said, "You three about done for the evening?"

Danielle looked at his name tag. "I don't appreciate your tone, Artie," she said, slowing her speech to articulate each word, a skill she'd perfected as an under-age drinker during her teen years. "My boyfriend and I are guests at this hotel. You can put our tab on the room and clear the table. We're done out there." She signalled Rory.

Rory didn't jump to his feet. "I just ordered a fresh beer," he whined. "Don't you want that rum and coke? You haven't touched it."

She gave Rory a withering look and he came running. "Oh, and Artie," Danielle said. "The woman on the couch is not with us. I think she was just some lonely person looking for someone to talk to."

"I've seen her before," said Artie. "She's okay."

"Well, she obviously had one too many tonight. It might be kind to let her sleep it off, but that's up to you." Danielle squared her shoulders and led Rory down the hall.

33

"THIS ISN'T GOOD,"STELLA told Joe as she hung up the phone. "Cassidy didn't come home from school today and her mother has no idea where she is. She'd told her mom she was staying at a friend's place, but Karen just ran into the girl's mother at the Capitol Theatre and she knew nothing about it."

Joe had been cleaning up after supper and he put down the dishcloth. "I saw Cassidy slip outside between classes today at about one o'clock. I should have mentioned it. She wanted to talk to a boy who doesn't go to the school. I recognized him as a kid I met in passing at the bike shop just before Jack died."

"Did you catch his name?"

Joe hesitated. "Oh man, that was weeks ago. Keagan, Keenan."

"Kieran Corcoran," Stella said. "I have to call Ben." Joe went back to washing the dishes, still on his best behaviour.

When Ben answered, Stella filled him in on the suspected runaways. "I'll talk to Cassidy's mother," he said.

"She called me from the Capitol so she could be at the station in minutes," Stella said. "Oh, and Cassidy used a text message to tell her about the bogus sleepover."

"Good," Ben said. "That'll help us locate her. Any word on Mrs. Ballard's condition?"

"She needed a serious operation but I don't know whether she's out of surgery and into the ICU yet. God, I hope she's going to be okay. Richard is a wreck. Pamela is friendly with Kieran, by the way. She told me on the QT that he'd been snooping around her property a couple of nights ago, showing an interest in Danielle's studio. Listen, I'm super afraid for Cassidy. If Kieran had anything to do with Ballard's death she could be in danger, particularly if she knows what happened up on Pulpit Rock."

"Take it easy now," Ben said. "Let's not get ahead of ourselves. We'll find the kids. I'll call you as soon as I have any news."

Her own passing reference to Danielle reminded Stella of Angie's call. She tried her number, and getting no response, sent a text message: *Sorry to cut you off earlier. Let's talk tomorrow. And don't let Danielle get you down – she's not worth the aggravation.* Stella added a heart emoji and pressed send.

* * *

Cassidy and Kieran ate the sandwiches bought in Crawford Bay then got back on their bikes and kept moving until they reached the general store at Gray Creek. Cassidy sat down to rest on the porch while Kieran went inside for energy drinks. When a friendly-looking lady came out of the store, Cassidy asked her how far it was to Creston. "A good seventy kilometres from here," she said. "Hope you aren't planning to get there tonight."

"Not sure how far we'll get," Cassidy said. She must have looked as tired as she felt, because the lady asked if they had a place to stay on the way to Creston. "Not really," Cassidy said, and the woman gave her a serious look.

"My cabin is ten clicks in the direction you're headed," she said. "It's close to the road – you can't miss it. Windsock on a post by the mailbox. I can give you a couple of blankets and let you camp on the deck."

"That would be amazing," Cassidy said.

Kieran came out with the drinks and the woman introduced herself as Nancy. She asked their names and Kieran quickly said, "I'm John and she's Katie." He didn't seem all that pleased about the plan to sleep at Nancy's place, but he agreed.

They must have been slowing down because it took about half an hour to cover the distance to the cabin. Nancy let Cassidy use the bathroom and gave them each a foamy and a blanket, and they lay down on opposite sides of a big covered deck, Kieran grumbling that they could have shared his sleeping bag. It was the middle of the night when Cassidy woke up and missed her mom really a lot; she sent her a text saying she'd had a fun evening with Chloe. Of course she wouldn't have been homesick if she actually had been at Chloe's house, but the uncertainty of the adventure was starting to wear on her.

Cassidy was still dead asleep when Kieran shook her shoulder at five o'clock the next morning and told her to get up. They left without even saying goodbye to Nancy.

* * *

"I knew there was a boy in the picture," Karen Pickering said. "She's been practically living at Max's." McKean had just told her about the seventeen-year-old Cassidy appeared to have run off with. Karen hadn't come to the station alone. A male friend who'd accompanied her to the play at the Capitol stayed in the background while McKean filled her in as best he could. He asked to see her cell phone and explained why. With her permission, the police would put a trace on Cassidy's phone.

Shortly after four that afternoon, Cassidy had texted her mother with the phony story about her whereabouts. At the time, Karen hadn't suspected a thing; she'd jotted a quick reply and heard nothing further. McKean suggested she send another message now. "The kids are likely on the move, so let's see if we can inspire her to get back to you. Let her think you still believe she's having a sleepover at Chloe's."

Karen sat down to compose the text. McKean left her with a colleague and drove up to Corcoran's rooming house. The landlord wasn't happy. Sometime during the previous twenty-four hours, Corcoran had cleared out his room and left without giving notice. McKean was already picturing a ground search, complete with a tracking dog. He put on a pair of gloves to fold and bag Corcoran's rumpled bedsheets and left his card with the landlord.

Back at the station, Karen had not received a reply to her latest message to Cassidy. "I'm dying to call her," she said. She was putting up a brave front, but the strain was evident in her face and voice.

"She might not have cell reception," McKean said, refraining from adding that Cassidy might not want to contact her mother in front of her boyfriend. "How about you go home?" he said. "Give us a shout as soon as you hear from her."

He messaged the RCMP dog handler to put him and his German Shepherd on alert for the following day, and copied the Chief. McKean was back at his basement suite, about to turn in, when he caught a call from a number he didn't recognize. "Yeah, it's me. Guy you talked to at that fancy joint up on Mill Street?" Corcoran's landlord was being ironic. "You might want to swing by again," he said. "Found a blood-stained towel in the garbage can."

The blood stain was no bigger than what might be expected from a mild nose bleed. The towel looked otherwise unused and it matched the lavender sheets from Kieran's bed. Now McKean had three items likely to be permeated with Kieran's scent – and possibly Cassidy's too. He was prepared to initiate a ground search, if it came to that.

McKean was on his way home from Kieran's boarding house for the second time when he caught a call from Stella. "Just had a thought," she said. "I wonder if Kieran contacted his uncle over on the East Shore. He and Cassidy could be holed up there as we speak."

McKean called the uncle and, apologizing for the lateness of the hour, asked if he'd seen or heard from Kieran. The man was evasive, but he loosened up when McKean said his nephew was likely on the run with a fifteen-year-old girl. "He didn't say anything about a girl," the uncle said.

"Go on," McKean said.

"Okay, so he wanted a number for a guy lives across the border."

"The border?" McKean said, trying to cover up his surprise. If the pair were carrying passports, maybe their plans hadn't been so spontaneous. "Any idea which crossing Kieran had in mind?"

The uncle paused. "Guess he'll be looking for what you might call an informal route into the States?" he said. "If I wanted to hook up with this particular gentleman across the line, guess I might make my way to Creston first."

McKean got the picture. Uncle and nephew were no strangers to the cross-border drug trade, and the urgency of catching up with the runaways had just been kicked up a notch. If the kids were on bikes, they would have avoided the mountain pass and taken the lower route to Creston via the Kootenay Lake Ferry. The first sailing to the East Shore was at 6:30 a.m. and McKean planned to be on it.

* * *

Stella spent a restless night plagued by images of Pamela, pale and bloody and confused. Richard sent a short update to say she was holding her own in the ICU, but she still had the breathing tube and hence wasn't able to talk. She certainly wasn't in any condition to use a keypad to communicate.

Stella kept thinking about Angie too, regretting she hadn't tried harder to get in touch after that distraught call. Danielle's drinking behavior certainly seemed bizarre. The woman hadn't been living in a cave; she had to be well aware of the dangers of fetal alcohol exposure. Later when Stella got up to use the bathroom, stepping around Joe who had opted to sleep on the floor, she was struck by a sudden thought: *Maybe Danielle wasn't pregnant.*

She might have faked the pregnancy to get Jack to marry her, a possibility that jibed with Pamela's take on Jack's dutiful proposal. Or maybe she'd simply missed a period and jumped to the wrong conclusion, keeping up the con after Jack's death for whatever reason. If Stella's hunch was correct, Danielle must be waiting for the right time to fake a miscarriage, possibly after she got the title to a house of her own.

God, it would have been good to talk to Pamela, but of course Pamela was in no shape to hear disturbing news. Which meant Stella would have to be strategic about when to confront Danielle. With little hope of getting back to sleep now, she tried to concentrate on a novel and came close to throwing it against a wall.

Stella was sure Angie would be interested in her fake-pregnancy theory, and at 7:45 a.m. she tried her number. She expected the Dark Angel to give her a hard time for calling so early, but Angie still wasn't picking up.

Joe got up around eight and offered to take the boys to their soccer games.

Stella was home alone, scrubbing a burnt pot left to soak overnight, when she caught an item on a local radio station. Early that morning, a woman's body had been discovered in the lobby of the Salmo Hotel. Police were not releasing further details or information about the victim's identity until next of kin could be notified. Stella turned off the faucet, her heart racing. The Salmo Hotel. That's where Angie had reported seeing Danielle last night, not long after Pamela's crash in the Mini.

Stella called Ben and his personal voicemail kicked in. "It's me," she said, "calling Saturday morning, a bit past nine. I hear police found the body of a woman at the hotel in Salmo this morning. Wondered if you knew anything about that. Danielle Stone was apparently at that hotel yesterday, perhaps not coincidentally the same day as Pamela's crash. Call when you can. Thanks."

Stella was still holding the phone when he called back. "Where are you?" she said.

"Hot on the trail of our young friends. Cassidy sent her mother a text around 5:30 this morning and Karen came right down to the station with her phone. I'd planned to catch the first ferry to the East Shore, but waited to find out Cassidy's location. She and Kieran are over there all right. When Karen caught the text, they were just south of Gray Creek, headed toward Creston. I'm on the second ferry, which should dock at Kootenay Bay in about ten minutes. Would you believe they might be planning an illegal crossing into the States? You gotta wonder what's going on in those hormone-addled brains. Oh, and to answer your question, the death in Salmo is under investigation – that's all I can tell you. I don't know how the hell that radio station sniffed it out."

"A hotel employee might have leaked it," Stella said. "Anyway, I want to help find those kids. I'm walking to my car. I'll go over the pass instead of taking the ferry. Maybe we'll meet in the middle."

Ben didn't try to discourage her. "For most of the East Shore route there aren't many options, but about twenty-three clicks north of Creston they might turn off at Lower Wynndel Road. It's less hilly than the highway. Why don't you take Lower Wynndel from your end? Find a pullout just north of the underpass, before the turnoff to the asparagus farm. That should be a good choke point if they slip past me."

Stella drove into Nelson, took the quickest course through town, and proceeded toward the Salmo-Creston Highway, tempting fate with an average speed fifteen clicks over the posted limit. When she slowed to drive through Salmo, she saw emergency vehicles in front of the hotel, police tape across the entrance, a few media types hanging around across the street. Well, under different circumstances, Stella might have been there too. Angie was likely down the road in Ymir, sleeping it off at home. Chances were Danielle and Rory were back at the studio, oblivious to the drama unfolding at one of their favourite watering holes. Stella hoped she was right on both counts.

Stella proceeded to the Salmo-Creston. She permitted herself a quick glance at the parking lot at Kootenay Pass, gateway to the scene of a crime of a domestic sort. But she pushed away thoughts of Joe and that damn woman from Search and Rescue. Today her priority was to stop Kieran before he dragged Cassidy into a heap of trouble.

34

THE THERMOMETER ON NANCY'S deck had registered a chilly six degrees Celsius when Cassidy followed Kieran down a dirt path to resume their ride along the narrow, winding highway to Creston. She was wearing everything she'd brought along, but still felt freezing cold and nervous too. Her heart pounded when two deer suddenly sprang in front of her bike, and she stopped to calm down, which is when she heard her phone ping. She must have just come out of a dead zone, because her mother had written the text last night. In it, her mom said she was glad Cassidy had a loyal, responsible friend like Chloe, and she hoped they would have a ball on their run Saturday morning. She couldn't wait to talk again, she said, and ended with a row of cute emojis. Fighting back tears, Cassidy replied: *Love you, Mom. Can't wait to talk too.*

She got back on the bike and pedalled hard, trying to warm up and bring on the good feelings that usually came with aerobic exercise. She was feeling kind of crampy though, and that made her worry about her period starting, which would be a disaster with only one pad in her gym bag. She finally caught up with Kieran at a little clearing on the side of the road where he'd stopped to wait. She hadn't even realized she was crying until she saw the look on his face.

They sat down on a log and cuddled as the sky grew lighter, her apologizing for not staying on the ferry yesterday and letting him flee alone. "I just wanted to be adventuresome and strong like you," she said, through shuddery sobs. "But I'm a wimp. A total loser."

"I'm the loser," he said, and for a few minutes he just held her and breathed into her hair. Then in a real quiet voice, he said, "I told you a fucking pack of lies. I never went to a fancy camp in Vancouver. I did time in a jail for young offenders. I've done some really stupid shit, and now I've hurt Mrs. Ballard, one of the few people besides you I truly respect. I lied about my mom too. She isn't exactly mother of the year, but she's not dead."

"Oh, babe," Cassidy said, stroking his cheek. "Maybe you've had some bad breaks, but you can't blame yourself for Mrs. Ballard's accident."

"There's where you're wrong," he said. "I am to blame. And the worst thing I did to Mrs. B – the worst thing I did in my stinking life – was to kill her stepson."

Cassidy jumped to her feet. "What are you talking about?" she said. "*I* killed Jack."

* * *

"It's bad, Stella," Ben said. "You might want to pull over. And this is strictly off the record, agreed?" He had disembarked from the ferry at Kootenay Bay, he said, and was now driving along Highway 3A on the lookout for Cassidy and Kieran. He'd just caught an update on his radio about the death in Salmo.

Stella was still on the Salmo-Creston, her cell phone mounted on the dashboard but she pulled over and turned off the engine. "Okay. I'll keep tight-lipped."

"The victim has been identified as Angela Maria Ludwar of Ymir, age forty. Single, no children. Leaves behind a mother." He paused. "Stella? You there?"

"I'm here."

"Your Dark Angel."

"The one and only. Did I tell you she called me yesterday? I was still at the hospital. She wanted to rave about Danielle and I cut her off."

"Don't beat yourself up, Stella. You had a lot going on."

"She really wanted to talk though, and I let her down. Last night I couldn't reach her and left voicemail. Checked off another item on my to-do list and moved on. I wonder if she was still alive when I left that message. Must be too soon to know the cause of death."

"No details on when the autopsy will be done. Danielle and Rory were still at the hotel this morning and they've been questioned, I know that much. Staff saw them talking to Angela in the pub last night. All three of them reportedly had a lot to drink. At some point

Danielle and Rory took a room and Angela crashed on a couch in the lobby. Later, the night manager couldn't rouse her and called 9-1-1."

"God, that's sad." Stella said. "Poor Angie. I should try to get hold of her mother. I'll do that when she's had time to talk to friends and family. But, listen, I better let you concentrate on finding those kids."

"Let me know when you get to your post. Drive safe."

Stella continued on her way. Soon she was on the final descent from the pass, nearing the turnoff to the Creston Wildlife Centre and the long, flat stretch of land the river meandered through. The vast fields were still lush and green, a few deciduous trees starting to drop their yellow and orange leaves. A flock of Canada geese flew in a V formation overhead, honking loud enough to be heard in the car. Angie would never experience a scene like this again, never speak or laugh or gossip about Jack and Danielle. It was sad to think how fixated she'd become on an unborn child who probably never existed.

Stella took the underpass to Lower Wynndel Road and steered into a pullout just short of the left-hand turn to the asparagus farm. She got out of the car to stretch her legs and rotate her injured ankle then leaned against the hood to check her phone. The ankle was healing nicely; she rarely felt pain or discomfort now. And again she thought of Angie and felt a strange blend of despair and elation she could only attribute to survivor guilt.

She got out and paced, trying not to check the time too often, trying to keep her head clear for what she hoped would be the imminent arrival of Ben's vehicle bearing Cassidy and Kieran. Would they be hostile or contrite? Or worse, tight-lipped? Stella had no sense of Kieran's opinion of her – they hadn't spoken for a long time. But she hoped Cassidy still considered her a friend.

While she waited she called Richard Ballard for an update on Pamela's condition. "She seems to drift in and out of consciousness," he said. "It's the pain meds, and she still has that bloody tube down her throat. I sit here and talk to her and hope she can hear me even when her eyes are closed. I told her about a silly project I had with Danielle, and apologized for keeping it from her. I don't know why the hell I did that. Nobody means more to me than Pammie."

"I'm sure it's a comfort to hear your voice," Stella said. "And Richard, take care of yourself too. Pamela would want you to. I'll come by as soon as she's ready for a visitor." Stella closed her eyes and said a little prayer for Pamela. At least Richard was fully there for her now.

Her heart beat a little faster when she saw the black and white Nelson Police pickup approach, two bikes in the cargo area, Ben at the wheel. He swung into the pullout and stopped nose-to-nose in front of her car. She walked over to the vehicle and looked into the backseat where two sullen faces tried to avoid her glance. Ben raised his eyebrows. He got out and walked Stella over to her car. "I'd like Cassidy to drive back to Nelson with you," he said. "She hasn't done anything wrong. No reason for her to ride into town in the back of a police car. She doesn't want to leave Kieran but I wouldn't mind separating them. I've spoken to her mother. She'll be waiting at the station."

Back at the police vehicle, Cassidy lifted her chin and said, "I'm staying with Kieran."

"Not an option, Cassidy," Ben said, firmly. "Ms. Mosconi will drive you back to the station. Your mom is waiting there for you."

Cassidy flounced over to the Pathfinder and, ignoring the front door Stella held open, climbed into the back seat.

Stella started the car. "Let's talk, Cassidy," she said. "We've been friends a long time, right?"

No response. The girl gazed out the car window.

Stella let a few minutes pass and tried again. "You and Kieran seem close, so I understand how hard this situation must be for you."

"I don't think you do understand actually," Cassidy said. "I love Kieran, and I'll never love anyone else. I doubt you can say the same about Joe."

Where the hell had that come from? "Listen Cassidy, we're not here to talk about Joe and me. The question is why you suddenly took off with Kieran. Obviously, he was the guy in the hoodie you saw the day Jack died. Why not talk to someone you trust about what really happened."

"No comment," she said.

"C'mon, Cassidy."

"I have nothing to say and that's final," she said.

Stella turned on the radio and stopped trying to engage for a while. Then she said, "Did you hear about Pamela Ballard's accident?"

Cassidy shifted in her seat but didn't say anything. It was a long drive back to Nelson.

At the station, Ben gave Cassidy and her mother a moment for a tearful reunion, then asked them to wait while he spoke to Kieran; a female officer led them to the station's least-threatening interview room. Ben showed Kieran into a bare-bones room with a metal table and chairs, but first he bent the rules again, stationing Stella behind a two-way mirror. When he was seated opposite the boy, he said, "You didn't say much during the drive, Kieran. How're you doing after a night on the road?"

"You don't care how I'm doing, so don't pretend to," he said. "Or I guess you care if I talk to you. Whatever. It's not like I'm free to get up and walk away."

Ben opened his notebook and started the recorder. "What made you and Cassidy take off yesterday."

"No comment," said Kieran.

"Okay. Let's go back to the day Jack Ballard died. Do you recall that day?"

Corcoran closed his eyes. "I wish I could fucking forget it. That day like split my life in two parts. Before and after."

Ben paused in his notetaking and looked up. He hadn't anticipated the kid to be so forthcoming. "What happened, Kieran?"

"I don't want to talk about it," he said, quietly.

"Let's pick up where we left off when I questioned you at the gym," Ben said. "Now that you've had time to think about it, do you remember seeing Ballard anywhere near Pulpit Rock on the day in question?"

"I might have seen him up there," Kieran said, adding quickly, "but I didn't see him fall."

"You're certain you didn't see Ballard go over the cliff?" Ben said.

"Aren't you listening?" Kieran said, raising his voice. He put his head down on the metal table.

Ben announced the time and turned off the recorder. "Okay, kid. Let's take a break. You hungry – want a burger or something?"

"Sure, whatever," Kieran said. "Uh, do you happen to know how Mrs. Ballard is doing? I heard she had an accident."

"I gather her injuries were serious. She had to have surgery."

Kieran nodded. Stella, still watching through the mirror, tried to read his expression.

When Ben came out of the interview room, Stella asked if she should try to talk to Cassidy again with her mother present. "Go for it," Ben said, and called over his colleague to order food for everyone.

Stella asked Karen if she could join her and Cassidy for lunch. The female officer interrupted to find out if they all ate red meat; all three agreed regular burgers would be fine.

"Good," she replied. "Sergeant McKean never thinks to ask if people are vegetarians."

* * *

The food order arrived and the officer passed out the burgers and left Stella with Karen and Cassidy. Cassidy opened her Styrofoam box and looked forlornly at the contents. Stella made small talk with Karen and put on a fresh pot of coffee. Then she said, "Now that you've had time to talk privately to your mom, Cassidy, I'd like to ask you a couple of questions. I don't think it will reflect badly on Kieran if you tell us why you two suddenly left town together."

"No comment."

"Oh, Cassidy," Karen said. "Stella is just trying to help."

"I doubt that very much," said the girl.

Stella folded her arms and leaned back in her chair. "Look, Cassidy. We know Kieran was the guy in the hoodie. Did you see him and Jack argue up at Pulpit that day?"

"Nope," Cassidy said. She delicately ate a single French fry then daubed her lips with a napkin.

Stella continued. "If Kieran was responsible for Jack's fall, the police will find evidence of that. Covering for him will only delay getting him the help he needs."

Cassidy forced a laugh. "Why do you assume Kieran is to blame? That's a real sexist attitude on your part, Stella."

"Cassidy – that's enough," Karen said. "There's no need to be rude."

Stella looked at Karen and shook her head slightly. She used a gentle tone when she spoke to Cassidy again. "Kieran has admitted to being up at the viewpoint that day."

Cassidy pounded a fist on the table. "No. If he said that, it was only to protect me."

Stella tried to reach out to her, but the girl shrugged away. "Tell me what happened, Cassidy," she said.

"I pushed Jack off that fucking cliff – and I'm not sorry I did."

Karen seemed to suppress a cry. "Cassidy. . ."

Cassidy jumped up and dumped the Styrofoam container and its contents into a wastebasket, then stormed across the room and leaned her forehead against a window before speaking again. "I'm sorry, Mommy. I was just *so* happy to see Jack up at Pulpit that day. I didn't know anything bad about him then. It was just the sweetest surprise, him standing there, looking at the view like he was waiting for somebody – waiting for me. I couldn't believe how lucky I was to get to talk to him the morning after his party. He called me over and I said 'Hi, how's it going' and he said, 'Excellent.' He said it was great to see me, and so great that even with all the rain, I was up there. He put his hand on my shoulder to point out a bunch of landmarks in town. He was like a little kid, showing me where everything was, laughing, almost hugging me." Cassidy pushed the heels of her hands against her eyes. Karen looked uncertainly at Stella and she shook her head again. After a moment, Cassidy dropped her hands and spoke directly to her mother. "Can you believe Jack had never gone up there before? I couldn't believe it. It seemed so special to be sharing that experience. We started talking about all the things we had in common, like exercising in any kind of weather because that's what you do when you truly love sports. He was so funny and fatherly, and it sounds lame, but time sort of stood still? It was like I'd been waiting forever to be with him like that." Cassidy sat down and closed her eyes.

Stella said, quietly, "And then. . ."

"And then the best moment of my life turned into the worst. He grabbed at me and it was nothing like a hug. His fingers dug into my arms and he groaned like an animal and leaned against me, and his breath – which I hadn't even noticed before – stunk of booze. I pushed him away, it was a reflex. It happened so fast and he fell. He fell right over the edge." Karen reached out to her daughter; Cassidy started to hiccough but she kept talking as her mom held her hand. "First I was too shocked to move then I called him but he didn't answer. I thought about climbing down to help but it was so steep and muddy I was afraid I'd fall too, so I just called 9-1-1. I didn't know what else to do."

Stella wished Ben could have heard all this but she hadn't wanted to interrupt Cassidy; now it seemed critical to respond to her without delay. "I want you to take some deep breaths, Cassidy," she said, "then listen very carefully to what I'm going to tell you. Are you listening? Jack died because he had an aneurysm that ruptured. Do you know what that means? A blood vessel in his chest burst – that's what killed him."

Karen quietly exhaled.

"No," Cassidy said, "He was fine until he started to touch me and I pushed him away. Mom, you said he was a serious flirt, a womanizer. When you told me that, I felt sick. Up till then I had just felt bad about what happened. But when I really thought about what he'd done . . . I mean, coming on to a teenager." Cassidy started to cry again.

According to Ben, the forensic pathologist had favoured the impact of the fall as the likely cause of the fatal rupture. But Stella had done some research of her own about aneurysms, double checking what she'd learned from online sources with a local cardiologist. Now she said, "Cassidy, look at me. Aneurysms can burst spontaneously. Jack's grabbing at you makes me think it must have burst right then, before he fell. Even if you hadn't been there, it might have happened that way. A rupture near his heart would explain the sudden change in his behaviour – one minute acting like his old self, the next minute groaning and grabbing at you."

"You're making excuses for me. He fell over the edge because I pushed him away. I caught him off balance."

"Cassidy, remember when we talked about swimming lessons and you told me I could trust you? Now I need you to trust me. I think Jack might have died even if he hadn't fallen over the edge." They sat together quietly for a few minutes, Cassidy wrapped up in her mother's arms now. Then Stella spoke again. "I'm curious about something you said about Jack being fatherly. You also used the word 'fatherly' when you wrote in his memory book at the funeral."

Cassidy wiped away her tears and looked into her mother's eyes. "I thought he was my real dad," she said.

* * *

After lunch, Stella and Ben had a quick confab in his office. She repeated what Cassidy had told her about Jack's fall, and apologized for telling the girl about the aneurysm. "I know you went out on a limb sharing confidential information," Stella said. "And I came to my own conclusion about when the aneurysm burst. But her description of Jack's dramatic shift in behaviour fits with information I got from reliable sources."

"Her story makes some sense," Ben said. "Antoniak also said aneurysms can burst spontaneously. But do you buy her complete about-face about what happened up there?"

"I'm not sure. She insists Kieran wasn't at the viewpoint. That he only claimed to be there to protect her from taking the blame for Jack's death. Yet she mentioned a trail runner the first time you interviewed her and we know now that was Kieran. I suppose he could have run straight up the mountain without detouring to Pulpit Rock – lots of people do."

"So basically, we don't know who's protecting whom," Ben said. "I think we should let Cassidy go home in her mother's care while I have another go at Kieran. His question about Mrs. Ballard came out of left field. I kind of let it go, but I wonder if there's a connection between him and the Ballard family that we're missing."

Stella repeated what Pamela had told her about Kieran snooping around the studio. Ben called Kieran back to the interview room and asked Stella to resume her post behind the mirror.

"Just to recap," Ben said to the boy, "you said you were up at Pulpit the day Jack Ballard died. But Cassidy was on the mountain that day too, and she claims to have pushed Mr. Ballard over the edge."

"That's bullshit," Kieran said. "She had nothing to do with it."

"So, tell me. How do you think Jack Ballard fell to his death?"

"I put a curse on him," Kieran said. "I cursed him to die. I had read about curses and talked to a friend about them, but I never really expected it to work." He fixed his eyes on a point just beyond Ben's face and started in on a rambling story. He said he'd caught up with Ballard near the viewpoint, although the meet-up had been unplanned. He and Ballard had argued and that's when Kieran uttered his curse.

Ben asked what the argument had been about.

"His girlfriend," Kieran said. "She was always coming on to me. He didn't like it. Thought I encouraged her."

"This would be his fiancée Danielle Stone?" Ben said.

"Yeah, that's her."

"Okay," Ben said. "What happened after you cursed him to die?"

"He just laughed and turned his back. I was pissed. I took off and went all the way to the CBC radio tower before I doubled back. I didn't even know the curse had worked until I was coming down the mountain later on. Then it was like a war zone, guys in uniform carrying a body bag. At the bottom, people all over the road, fire trucks, police cars."

Stella opened her phone and tapped out a text: *Ask him if he's ever cursed anyone else.*

Ben glanced down at his phone. "I'm still trying to get my head around this cursing business," he said to Kieran. "Did you ever put a curse on anyone besides Ballard?"

The boy raked his fingers through his hair. "Jack was the first. Too bad I didn't stop there."

Ben waited. "Mrs. Ballard's accident should never have happened. I just wanted to scare that evil bitch who was ruining her life."

"And who is this evil bitch?" Ben said.

"Danielle Stone," Corcoran said, in a tone that implied Ben was slow to catch on. "If you ever met her you wouldn't have to ask. Mrs. B should never have gotten into that Mini."

"Wait a sec, Kieran," Ben said. "Did you tamper with the Mini?"

"Don't insult my intelligence. I know cops can tell when a car's been fucked with. I didn't touch it. Hela must have scared her."

"Hela?"

"A Chilean Rose tarantula. And now she's gone too."

"Let's take another break," Ben said. He glanced under the table. "Are those the shoes you wore up to Pulpit Rock? I'd like to borrow them for a couple minutes."

"Go ahead," Kieran said, kicking off the shoes and passing them to McKean. "I know how these things work. You have to check my footprints to see if I really was up at the viewpoint that day."

After showing Kieran where he could get a coffee, Ben met Stella in his office. Kieran's left running shoe matched a plaster cast taken up at Pulpit the day of Jack's fall. "So where does this leave us?" Stella said.

"With two half-baked confessions," Ben said.

"But Cassidy's story has a ring of truth," Stella said. "Kieran's curses didn't kill anybody. But if he put a tarantula in the Mini to try to scare Danielle, that could have scared Pamela enough to run the car off the road. And one thing I'll say for Kieran, he's a pretty good judge of character, at least in the case of Danielle Stone. On top of everything else, I think she might be faking the pregnancy."

35

"SHE'S PERKING UP," RICHARD said over the phone. "They've taken out the breathing tube."

Stella felt a great weight lift from her shoulders. Richard would have a short time to be grateful and happy before he heard the devastating news that Danielle had faked the pregnancy – if indeed she had. Stella's next task was to find out. It was Sunday morning and she told Joe and the boys she had an errand to run. She got in her car and drove up Lucky Jack Road to the Ballard residence, mounted the stairs to the studio, and rapped on Danielle's door.

Within there was silence, then muted conversation. Danielle opened the door as far as the chain permitted and said, "What do *you* want?"

"Hey, good morning to you too," Stella said. "We need to talk. Do you want to come out, or shall I come in?"

Danielle unlatched the chain and swung open the door. Rory was stretched out on top of the bed in his boxers, reading the *Nelson Times.* "Hi, Rory," Stella said. "This might be a good time to put on some pants and go get some coffee."

Rory looked at Danielle.

Danielle said, "Go home. I'll call when I want you to come back."

Rory grabbed his pants and shoes and departed barefoot.

"I'm curious about something, Danielle," Stella said. "When were you planning to fake a miscarriage? I guess you wanted Richard to buy you a house first, but the car crash will have put that on hold."

"You're bonkers." She pointed to the open door. "Go away."

"I can only speculate," Stella said, shoving aside magazines and cushions and sinking comfortably into a beanbag chair. "But I don't think you're pregnant and I doubt you ever were. Maybe if Jack hadn't died, the farce would have ended sooner. But manipulating

Richard to buy you a house – and without Pamela's knowledge – that was low."

"You know nothing. Less than nothing. Jack would have wanted them to take care of me. Richard said so himself."

So, she wasn't denying the hoax. Stella carried on. "The point is though, you lied about being pregnant and you used Richard and Pamela. I expect there'll be an investigation into the crash, which maybe not coincidentally involved your car."

"You think that didn't freak me out?" Danielle said. "Tell me how it's my fault Pamela took my car without permission and drove it into the fucking pond? If the insurance company writes of that Mini, I'd better be compensated."

"Funny how when trouble happens, there you are. Seems you had a strange connection with Angie and she ended up dead. Were you jealous of her? She was Jack's first love, and that's something nobody can take way. You lied about the pregnancy, but I still don't understand what you were trying to cover up about Jack's death."

"Oh, right. You and your fuckbuddy must have wracked your tiny brains. McKean goes after Jack's medical records, and you get Pamela to spy on me. I knew you two were trying to incriminate me. If you hadn't been sniffing around I'd a been long gone from this hick town. The house was Richard's idea. I never even thought of him buying me a house. I figured they'd give me money to go away, but I didn't think I'd have to hang around and fight to prove my innocence. My sex life with my fiancé was our business. And, for the record, nothing we did in private affected his health. He had the heart and body of an elite athlete." She reached down and grabbed the lapels of Stella's jacket, pulling her to her feet. "Now *fuck off*." She shoved Stella through the open doorway.

Stella straightened her clothes and considered Danielle's little speech. Was it as simple as that? The mighty Dom thought she had harmed Jack during sex and was afraid his medical records might implicate her in his death?

Danielle stepped out onto the balcony and gave Stella another shove. "Why are you still here? *Go.*"

Stella was careful not to stand too close to the top of the stairs. "Watch it, Danielle," she said. "With all the trouble you're in, hurting me wouldn't look good. I'll be on my way, but you have twenty-four hours to tell Richard the truth or I'll tell him myself. He deserves to know you're not pregnant and you never were."

"That would kill him, you bitch! Richard *needs* me to be pregnant."

"No, I don't think he does. Not anymore. He'll be sad to give up hope on that last possible link with Jack, but he'll be all right. Pamela is recovering, and even while she was unconscious she was more of a comfort to him than you ever were."

Danielle slapped her face.

Stella stumbled a little but found her footing. She held onto the railing and carefully descended each stair, then climbed a little shakily into her car. She checked her face in the rear-view. Her cheek was red, but the skin wasn't broken. She took a moment to calm down before she started the car. Yes, the truth about the pregnancy was going to be a blow to Richard, but he would come to terms with the disappointment. And Danielle's admission would remove any obligation he and Pamela might have felt to support her.

* * *

When Stella got back to the cabin, she noticed a mysterious hum of activity. Matt was lugging a cooler out to the Subaru, Nicky was trying to corral Snickers into his kennel, and Joe was standing in front of the ironing board with a rumpled blue-and-white checked table cloth that hadn't been used in months. Stella said, "Who are you and what have you done with my husband?" Joe's expression softened, probably at the old familiar turn of phrase. Stella had surprised herself a little too. "What's all this about?" she added.

"Kidnap picnic," Joe said. "The guys and I are going to spirit you off to Kokanee Creek Park for a simple, yet elegant, deli lunch. The food's packed. Wine's disguised in a plain paper bag. And I just have to press this thing."

When they got to the park, the boys tore off toward one of the playgrounds, kicking up fallen leaves as Snickers bounded along beside them. Joe urged Stella to sit and enjoy the view of the mountains while he laid everything out. At the far end of the lake, a skiff of snow on Sphinx Peak foreshadowed the winter ahead. In a week or two they'd put away all the bicycles and before long another ski season would begin. Stella idly wondered if Matt had outgrown his equipment then caught herself. Family ski gear would be the least of their concerns if she and Joe weren't able to salvage their marriage.

The picnic table had been marked "Reserved," a little joke on Joe's part. Earlier he and the boys had driven over to tape the hand-lettered sign in place, even though on this crisp fall day there was little competition for tables. Only a few people were at the park, most of them walking dogs along the shoreline of the lake. Now Joe spread the tablecloth and opened the contraband Cabernet Sauvignon. He filled two plastic cups and proposed a toast. "To my wife," he said, raising his glass. "I want to spend the rest of our lives sharing times like this."

"Cheers," she said. "I appreciate the effort, Joe, and the thought behind it."

That seemed to be enough sentiment for him. "So hey, let's eat," he said. He whistled and the boys and dog came running.

Later, Matt and Nicky went back to the playground, and Stella stood up and corked the remainder of the wine, stacked the empty deli containers, and began to gather plates and cutlery. "Regarding SAR," Joe said. "I have a suggestion I'd like you to think about."

Stella stopped clearing up and looked at him.

"How about I ask for a leave of absence for a couple months?" he said. "Maybe till after Christmas."

Stella didn't jump in with a response.

"I know you want me to quit," he continued, "but it would mean a lot to me if you'd consider a compromise."

Stella nodded. "Okay, fair enough. But just so you know, I'm not sure a break will solve the problem."

"Can we take it a day at a time?" Joe said.

Stella folded the tablecloth. "Let's give that a try."

The boys were on the beach tossing sticks to Snickers when Joe hefted the cooler and started for the car. Stella caught up with him and rested her hand on his shoulder. He put the cooler down and wrapped her in a tight hug.

* * *

That night when everyone was asleep in their small cabin by Kootenay Lake, Stella went outside to call her dad. The last time she'd heard his voice, he had talked about a possible move to Cranbrook, the chance of a job at the Honda dealership.

"Hi, darlin,'" he said. "Been meaning to call."

"Too busy selling Hondas?"

He graced her with a bark of laughter. "Didn't get the job. But I traded in my Hyundai for a late model CR-V. Crazy, eh? If I can't work at the dealership at least I can drive one of their cars. Point of pride, I guess. Decided to take a trip, see the country at my own speed. I'm thinking of wintering in Newfoundland. How does that sound?"

"It sounds cold, and far away," Stella said. "And just when we were getting to know each other again."

"That part I don't like. It's been good to reconnect, Stella."

"Is this how it's going to be then? Touch base, move on."

"Hey, let's talk right now. We don't need to be in the same room to have a conversation. What do you want to talk about?" he said.

"I still think about the canoe incident," Stella said. "It was my fault."

"Stellarina – you were a child! Your mom and me, we were responsible."

Stella went silent.

"It wasn't your fault, baby girl," he said. "You must be having one of those false memories people talk about."

"I don't think a person misremembers that sort of thing. The big stuff stays with you."

"Don't talk like that, Stella. The past is the past, right? Didn't we agree there's no point hashing over old news?"

"I guess we did," Stella said.

"Listen, darlin,' you gonna be okay? Because I'm real sorry but I gotta run. Next time I'll call you. What do you say? Do we have a deal?"

"Sure," Stella said, knowing next time wouldn't be anytime soon.

36

IT WAS EARLY ON the final day of Stella's suspension, when she received a text from her publisher. *It is my pleasure to reinstate you as a full-time reporter, effective immediately. Welcome back!*

Stella called Patrick at home. "Apologies for the wake-up call, but I've been summoned back to work one day early. What's up? Can't you guys live without me?"

"It's been hell," Patrick said. "Jade took job action to protest your suspension. She called in sick three times last week."

"Never figured Jade as a booster," Stella said.

"You kidding me? She stopped bringing in biscuits for the Bichon Frise. One day she referred to you as a role model and mentor in front of the publisher. I thought I'd wandered into the wrong newsroom."

"I stand amazed and flattered. It'll be great to get back to work, but I have some things I have to wrap up today. Might not make it in till the afternoon."

"Whenever," Patrick said. "You're the anointed, at least for the moment. While you're wrapping things up, you might want to swing by the rec centre and snap a few pics of the pool. Somebody in admin emailed to say the renos are pretty much complete."

"I can do that," Stella said. She wondered if she could talk Cassidy into joining her.

Later the girl had an appointment at the Nelson Police Department to make a formal statement regarding her final encounter with Jack Ballard, and her mother had asked Stella to be present. But first Stella had to make a quick trip to Trail. Pamela herself had called from the hospital – a first since the accident. She'd been moved from the ICU to a regular ward, and seemed in good spirits.

Stella found Pamela's room and peeked around the door to find her sitting up in bed with a breakfast tray in front of her. "Come in, come in," Richard said, jumping up to hug Stella. "I'll go get you a coffee."

"That's okay, Richard. Please, sit down." Stella walked over to take Pamela's hand. "And how are you, my friend?" she said.

"I'm fine, Stella." Her voice was hoarse after having a breathing tube down her throat for several days, but her smile was as bright and warm as ever. "I've been looking forward to catching up, and to thanking you for risking your life to rescue me."

"Richard has been exaggerating," Stella said. "But it's wonderful to see you looking so well. Richard, how are you doing?"

"Fine, Stella, just fine," he said. "Take a seat. You have something on your mind. Is Danielle making a fuss about the car?"

"I gather you haven't heard from her." Stella squeezed Pamela's hand and sat down on a chair next to the bed. "Richard, I'm sorry, but I have something to tell you both that's going to be hard to hear." She paused a second. "Danielle isn't pregnant, and I don't think she ever was."

"Good God," Pamela said.

"So she played us," Richard said, quietly.

"She might have believed she was pregnant in the beginning. I suspect she wouldn't have kept up the pretext if Jack hadn't died."

"If Jack had lived, she wouldn't have needed us," Richard said. "We weren't that close to her until we lost our boy."

"My poor darling," Pamela said, reaching for Richard's hand and pulling him close to her. "My poor, poor darling."

Stella asked them to excuse her for a moment, and left to give them some time alone to process the news. She went to the coffee shop in the lobby and picked up a copy of the Trail newspaper and three cups of locally roasted coffee.

When she returned to the hospital room, Pamela and Richard were still holding hands. They'd been talking about Danielle and comparing notes. "Even with all my doubts about Danielle, I didn't see this one coming," Pamela said. "The baby had become real to us. It's going to take a while for it to sink in that we'll never have that grandchild. Danielle's dishonesty seems like a terrible betrayal of Jack."

"I can't disagree," Richard said. "But I was complicit, and I've asked Pamela to forgive me for that. We have to move on together now. I expect I'll have to properly grieve the loss of that imaginary child. But I didn't lose my sweetheart, and I'll be by her side through her recovery and always."

Pamela squeezed his hand. Then she asked Stella about Kieran. "I half-expected to hear from him after the accident," she said "We'd become quite friendly."

"Oh, dear," Stella said. "I'm afraid that's a long story." She recounted everything she knew about Kieran, as accurately as she could. "I think the poor guy is somewhat deluded, Pamela, but he seems to think the world of you. And he was correct in sensing that Danielle was making you unhappy."

"Yes, he got that right," Pamela said. "He's a good kid, you know." She took a sip of coffee and cleared her throat; Stella made a mental note not to keep her talking too long. Now Pamela turned to Richard and said, "Listen, darling, I'd like to help Kieran. He's got himself in a bit of a mess, but when he comes out the other end, why not let him stay at the studio. I don't think he's had a lot of advantages. He deserves a fresh start."

"It's generous of you to want to help Kieran," Stella put in. "Considering you likely wouldn't be lying in a hospital bed if he hadn't put a tarantula in Danielle's car."

"Well, that thing startled me, all right." Pamela shuddered. "I saw the box on the seat and left it alone. But when I took a curve a little too fast, it slid onto the floor. Out popped the spider and I took my eyes off the road. But Kieran couldn't have predicted that. I don't think he meant to harm anyone, not even Danielle."

"I've never met the kid," Richard said. "But I don't mind giving him a hand. I think Jack would have approved. I'll email Ms. Stone to give her notice on the studio."

* * *

When Rory turned up at the studio with two cups of black coffee, Danielle was tossing a big plastic garbage bag over the railing of the balcony. It landed on the driveway with a splat but remained intact. "Whassup?" he said. "You packing already?"

"I can't leave until the frigging car business is settled, but as soon as I have my own ride again, I'm out of here. I sure as hell don't want to be around when Richard brings the Queen home from the hospital."

"So, what happened after the reporter went to see them? Did Richard call and throw you out?"

"He sent a cold, impersonal email. I'm surprised it didn't begin 'to whom it may concern.' It hurt my feelings. Richard is the most decent man I've ever known – I loved him like a dad and he loved me too. I know he did. That fucking reporter turned him against me." Danielle took a second to run her fingers under her eyes to protect her mascara. "He said he was disappointed I led them on about the baby. But he didn't throw me out, for your information. He never would have done that to me. The Queen must have made him give me notice. He said 'Pammie' had plans for the studio. Only the Queen would think about redecorating while she was lying in a freaking hospital bed, barely conscious. *Christ.*" She reached for another bag. "Hey, did you tell your parents about our move to Cincinnati?"

"Uh, not really. I don't think that's going to work out for me actually."

"What are you talking about? Of course it's going to work out for you. For us. You'll cross the border as a tourist and we'll take it from there. If you're worried about money, don't be. You can work as a shampoo boy at my mom's salon until something better comes along. Her little old lady clients will totally dig you."

"Yeah, but like, the thing is, I'm not really into big cities? And I have to think about my parents. They're not getting any younger and Cincinnati is friggin' far away."

"Rory, look at me. Your parents are in their fifties. What? – they need your help to get around the golf course? I don't think so."

"Another thing, I can't really see myself living in the States. I guess I'm a Canuck through and through."

"You're breaking up with me over politics?"

"Uh . . ."

"You disgust me," Danielle said quietly. She should have trounced him, but she didn't have it in her to fight anymore. She was just so fucking tired. "Go," she said. "Get out of here, you useless piece of shit. *Go.*" She slammed the door behind him before she allowed herself to break down.

* * *

On the drive back from Trail, Stella called Cassidy. "How would you like to make a quick stop at the pool before we meet with Sergeant McKean?" she said. "I have it on good authority the repairs are almost done."

Cassidy said, "Oh, the pool. I haven't given much thought to swimming lately. But, yeah, I wouldn't mind seeing how it looks."

Stella smiled to herself. "I'll be entering Nelson in about twenty minutes. I'll swing by and pick you up. Tell your mom we'll meet her at the police station at ten."

At the rec centre, Stella and Cassidy were permitted entry to the construction zone. The contractor provided each of them with a hardhat and led them around the deck, rhyming off all the improvements that had been made. Stella caught it all on her recorder and snapped lots of photos. There was still some scaffolding to take down and the pool was empty, but it would be filled with water in time for a grand opening to be held the following weekend.

She asked Cassidy if she was excited about getting back in the pool. The girl shrugged. "I don't know how Kieran feels about swimming," she said. "But I know he hates the guys from swim club I used to hang out with. I guess those idiots will start working out here again when the fitness room re-opens, thank God."

Neither of them mentioned the swim lessons Cassidy had once offered to give Stella.

They walked over to the police station where the receptionist led them to the pastel interview room. Ben and Karen were already there. Karen gave her daughter a quick hug before everyone sat down.

Ben asked Cassidy to repeat everything she'd told Stella about the incident at Pulpit Rock. He listened without interruption and recorded what she said. When she finished saying her piece, Ben asked if she had anything to add. She shook her head. Then he asked Karen if she wished to comment. "Cassidy is a good girl," she said. "She normally wouldn't do anything to harm or deceive anyone. I think she realizes now she should have spoken up sooner. That would have saved a lot of trouble for you and others."

Ben said, "Your mother's right, Cassidy. If you'd told us what happened between you and Jack Ballard – and if you'd been more forthcoming about Kieran being the guy in the hoodie, a number of consequences might have been prevented, including Mrs. Ballard's car crash. Kieran would have realized his curse hadn't killed Jack Ballard, and he wouldn't have had any reason to feel guilty and protective about Mrs. Ballard. A lot of time and energy was wasted trying to get to the bottom of what really happened, and the uncertainty also caused anxiety and pain for some people."

Cassidy looked stricken. "Will I be sent to a youth custody centre?" she said.

"That's unlikely," Ben said. "But I expect the new evidence will result in an inquest into Jack Ballard's death, and if so, you may be asked to testify. That would mean repeating what you've told me today. An inquest doesn't assign blame. It aims at getting at the truth of what happened. Does that make sense to you?"

"Yes. But, um, what about Kieran? Is he in a lot of trouble?"

"At this point, I can't say," Ben said. "First and foremost, Kieran needs help, and I'll do what I can to make sure he gets it. I recommend you get some counselling too, Cassidy. It seems to me you've been on an emotional roller coaster from the moment you came across Jack Ballard up at that viewpoint. Would you agree?"

"Yes," Cassidy said. Her mother nodded. A very subdued family of two said their goodbyes and left the interview room.

Stella collected her coat and bag. "Let's go to my office," Ben said. "I'll make you a bad cup of coffee and bring you up to speed on the situation in Salmo."

While he put on the coffee, Stella sank into a visitor chair. "This case has been a disaster from start to finish," she said. "Jack Ballard partied hard, trudged up a mountain, and toppled over a cliff. If he hadn't gone up Elephant Mountain that morning, maybe that aneurysm would have ruptured while he was lying in bed or sitting in a coffee shop, if it ruptured at all. In any case, no one would have felt implicated in his death. Cassidy and Kieran both held themselves responsible, and even Danielle the Overzealous Dom was afraid she'd harmed him. I had twinges of guilt myself. In the last conversation I had with Ballard, he talked about climbing mountains, implying that might please me. I didn't like the coincidence of his going up to the viewpoint the next morning for the first time in his life. And it sure would have been nice if Danielle had dropped the pregnancy ruse and gone back to the US before Angela got all bent out of shape about her drinking. Poor Angie. I wonder if she'd still be alive if all this hadn't happened. You were going to bring me up to speed about the scene in Salmo."

"Looks like your Dark Angel died of a fentanyl overdose, with alcohol a possible contributing factor. Sorry, Stella."

"Angie liked her beer, and I heard she might have used cocaine. But I didn't see her as an addict." She closed her eyes a moment. "Any evidence someone might have tampered with her drink?"

"By the time the police got there, the table had long been cleared, the glasses run through a commercial dishwasher. Angela's purse contained a small packet of fentanyl. She might have doctored her drink to enhance her high, but it looks like her death will be classified as accidental."

Stella was quiet a moment, recalling something Angie had said about Jack. *I'm surprised more people don't jump. Or take pills. Just drift off to sleep, good bye world.* Stella didn't repeat this to Ben. To pass on hearsay that might point to suicide as a cause of Angie's death seemed unfair to her memory and to her mother.

Ben stood up and stretched. "Glad to hear Pamela Ballard is doing better," he said.

"God, yes. That's the silver lining in all this," Stella said. "Pamela hasn't fully recovered but Richard will be there for her as she convalesces. He's hurting too, over the loss of that phantom grandchild." Stella put down her coffee cup. "Guess I'd better get back to work. My suspension has been cut short by one day. Apparently, I'm back in favour with the publisher."

"Good. I can start reading the *Times* again," Ben said.

"We've managed to steer clear of anything personal, and I'm fine with that," Stella said. "But I want you to know I'm sorry about your troubles at home. I hope things work out in a way that's right for you."

"Thanks. Maybe I'll keep you informed, in case you don't have enough drama in your life already." He stood up to open the door for her and squeezed her hand as she slipped past him.

37

ANOTHER SATURDAY MORNING IN Nelson, and when Joe took the boys to their soccer games, Stella made a bold move. She called Ben and suggested they hike up Elephant Mountain together. It seemed a fitting end to the bizarre investigation that had preoccupied them for weeks. No charges had been laid in the deaths of Jack Ballard and Angela Ludwar. Yet crimes, big and small, had been committed. Most, but not all of them, unintentional. When Stella and Ben reached Pulpit Rock, they sat down to rest on a bench unnervingly close to the place Jack Ballard had fallen.

Ben put his arm across the back of the bench as they gazed down on the deceptively peaceful-looking town they lived in. The big orange bridge across Kootenay Lake glinted in the autumn sunlight. On an easterly hill above the bridge, stood their old alma mater, where Cassidy had returned to her tenth-grade classes and Joe continued to teach science and biology. With the community pool open again, the parking lot over at the rec centre was full. Down in Railtown, the restored train station that housed the *Nelson Times* probably looked much the same as it had decades ago when passenger trains still ran. One block up from Baker Street, the unassuming building that was home to the Nelson Police Department sat a stone's throw away from the public health centre where Cassidy and Kieran had found supportive mental health counsellors. On the waterfront, kids' soccer games were in progress and Stella tried to pick out Matt and Nicky from among their teammates.

"Well," she said. "I guess we can finally lay to rest the enigma that was Jack Ballard."

"Figured him out, have you?" Ben said. "As I recall you weren't his biggest fan."

"Did you know I dated him briefly in grade ten?"

"If I'd known at the time, I would have been green with envy."

Stella laughed. "I had a crush on you too. Too bad we were both too shy to do anything about it."

Ben squeezed her shoulder. "My single biggest regret."

"We wouldn't want to wish away three special little boys though," Stella said.

"No, we wouldn't," he said. "But what happened with you and Ballard back then – how come you dated only briefly?"

Stella hesitated. "He got aggressive and that scared me off. More recently he half-heartedly tried to make amends, but I still didn't trust him. I guess Angie helped me understand him better than anyone. Funny thing is, if I'd given any thought to BDSM before I got involved in this case, I wouldn't have pegged Jack as a Sub. Maybe as adult he just wanted to please the women in his life. In my case, that made me suspicious. I guess that says something about me."

"That you're nobody's fool?"

"If only." She watched as two red kayaks skimmed under the bridge, one ahead of the other. "I called Angie's mother the other day. She's holding a memorial for her on Remembrance Day when some relatives can drive in from Medicine Hat. She asked me to say a few words at the service, which kind of threw me. She seemed to think Angie had looked up to me. If that was true, she sure hid it well."

"What will you say about your Dark Angel?"

Stella thought for a moment. "Well, she was fiercely loyal to old friends. And, let's see . . . She was willing to speak up on behalf of those unable to speak for themselves, notably Danielle's phantom baby." Stella closed her eyes for a moment. "Hey, should we keep going? See if we can make it all the way to the flagpole?"

"Sure," Ben said. "Your ankle up to it?"

"Absolutely."

They walked to the place the trail split in two and chose the more challenging "Black Diamond" route to the flagpole. The effort of clambering over big slabs of rock temporarily curbed the conversation. After a while, Stella spoke again. "Too bad Cassidy and Kieran weren't more open with each other."

Ben said, "A lot came down to Cassidy and Kieran circling each other, afraid to come clean about what each of them had done.

Guess we can chalk that up to lack of maturity. Even Kieran seems remarkably naïve despite the edgy image he tries to project."

"Well, you and I still pussyfoot around each other," Stella said. "You haven't said much about your split with Miranda, for example."

"Not much to say."

"Joe slept with another woman."

Ben stopped and looked at her.

"Yeah. Only happened once, he says. Never again, yada, yada."

"How do you feel about that?"

"We've come to an agreement. A compromise, which I don't have much faith in, to tell you the truth. And Ben, let's be honest. There was a time you and I might have gone down that road. I don't feel entirely justified in claiming the moral high ground with Joe." They high-stepped it through a narrow passage.

"So, where do we go from here?" Ben said.

"Race you to the top?"

"I was speaking metaphorically," Ben said. "But I'm game. I'll give you a five-minute head start, then I'm coming after you."

Stella turned and ran.

Acknowledgments

This is a work of fiction and all characters and events are imaginary. Beautiful Nelson, British Columbia, inspires the setting for the Stella Mosconi Mysteries, although I take liberties with the geography and other features of the place when it serves the story to do so.

Stella's life as a reporter is influenced by what I've learned from real-life journalists, including the editorial staff of the *Nelson Star* – at present, Tyler Harper, Bill Metcalfe, and Greg Nesteroff – who at times have invited me into the newsroom to watch them in action.

Online research only gets an author so far, and I'm grateful to the experts who advised me on this book. Chief Constable Paul Burkart of the Nelson Police Department kindly answered my questions on police procedures. For information about BC Search and Rescue, I'm obliged to Darcey Lutz, paramedic and former Nelson team member, as well as Barry Blair of Arrowsmith Search and Rescue and Lisa Nothling, a former SAR team member based on Vancouver Island. Dr. Sarah Merriman answered my questions related to Stella's experience in the ER, while Dr. Brad Merriman gave me advice on Pamela Ballard's injuries and medical treatment related to her car crash. Errors in any of these matters are entirely my own.

I'm fortunate to be represented by Morty Mint, whom I count as a friend as well as an agent, and to be published by Mosaic Press. My thanks to Publisher Howard Aster, Senior Editor Michael Walsh, Publication Coordinator Brianna Wodabek, and editor extraordinaire Matthew Goody, who showed me the path when I lost my way. I'm also grateful to author/editor Linda L Richards for helpful advice on the manuscript.

Finally, heartfelt thanks to my support team of David, Erica, and Sarah, my sister Jennifer Steeksma, and fellow crime writers RM Greenaway (who has been there for me from the start), Iona Whishaw, and AJ Devlin.

About the Author

JG Toews is a former health professional and non-fiction author turned crime writer. *Lucky Jack Road*, is her second Stella Mosconi Mystery and a sequel to *Give Out Creek*, a finalist for the 2016 Arthur Ellis Award for Best Unpublished Crime Novel and the 2019 Lefty for Best Debut Mystery Novel. Judy lives in Nelson, British Columbia, Canada. Visit her at www.jgtoews.com or follow her on Instagram and Facebook @JG Toews and Twitter @judytoews.

Photo credit: Lisa Seyfried Photography